PRAISE FOR TH_

"A thrilling and fast paced science fiction story that takes depth of feeling as one of its core principles and combines that with pyrotechnic grace. I like here the ability to rethink genre trope, to add something new – to tell Caeli's story in a way that makes the whole enterprise feel fresh and invigorating instead of just going through the same old motions."

—*Writer's Digest*

"If you insist on depth, action, integrity, and great writing in your science fiction that doesn't overpower the message of the story. Stop. Buy. Read. Enjoy. Period."

—*Book Club Babble*

"Tabitha Lord took the bold step of writing a strong female character who is an empath in a genre that usually resorts to violence as the primary way to win the day."

—*Muriel Stockdale,*
author of Gabriel Born

"Ms. Lord weaves a tale of moral strength and courage under fire. As an added bonus the action scenes will leave you breathless!"

—*Heather Rigney,*
Amazon Bestselling author of the
historical fantasy Waking the Merrow

"Five Stars for INFINITY...and the next book please!"

—*Whiskey With My Book Reviews*

Also by Tabitha Lord:

HORIZON

INFINITY

To Amy,
Enjoy this final
adventure!
Thank you for
years of support &
friendship.
Love,
Tabitha

EQUINOX

BY

TABITHA LORD

ISBN 13: 978-1-63489-241-4
eISBN: 978-1-63489-244-5

Printed in the United States of America
First Printing: 2019

23 22 21 20 19   5 4 3 2 1

Cover and interior design by Steven Meyer-Rassow

Wise Ink Creative Publishing
807 Broadway St. NE, Suite 46
Minneapolis, MN 55413
www.wiseink.com

For Nicholas. I'm so privileged to be your mom.

DEREK

CHAPTER 1

Derek checked his oxygen level, secured his helmet, and tapped a gloved thumb against the protective fabric of his suit.

"Captain, we are aligned with the *Carina*." He heard the pilot's voice through the com in his ear. "Extending the docking port now."

A hum vibrated under his feet, followed by a thud. "Port attached. The seal is good."

"Roger that," he answered robotically.

Derek knew it wasn't a good idea for him to lead the boarding team, but he was in charge of Almagest's newly minted space fleet. No one outranked him, and no one could countermand his orders. He had to be the first one on board.

If she was dead, he had to be the first to see her, the first to stand in the last place she stood.

His brain felt numb, his emotions dull and distant. "Give me a few minutes," he said to the team suited up next to him. A chorus of subdued "yes, sirs" answered.

He tapped the control panel, and the door in front of him slid open. Closing his eyes, Derek tried to steady his breath before stepping onto the deck of the *Carina*.

She was a small ship, a long-range shuttle with an enhanced weapons system. Fast and maneuverable, she was the vessel of choice for delivering high-profile diplomats to distant worlds. On approach, Derek had seen the gaping hole where the attacking ship had latched onto her side and ripped through her hull.

The thought of what he might find on board made his stomach churn. Swallowing back the bile in his throat, he forced himself to put one foot in front of the other. He repeated her name over and over in his mind, as if the power of his thoughts could will her to live.

As soon as he stepped into the dimly lit corridor, Derek could tell that the gravitational system was still functioning. *Carina's* emergency systems had kicked in, sealing off compartments and shunting emergency power to life support. From where Derek stood, nothing looked amiss. He passed by the empty crew quarters, catching a glimpse of Caeli's travel bag resting on one of the bunks.

Once he'd made his way to the bridge, he stood, hesitant, outside the closed door. This was where she'd be. For him, space travel was a part of life, but for Caeli, who'd never known a world outside her own until adulthood, it was magical. Every launch thrilled her, and she could spend hours gazing at the stars.

Taking a deep breath, he punched the override code into the lock.

When the doors slid open, carnage assaulted him. Blood splattered the control panel and pooled in sticky puddles on the floor. A body lay contorted over the pilot's seat, another sprawled face down on the floor. But there was no sign of Caeli.

She wasn't here. Maybe she wasn't dead.

He leaned heavily against the doorframe, a warm rush of relief spreading through his body. He could deal with anything but dead.

The fog that had engulfed him since he'd received the distress call from *Carina* twelve hours earlier lifted. Mind racing, he barked into the com, "Evans, get the team in here."

Moments later, the group appeared.

"Process every inch of this ship. Transfer all sensor data, cockpit recordings, and video feed directly to the command center. Get the bodies ready for transport," he instructed, the paralysis that had gripped him completely dispelled.

***

Six hours later, Derek was back on Almagest. He hadn't slept, but he'd managed to shower. Running a hand through his damp hair, he sat at a workstation in the mission control center. The information scrolling across his screen told a familiar story of a ship materializing out of nowhere, launching a quick and dirty attack, and then disappearing. Even before all the data could be analyzed, he knew it was the Drokarans.

He had a communication scheduled with Admiral Reyes in less than an hour, so he wasted no time playing back the cockpit video recordings. White-knuckling the armrests of his chair, he watched the pilot's chest explode in a red haze. When he heard Caeli's screams, he slammed his fist onto the desk. He played the feed of the enemy soldier carrying her unconscious body out of the ship over and over until finally a soft knock sounded behind him.

Finn stood in the doorway. The dark circles under the younger man's eyes told Derek that he hadn't been sleeping either.

"Find anything useful?" Finn asked.

Derek sighed and rubbed his hands over his face before answering. "Not really. It was definitely a Drokaran attack, but we suspected that already."

"She's alive, though?" Finn asked, voice pleading for confirmation.

Finn had been Caeli's friend before he became Derek's. An Amathi soldier turned resistance fighter in the recent civil war, he had befriended Caeli and then recruited her to the cause. When the resistance finally defeated the ruling regime, Finn and Caeli shared transitional leadership roles in the construction of their new government. Now, Finn retained control of Almagest's military forces while Derek helped him build a space fleet, train the pilots, and move the planet from a vulnerable, rogue world to a protected, integrated member of the Inter-Planetary Alliance.

Caeli's ship had been en route to Cor Leon, seat of the Inter-Planetary Alliance, to formally accept Almagest's membership into that body when the Drokarans attacked.

"She was alive when they took her," Derek answered.

Finn visibly relaxed, tension draining from his body. "What do they want with her?"

Derek drummed his fingers on the desk. "When Marcus was selling the Novali kids, my team on *Horizon* tried to track down the crew he was dealing with." Marcus, the dictator in power before the war, had begun selling gifted Novali children on the black market in return for weapons, advanced technology, and information.

"I remember," Finn replied.

"We found the mercenary crew and one of the Novali girls, but before we could rescue her, she was sold to someone else, someone we knew had worked with the Drokarans."

"If the Drokarans got ahold of the Novali girl and realized there were others like her, they'd be looking for the source."

Derek nodded. "And Caeli joined us on-mission once while she was aboard the *Horizon*. She interrogated a Drokaran using her gift. He escaped, and I'm sure they've started putting the pieces together."

"The Drokarans knew Caeli was on the *Carina*. That means they know the Novali are from Almagest," Finn said.

Derek met Finn's worried gaze. "I believe they do now. But the *Aquila* is still patrolling Almagest's airspace, and we have a first line of defense ready. I'm about to talk to the Admiral of the Inter-Allied Forces and brief him on the situation. Even though Caeli didn't make it to Cor Leon, Almagest is now a member world. We'll protect this planet," he promised in the most assuring tone he could muster.

The Drokarans were a fearsome enemy. Despite Alliance intervention in the past, they'd taken whole worlds. Derek could only take comfort knowing that at least Almagest had some warning.

"What about Caeli?" Finn asked.

Derek opened his mouth to speak and then closed it again. When he could finally make his voice work, he said, "I'll find her. Whatever it takes."

CΛELI

CHΛPTER 2

Caeli huddled in the corner of the cell, arms wrapped protectively around her knees. Bone-deep exhaustion and a blinding headache threatened to pull her into unconsciousness. She longed to give in, to surrender to the darkness, but with a meager shred of mental strength, she fought the urge.

Scanning the stark room, she couldn't find any weaknesses. The cell door locked from the outside, and the ventilation tube over her head hovered well out of reach. Essentially, she was imprisoned in a steel box.

Under the glaring artificial lights, day and night were indistinguishable, and she knew she'd lost huge chunks of time. Her memories tried to return. She fought to make sense of bits and pieces of hazy images, but they remained incoherent and out of focus, like a long-range transmission interrupted by an electromagnetic storm. The last clear memory she had was of the *Carina*'s pilot, Lieutenant Riggs, informing her they'd just cleared the Almagest system.

Her belly churned with both excitement and nervousness. This mission was the culmination of her hard work and the determination of so many other good people. She'd barely survived the devastating war that ripped through her civilization when so many others hadn't. The trauma of loss felt like an old scar, noticeable and sore, a permanent mark on her body, but one she'd learned to live with.

When her people had finally found true peace, they'd grieved together, healed as best they could, and then labored to build a new, unified government. That government was now strong enough to participate in and receive protection from the Inter-Planetary Alliance. Seated behind the crew in the cockpit of the Carina, Caeli felt deep satisfaction. This gift of belonging was something they had all earned.

And now, finally, Caeli had dreams of her own again. She and Derek were building a life together. He'd asked her to marry him.

A blast jolted her from her thoughts. If she hadn't been harnessed into her seat, she would have been thrown out of it. Alarms blared. She heard herself scream.

Riggs, well-seasoned and handpicked by Derek, spoke into the com. "Almagest control, this is the Carina. We are under attack. We've lost thrusters and weapons."

Another jolt, followed by the scraping sound of metal on metal, rattled her teeth. She gripped the armrests, frozen in terror.

"They've breached the hull!" The pilot's voice rang with alarm.

He reached under his seat for his sidearm and unbuckled his safety harness, his copilot doing the same. When the aft compartment door slid open, they fired at the incoming enemy, but to no avail. Armor protected tall bodies, helmets covered heads and faces.

When the first figure raised his weapon, Caeli screamed again. Time slowed. She watched each action occur as if it were a single event. The insurgent's gun fired. A hole appeared in Riggs's chest. Blood sprayed the control console behind him. His body fell heavily backward. One more shot. The copilot's body spun around. Crashed against the panel. Slid to the floor. Blood pooled around him, crimson against steel gray.

Caeli's throat was raw from screaming. Her chest heaved and

*she squeezed her eyes shut, expecting that the next shot would be for
her. But it never came. Instead, when she opened her eyes, a gloved
hand held a syringe to her neck. The tiny needle punctured her skin.
Numbing warmth spread from her chest to her belly to her limbs. Her
vision blurred, and she tipped into darkness.*

She attributed the pounding in her skull to the side effects
of whatever drug they'd used on her. Her stomach roiled from
the pain, from the recurring vision of Riggs's stunned face as he
tumbled backward in death. He had a family. She'd met them.

Leaning her head against the cold wall, she tried to make
sense of what had happened to the *Carina*. And only one thing
made sense.

When the cell door finally slid open, she wasn't surprised to
see a Drokaran staring down at her, but she was surprised to
see this *particular* Drokaran. A chill rippled up her spine.

Years ago, she'd interrogated this man. She'd searched his
mind for information to stop a deadly terrorist attack and
found what she was looking for. But the experience had left
her shaken and agitated, his mind difficult to penetrate, the
connection, once established, disorienting.

As he stepped into the room, she involuntarily shrank
backward, pressing her body against the wall. Expressionless,
he spoke. "Come with me."

Two more men stood behind him, their postures
nonthreatening, but she wasn't fooled. Daksha Karan, her
Drokaran captor, knew about her abilities.

She pulled herself to her feet, legs shaking, and followed
him out of the cell. Recessed windows near the ceiling let in
sunlight. She was no longer on a ship.

Caeli tried to pay attention to her surroundings, to the path
they took through sterile hallways, in case she might have

to navigate them on her own. She'd escaped from a military prison once before, and although she had no real idea where she was now, she had to do something. She had to act like her attention to detail might prove worthwhile, or else she'd lose hold of her tiny thread of composure and spiral into a panic.

But when Karan led her into the laboratory, when she saw the metal table with wrist and ankle restraints attached, her self-control dissolved anyway. She stumbled into her captor, who grabbed her firmly by the back of the neck and propelled her forward.

"What are you doing?" Fear made her voice catch.

Karan didn't speak. His two guards trained their weapons on her while he maneuvered her onto the table and fastened the restraints. As she pulled uselessly against them, her mind clouded in terror. Caeli's eyes darted around the room, looking for something, anything to help her escape. But even if she could incapacitate Karan, she'd never get past the guards.

When her eyes met Karan's, she desperately tried to push her mind into his. But his consciousness was sealed off to her, and without physical contact, she couldn't breach his mental barrier.

"Please, don't," she begged.

He stepped away from her and spoke to one of the guards. "Tell the team she's secure. They can begin."

The Drokaran stood in front of a workstation. Caeli strained to see what he was doing and to take stock of the room's contents. It looked like a medical laboratory, the equipment familiar and the space neatly organized.

When the door slid open a few minutes later, three people entered. The first, a woman, approached Caeli, pushing an equipment cart to the side of the table. Caeli's heart thudded in her chest, sweat beading at her scalp.

While the woman worked, Caeli followed her every movement. Wordlessly, the Drokaran attached monitors to Caeli's chest and forehead. She took blood samples and DNA swabs, measured heart rate, breathing, and blood pressure. Nothing beyond what might happen at a normal physical examination.

As she worked, the Drokaran woman spoke to her colleagues in a clipped, authoritative voice, and they followed her directions impeccably. Her lithe body moved with economical grace, nothing wasted, neither an errant motion nor an unintentional expression. Thick, dark hair swept into a tight knot at the base of her elegant neck. Piercing brown eyes, several shades darker than her flawless skin, reflected a sharp intelligence.

When finished, she packed away her samples and for a brief moment stood staring over Caeli. Caeli tried to push her mind into the woman's, survival instinct and blinding terror ignoring the voice in her head that recoiled at violating someone else's thoughts. But, as with Karan, she couldn't gain access.

When the woman and her assistants were gone, Karan unfastened the restraints and motioned for Caeli to stand.

"Why are you doing this?"

He stared back at her for so long she thought he wouldn't answer. Finally, he asked, "You don't know?" She heard a note of surprise in his voice, the first glimpse of emotion she'd seen from him.

She shook her head, but dread gnawed at her.

CHAPTER 3

She lay on the cot in her cell after a meal of unidentifiable protein and a jug of water. Her stomach rebelled at the food, but she drank down the water in greedy gulps. Desperate to find some piece of useful information, she pushed her mind out as far as it would go. The pulsing life force of strangers, the tangle of their distant thoughts, hummed back against Caeli's own.

She sat up in surprise. The minds she felt weren't Drokaran. The Drokarans had invaded and now occupied several Alliance worlds. Maybe she was on one of them. She tried to sort through the background noise, to find some clue, but the voices were too distant. With the adrenaline gone from her body, she fell into a fitful sleep.

When Karan came for her again, she stumbled, bleary-eyed, down the same hallway. This time, as soon as she could string a coherent sentence together, she rushed to question him. "Where are we? Can't you at least tell me what planet we're on? Please." This was met by his familiar stony silence.

He and the security detail marched her back to the lab. Despite the relatively benign earlier session in the laboratory, Caeli spiraled into a panic when Karan secured her to the table. Squeezing her eyes shut, she counted her own breaths, fighting against the darkness that hovered at the edge of her consciousness.

The Drokaran woman and her team entered and attached leads to Caeli's temples and chest. Data from her body transmitted to several monitors and processing units cluttering the room. Instead of taking her blood as she'd done the day before, the woman injected Caeli with a vial of clear liquid.

At first, Caeli didn't feel anything other than the negligible sting of the needle penetrating her skin. But slowly, the background noise in her mind disappeared. Her ability to sense others, to hear them, was gone. That part of her mind felt numb and sluggish, and its silence terrified her.

Her eyes darted around the room. The woman checked the monitors and tapped notes on a keyboard, otherwise occupied, but Caeli found Karan staring at her.

"What did you do to me?"

Karan stepped closer to her, but his eyes wandered over to the monitor.

"Please," she begged. The loss of her gift was like being blinded, the silence in her mind a gaping hole. "What's happening?"

Her body trembled and black spots danced in her peripheral vision. Sweat slid down her forehead. She couldn't pull enough air into her lungs. As the seconds stretched to minutes, Caeli retreated into the quiet, dark recesses of her mind.

Finally, distant voices cut into the silence, and once again, the warm flow of life, not from her own body, flooded into Caeli's brain. She choked out a sob of relief.

"Activity is increasing in the right parahippocampal gyrus," the woman said. Karan nodded. "Once it normalizes, proceed with phase two."

At Karan's words, Caeli's relief drained away, an icy chill of dread taking its place.

The next injection worked quickly. Instead of fading to silence, the voices grew in volume and clarity. She couldn't filter them out. The intensity of the noise seared her brain. Her body jerked against the restraints, and she heard herself screaming, begging her captors to make it stop.

Standing nearby, Karan watched. Caeli locked her gaze onto him and, without thinking, pushed her mind against his. This time her consciousness slid through, like wind parting blades of grass. Karan's eyes widened.

Caeli manically scoured his thoughts, tearing through his mind with brutal disregard for the damage she might be doing. She had to make him stop the noise, stop this agony.

Images, places, battles, even the memory of their last meeting, burned a pathway through Caeli's brain as if the thoughts were her own. Karan clutched his head and backed away from her.

"Laina!" he shouted, and the woman approached Caeli, something in her hand.

Caeli turned on her. "No!" she screamed.

The woman staggered back and collapsed to the floor, convulsing. Blood streamed from her nose and ears, a crimson stain pooling around her head.

More bodies filled the room, the chaos of their thoughts flooding Caeli's brain. She squeezed her eyes shut, trying to drown out the roar, but their panic was now her own. She screamed and twisted against the restraints until something covered her nose and mouth and the world went dark.

***

She awoke in the cell. Blinking in the dim light, she tried to focus on the still figure seated next to her. When she lifted her head, stabbing pain shot through her brain. Gasping, she lay motionless.

"I have something for the pain." Caeli recognized Karan's voice. He held a tiny vial out to her. "Squeeze it under your tongue," he instructed.

She complied, and almost immediately the throbbing eased. Karan leaned back in his chair, waiting.

Carefully, Caeli sat up, pulling her knees to her chest and hugging them tightly against her body. Her mind felt normal, with discordant voices whispering at a distance. She could choose to focus on them or let them linger passively in the background.

Her body ached and her head felt cloudy. It felt anything *but* normal. Memories fought to surface. She held them off as long as she could until finally, hanging her head, she said, "I killed her."

Her chest constricted and sweat ran down her back. Bile rose in the back of her throat. She clamped a hand over her mouth and swallowed it back.

"Yes," Karan answered.

"I didn't mean to."

"I know."

Caeli looked at Karan, trying to determine if something in his voice bordered on sympathy. He held his expression blank, and when she searched his face, he looked away.

Just beneath the surface of her own memories, others churned. She knew they were his, the ones she had torn from him in a panic. Now they formed images in her mind, discrete and vivid, but out of context and confusing. The corresponding emotions in most cases were cold, restrained, calculating. But layered under those were others. Pride, loyalty, desperation.

The last time she'd been in his head, she'd managed to pull out pertinent information, and yet she knew he'd managed to hide his deepest emotions from her. Now, she had some of them.

Under normal circumstances, she had a great deal of control over an empathic exchange, but under stress, it could be messy, inexact. When, years ago, she'd healed Derek after he'd crash-landed on her planet, she'd inadvertently stumbled onto some of his powerful memories and in turn had left her own behind. Both of them had been disoriented, knowing they shared intimate details from each other's lives but without really understanding the context. He'd had a brain injury, though, and if she'd hesitated, he'd have died.

Her thoughts lingered on Derek. The ache of missing him was a physical thing, squeezing her chest and leaving her momentarily breathless. He'd know she was still alive. He'd be searching for her. But despite all the resources he could access, all his skill as an officer with the Alliance, he might never find her.

She wanted to go home. Rage, cold and violent and directed at Karan, flared briefly in her mind. In that second, if she could, she'd have killed him to have her life back.

When Karan looked up at her again, he flinched slightly before carefully arranging his features. "You're dangerous."

"So are you," she answered.

"We are two parts of a whole."

Caeli froze.

"What have you learned about your history? About where you came from?" he asked.

She swallowed hard, her thoughts racing.

He didn't wait for her answer. "Drokarans are taught who

we are and where we come from since childhood. We've never lost our history."

"I don't . . ." she began, and then stopped, shaking her head.

"Yes, you do," Karan said. "There was a war on your home world. Not the recent one, but another, a millennium ago."

"It essentially ended our civilization. We lost all the records. We didn't know who we were," she whispered.

"But I think now you do," he said.

"The Novali, the people like me who could do things with our minds, we were an experiment," she replied, staring blankly ahead, remembering.

The resistance had found an underground bunker, a safe hideout to weather the winter. Well-preserved, the bunker had been a laboratory facility from the first civilization on the planet, the original colony. Eager to learn what they could, Caeli and her group had attempted to find any information left behind.

And find it they had, in the form of a huge data library. From log books to lab records, a story emerged of a struggling young colony and an illicit genetic experiment to control the next step in human evolution, all leading to a planet-wide war.

"The Novali were the result of a terrible, unethical human experiment," Caeli repeated.

Karan stayed silent, but he leaned forward, waiting for her to continue.

"The intention was to improve the human mind and body, make us stronger, smarter, healthier. But not everyone exhibited those kinds of changes. Some turned out to be empathic, telepathic."

"The beta group," Karan finished.

Heat flushed Caeli's face. She leaned back against the cold

wall as tears streaked down her cheeks. All the pieces of the puzzle finally clicked into place.

When the war they'd started had nearly decimated Almagest, some Novali had escaped, fled in defeat to find a new home.

But the beta group, the empathic people like Caeli, had been discarded like worthless trash.

"You left us to die," she whispered.

DEREK

CHAPTER 4

The landing fields in Alamath had been expanded and updated to accommodate the growing fleet of spacecraft. Derek waited alone on the edge of the south field for the *Solstice* to arrive, watching the sun set behind green hills. He would have appreciated the stunning display of color on the horizon if he'd been able to do anything but worry.

A cool evening breeze brought with it the smells of spring, new grass, and damp earth. The fragrance triggered vivid memories of recovering at Caeli's hidden camp in the forest after his crash years ago. He closed his eyes and she appeared in his mind, thinner and haunted, but still beautiful. Her face was the first thing he'd seen when he woke up, scared and in pain and very far from home. He could still picture her smile of relief when she knew she'd saved his life.

The image quickly transformed. Now she was screaming in horror as the Drokarans boarded her ship and killed her crew. He clenched his fists at his sides, furious at his inability to do anything, terrified at what might be happening to her.

A few moments later, a dark speck appeared in the amber-streaked sky, growing larger by the second. Derek tracked its smooth descent and watched it gently touch down on the landing field. Eighteen months ago, this same ship had left him here to start his new command, building Almagest's fleet. He'd spent over a decade as an intelligence agent for the Alliance, but his work now presented a completely new kind of venture. He'd tackled it with enthusiasm, the challenge of creating something a stark contrast to his previous job of impersonating criminals and preventing disasters.

At first, he worried that he'd become addicted to the game, that he'd miss the rush of danger, and sometimes he did. But mostly, he felt satisfied and pleasantly exhausted at the end of each day.

Somewhere in the back of his mind, though, as an Alliance soldier, he knew his other job wasn't really finished, not while the Drokarans posed such an imminent threat. Now that threat was at his doorstep. He needed to get back into the fight.

A figure emerged from *Solstice*, one Derek instantly recognized as Kat. *Of course she would come herself.* Derek had met Kat when they'd both first joined the Alliance. A talented pilot and an even more talented field operative, she'd been his pick for his team when he'd been assigned to *Horizon*. Their friendship spanned decades, and their loyalty to one another ran deep.

She started to walk toward him and then broke into a jog, unabashedly throwing her arms around him when she reached him. Derek buried his head in her shoulder, grateful for this one private moment when he didn't have to hold himself together.

"We'll find her," Kat whispered into his ear.

***

Derek had already greeted his crewmates and settled into his quarters. Several of those familiar and welcome faces now surrounded him at the conference table, and he was eager to dive into the briefing.

Captain Donovan sat at the head, with Kat and Drew Chase across from him. At his left side, Derek was surprised to see the agent he'd previously worked with during the attempted rescue of the Novali child from human traffickers.

"Lieutenant Commander Sean Asher is on loan to us for the duration of our mission to find and rescue Dr. Crys," Donovan began. "He's been busy over the last eighteen months and has vital intel."

"Good to see you," Derek said.

"Likewise," replied Sean with a nod.

"I'll let him catch you up, Derek," Donovan said.

Sean cleared his throat. "After we parted ways on Elista, I promised to keep looking for the Novali girl, and that became my official order anyway. Command suspected that trail would lead us to the Drokarans somewhere along the line, so there was potentially even more to be gained in the process. I'll spare you the details, but bottom line, the mercenary who kidnapped the girl was taking her to Mira."

Derek sat back in his chair, his thoughts churning. Mira was an Alliance world that had fallen victim to a massive Drokaran invasion force and remained occupied. It was also Drew Chase's home planet. Derek threw a quick glance in Drew's direction, but the younger man didn't react. Drew nearly always looked unperturbed, keeping his emotions well in check, a necessary skill for an explosives expert.

"Did they make it to Mira?" Derek asked, returning his attention to Sean.

Hesitating for a moment, Sean shook his head. "No. I'd intended to grab the girl on Baishan, but somehow they caught wind of my tail and made it to their ship. I followed them out of the system and fired, just a shot to slow them down. Turns out it was a lucky shot, or a very unlucky one, because it caused a chain reaction and blew the core."

"Damn," Derek said, rubbing his hands over his face.

"Yeah, it was a bad day." Sean stared down at the table, a muscle in his jaw twitching.

"Her name was Nysa," Kat said softly, giving Derek a somber look.

A heaviness weighed on the room. Captain Donovan waited, giving his crew time to process the information. Leaving that girl behind had haunted Derek, and until this moment, he'd held out hope she'd be rescued. Now, he'd have to tell her brother she was dead.

After several heartbeats, Sean spoke again. "I think Mira is where they'll have taken Caeli."

Derek's stare met Sean's, his thoughts racing. If that's where they were taking Nysa, it made sense it was where they'd take Caeli. His rush of excitement over this new piece of information was immediately tempered by the impossibility of reaching her there. "There's been no intel out of Mira since we surrendered the planet a decade ago. The Alliance operatives who stayed behind were never heard from again."

"I know," the agent replied. "But the Alliance has reason to think the Drokaran hold on Mira might be weakening. Maybe they're stretched too thin. Maybe the Mirans are finding a way to harass them from the inside. Whatever the case, I'm supposed to find out."

"Admiral Reyes had Commander Asher rendezvous with

Horizon when we realized that Caeli might be on Mira," Captain Donovan said.

Derek sat back in his chair, putting the pieces of information together in his mind. "How much intel do you have so far?"

Sean shrugged. "Not much yet, but I may have a way of getting onto the planet."

Derek glanced between Kat and Drew. All three of them had been on Mira during the war. All three had witnessed firsthand the brutality of the Drokaran invasion force. And now they'd be sneaking back in behind enemy lines, essentially blind. His gut knotted. But to find Caeli, he'd do it. He'd do anything.

CAELI

CHAPTER 5

"Get up."

The sharp command woke Caeli from a sound sleep. She sat up, heart thudding in her chest, as bright light flooded her cell.

Aside from the guards who brought her meals, Caeli had been left alone. Without any natural light filtering into the isolated chamber, she couldn't be sure how much time had passed. During the solitary hours, she alternated between relief that she wasn't being tortured with the drugs and despair so deep she thought she might never find her way out of it.

Karan's imposing figure in the open doorway sent a coil of dread snaking up her spine. "Move," he ordered.

Standing on shaking legs, she forced herself to follow him. When they passed the medical lab without pause, the trembling in Caeli's body subsided, a portion of her terror transforming to curiosity. They approached a security checkpoint leading out of the building. A guard nodded once at Karan, and he strode out with Caeli on his heels.

A chill breeze lifted the limp curls from her forehead. She took a deep breath, inhaling the faint scent of saltwater that hung in the air. It was nighttime. Spotlights illuminated the exterior of the building and surrounding grounds, but the sky was dark. Stars twinkled overhead in an unfamiliar pattern. Caeli stared up at them, disoriented.

Karan motioned for Caeli to get into a waiting vehicle and then slid in beside her. "Go," he ordered the driver.

The vehicle wove its way onto the multileveled highway system, Caeli's attention riveted out the window. Squinting at the darkness, she tried to gather a glimmer of information about her surroundings, but the vehicle moved too quickly and the outside world sped by in a dark blur.

She glanced at Karan, who wore his familiar stony expression. Now, however, she could feel the tension vibrating just beneath his still exterior. It was like she could tune into him. She held her expression blank as she tried to make sense of it. Making the empathic connection with him while drugged must have given her access to his mind.

"Where are we going?" she asked, careful not to let her consciousness touch his, afraid he would discover this secret.

"My residence," he answered.

Immediately, an image formed in her mind. A dark-haired child playing with a stack of blocks. Intelligent eyes. Fragile body. This was Karan's memory, unintentionally stolen during that one violent moment in the lab. Caeli turned her head away, stunned by the clarity of her vision and the intensity of the emotion attached to it.

Moments later, they came to a stop and Karan rushed out. Caeli followed. Motion-sensing lights flicked on, illuminating the entryway of a single-story house. Karan placed his hand on a flat panel to the right of the door, and it clicked open.

"Marta!" he shouted.

"In here," a softer voice answered.

Caeli trotted after Karan, through the entryway and kitchen area to a living room. The young boy from Caeli's vision was here, lying still on a sofa. An older woman sat on a chair pulled up next to the couch, stroking the boy's head.

"You were supposed to keep him safe!" Karan barked.

The boy's eyes flew open and the woman flinched, but she kept a gentle hand on the child's head and answered with a steady voice. "He is a little boy, Daksha. They fall. You'll scare him if you raise your voice."

Karan turned to Caeli. "Help him," he ordered.

Caeli approached the sofa and knelt down. "Marta?" she asked.

The woman nodded.

"I'm Dr. Caeli Crys. Can you tell me what happened?"

Marta's forehead creased with concern and unspoken curiosity, but she locked eyes with Caeli and answered, "He's only two and a half. He tripped on his own feet. But his bones break easily. Too easily. He fractured his left arm." She turned her attention back to the boy, whose lips were trembling. "His name is Navi."

"All right, let me have a look," Caeli said, peeling back a soft blanket. The boy's left arm was cocooned in a makeshift yet functional splint and held against his chest with a cloth wrapping.

"Navi, my name is Caeli." She placed her hand on the boy's shoulder. With her inner vision, she followed the line of his bones from shoulder to wrist, her mind snagging on fractures and tiny bone fragments. The injury was much worse than it should have been for a simple fall. Caeli could feel that his bones were abnormal, porous and brittle when they should have been elastic and firm.

She could heal the breaks with her mind, but not the underlying disease. She imagined Karan knew this already.

Caeli had been on *Horizon* when she'd first suspected the Drokarans were sick. She'd examined tissue samples from a Drokaran who'd been killed during an Alliance mission. She and the ship's doctor had hypothesized that the Drokarans invaded populated worlds for the resources and territory, but more importantly because they needed people, healthy people, in order to run large-scale drug trials, possibly even to harvest healthy DNA.

"Do you have painkillers for him?" she asked.

"He is brave," Karan answered.

"He is a baby!" Caeli snapped back.

Karan's fear, and his own pain at the child's suffering, hit her like a wave. Softening her tone, she said, "I can help him."

Marta stood. "I have his medicine. This happens."

Caeli watched Marta cross the room, her thick, dark braid laced with silver swinging at her back. She pulled open a set of doors built into the living room wall. Drawers and storage cabinets, filled with neatly organized medical supplies and drugs, opened outward. Marta took something from a shelf and returned.

"Here, Navi. Under your tongue. You know what to do." Marta gently lifted the boy's head. "There we go," she said soothingly as he swallowed the medicine. When he finished, she wiped a stray tear from his cheek and smiled at him.

Seconds later, his big brown eyes glanced fearfully at Caeli before fluttering closed.

"Let's get the splint off," Caeli said, turning to Marta. The other woman held the boy's limp body in a seated position while Caeli unwound the material. Delicately, they removed his shirt.

As Caeli sat back on her heels and placed her hands on the boy, Marta's worried stare made her spine tingle. Karan moved a step closer. Ignoring them both, she closed her eyes, took a deep breath, and began her silent healing.

With her mind, she moved misaligned bones back into place and then coaxed them to knit together. She sealed fragments, like puzzle pieces, and freed nerves constricted by the damage. The boy whimpered once during her ministrations, and Caeli stopped to soothe him with gentle words.

When she was satisfied that she'd repaired everything, she wiped a hand across her sweaty brow and nodded at Karan. Marta helped her replace the splint, and they covered the sleeping boy with the blanket. The older woman glanced at Caeli with barely concealed astonishment.

Gripping the side of the couch, Caeli wearily pulled herself to her feet. Karan took a hesitant step toward her, his eyes moving between her and Navi. He didn't try to hide his angst.

"The arm is mending nicely. There won't be any permanent damage from this break, but . . ." She let the thought hang between them.

Ignoring the unasked question, he nodded and walked into the next room. The door thudded closed behind him.

Caeli blinked at his abrupt disappearance and then swayed on her feet. Healing depleted her energy. While Navi's injuries weren't anywhere close to others she'd tackled, this exertion on top of the stress of the last several days had her dangerously close to passing out.

Marta put a comforting arm around Caeli's shoulder and led her to the table. Caeli sank into the chair and rubbed her temples. A headache threatened, and she longed to close her eyes.

"Here," Marta said. She handed Caeli a cup of water and sat down across from her.

Holding the cup with shaking hands, Caeli sipped. "Where am I?" she asked, whispering.

"I believe this was the home of a former town councilor. After the war, the Drokarans confiscated property and moved their own leadership into place," Marta answered with an equally soft voice, glancing at the room into which Karan had just disappeared.

She took in that piece of information. This *was* an occupied world. Likely a former Alliance world. "Which planet?" she asked.

"Mira."

"Mira," Caeli repeated. She knew little about the planet, only that it had experienced some sort of civil unrest and had caught the attention of the Drokarans. They'd invaded and remained the occupying force, cutting the planet off from the Alliance. "You're Miran, not Drokaran."

Marta nodded. "My own children left with their families years before the invasion, when the first drought decimated much of this continent's food supply. They migrated back to Erithos. I understood. I probably would have done the same years ago when they were young. But I'm a teacher, and many of my students' families didn't have the means to leave. I couldn't abandon them. I thought we would weather the upheavals, find solutions. No one anticipated the Drokarans," she said.

Caeli leaned forward, intent on learning everything she could. "How did you end up here, taking care of Navi?"

"After the war, while the Drokarans were restructuring our government and installing their own people, Karan found me. He'd heard I'd been a teacher and requested I care for his young son." She paused and gave Caeli a small smile. "*Request* is probably the wrong word. But that little boy is innocent. And he's sick. So, I do my best for him."

Finished speaking, Marta lapsed into silence.

Caeli felt the woman's curiosity and met her expectant gaze. "I'm from a planet called Almagest. Some of my people are empaths and telepaths. We can do things with our minds, like heal. We're recovering from our own civil war, rebuilding. I was on my way to Cor Leon to formalize our membership in the Alliance when Karan's crew attacked my ship and brought me here."

"He must have had a reason for targeting you specifically."

Caeli nodded. "I've encountered him before. I questioned him using my gift. It's not something I would ever do lightly, but the Drokarans had planned an attack on another world, and I had an opportunity to help stop them. We successfully prevented the attack, but Karan escaped."

She nearly told Marta the truth about her people and the Drokarans, how they were all from the same colony, the same heritage, but she couldn't bring herself to say the words out loud. She stopped speaking and stared down at her lap, her eyes suddenly so heavy she could barely keep them open.

"You should rest," Marta said. Grateful, Caeli followed her into a bedroom and collapsed onto the plush bedding.

***

For the first time since her ship had been attacked, Caeli awoke feeling rested. Stretching, she appreciated the comfortable bed, a stark contrast to the stiff cot in her cell. She had no idea how long she'd been asleep, but the muffled sounds of the household outside her closed door told her it was daytime.

Her clothing stuck to her body, sweaty from sleep and sour-smelling from days of stress. But hunger gnawed at her belly, and the more pleasant aromas of cooking food drew her into the kitchen.

She found Marta seated at the table next to Navi. The little boy spooned hot cereal from a bowl, spilling as much on the table as he shoveled into his mouth. Caeli couldn't help but smile when he gave up on the utensil entirely and began licking his fingers.

Marta noticed Caeli and gestured for her to sit. "You must be starving," she said, moving about the kitchen to prepare another breakfast.

"It smells wonderful," Caeli answered.

"Navi's arm seems to be well healed. He's favoring it a little, but he tugged off the splint," Marta observed, handing Caeli a steaming bowl.

"That's a good sign." Carefully, she took a bite of her steaming breakfast.

"It's amazing," Marta said quietly.

"Where's Karan?" Caeli asked between bites.

"He's left for the day. He wanted you here in case Navi needs anything."

Caeli's spoon stopped halfway to her mouth. "He left us here alone?"

Marta gave a short laugh. "No. This house is a well-guarded fortress. I believe Karan is a rather high-ranking Drokaran officer."

Caeli silently continued eating. A windowless cell in the middle of a Drokaran command center felt like a fortress. This house, no matter how well guarded, didn't.

DEREK

CHAPTER 6

It had taken too long and cost too much to arrange this meeting. Derek sat tapping a thumb against his thigh, sweating. The loud, pulsing music irritated him, but the crowd of gyrating bodies on the dance floor and the dim overhead lighting made this particular club an ideal place to conduct illicit business in plain sight.

He spotted Drew and Kat on the dance floor, their bodies pressed together, attention seemingly riveted on one another. He knew better. Neither would miss a thing. And nearby, although Derek couldn't see him, Sean Asher prowled through the crowd, keeping an eye on the exits.

As he sipped his drink and waited, Derek unobtrusively scanned the room for his contact. He hadn't met her yet, but the deep-cover Alliance operative who'd set up the meeting had assured him she'd be here.

Although it had been almost two years since Derek's last mission on Baishan, it felt like yesterday. The sweltering heat, the congested bars filled with questionable characters conducting questionable business, the undertone of violence everywhere, all made it one of his least favorite places. But it was also a hub of scientific research for those who liked to work on cutting-edge, often morally ambiguous projects and were willing to sell their discoveries to the highest bidder. The Alliance had brokered deals here before, indirectly, of course, and would undoubtedly do so again.

A woman approached the bar, sat at a high stool, and ordered a drink. From his table, Derek had a clear view, so he watched her for a few moments before standing. High, angular cheekbones, short, dark hair, lithe, athletic body. Confident, almost arrogant mannerisms as she dealt with the bartender.

Eventually, he made his way over and leaned in next to her. "Join me at my table," he said, more order than invitation.

She turned to him and raised a perfectly sculpted eyebrow.

Grinning, he added, "Please."

She looked him up and down appraisingly and tilted her head. "Maybe I will." Grabbing her drink, she followed.

When they were both seated, he addressed her by name and title. "Dr. Irina Tate. I think we might be able to conduct some business." He swirled the liquid in his glass and waited for her to answer.

"You don't waste any time, do you?" she said. He thought he heard a note of disappointment in her voice.

"Unfortunately, I'm on a tight schedule this trip."

She gave a slight nod. "Nico says you want in on the Mira trade deals?"

"I do. I understand the occupying force is paying a premium for your cocktail specifically."

Her lips turned up in a smile. "My drugs have been the most effective at suppressing symptoms and slowing an array of degenerative diseases." After a long swallow of her drink, she added, "But I already have a distributor."

"Would you consider siphoning off some of your product for a one-time deal? If the price was right?" he asked.

She looked at him, puzzled, but knew better than to question his motives. "How much?"

"I'll pay triple the cost for one shipment. And the offer's firm. I don't have time to negotiate."

Raising her eyebrows, she said, "My distributor isn't going to like this."

But when she didn't outright refuse, Derek knew she was going to take the deal. "Tell him the batch got corrupted and you're making more. He'll never know. I'm discreet," he said, shrugging and tossing back the last of his own drink.

"And mysterious," she replied, looking him up and down.

He grinned. "Not mysterious. Just opportunistic. Where should I meet you to take delivery?"

She paused for a fraction of a second, and then gave him the information.

***

Derek stared at the control panel, Kat next to him in the pilot's seat. From the aft quarters, his crew chatted, their voices humming in the background. All of it was comfortingly familiar. He needed that now.

He was used to working under stress, with a ticking clock and lives hanging in the balance. He'd done it for years as an Alliance operative. He'd even done it with Caeli by his side, first when she'd helped his team on Tharsis, and later when his mission became saving her world. He'd worried then that neither of them would live to see their future, but they'd been facing those fights together. Not knowing where she was or what was happening to her was something else entirely.

Dread filled his dreams, accosted him when he woke up, and gnawed at his thoughts during every waking moment. His solution was to keep moving, keep busy, but the dull hours of space travel now made that impossible. Despite his worry over Caeli, he knew he had to keep his head in the game, or he risked getting someone else killed.

As if reading his thoughts, Kat said, "We've got your back."

Squeezing his eyes shut and rubbing a hand over his face, he replied, "It's the only thing keeping me going right now." He'd never admit that to the other members of his team, but Kat knew him almost as well as he knew himself. "How's Drew about going back to Mira?" he asked, partly to distract himself, partly out of genuine concern.

"I think he's dying to get back there. You know him, though. He won't say much."

Derek knew Drew had been born on Mira, had spent his childhood there, and had left with his family as a young teenager. The Drokaran invasion had happened a few years later, after Drew had joined the Alliance. Although the *Horizon* team had been part of the battle for Mira, the bloody, decisive fight had ended almost as quickly as it began. The loss of Mira had dealt a devastating blow to the Alliance, and to Drew, who still considered the planet his home.

"I wonder what we're going to find down there," Kat said, throwing Derek a worried glance.

He didn't have a good answer.

When they entered the Miran system an hour later, what they did find was a planet-wide defensive shield array. "I can't see anything, but the ship knows it's there," Kat said.

"Okay, open all communication channels and let's sit and listen. See if we can't figure out the protocol," Derek ordered.

There was a good bit of chatter from ships coming and going. When he'd heard enough, Derek initiated contact. "Mira control, this is the *Kairos* requesting permission to land. We have our cargo manifest and identification code ready to transmit."

"Stand by, *Kairos*," a voice answered immediately.

Derek's heart raced. Kat sat still beside him, jaw clenched and forehead furrowed.

"*Kairos*, transmit manifest and code."

Derek sent the information and held his breath.

In seconds, the disembodied voice replied, "*Kairos*, you are cleared to land. Queue at these coordinates and wait for the next cycle."

Kat leaned back in her chair and closed her eyes. "We are actually going to land on Mira."

"Looks like," Derek answered, the tightness in his chest loosening a few degrees.

Kat flew *Kairos* into the queue and waited. When the sensor indicated shielding had dropped, she followed the other ships into the planet's upper atmosphere. Immediately, another set of coordinates appeared on her display console, along with a message. "All ships, do not deviate from this course or you will be fired upon."

"Friendly," she mumbled.

"How many Drokaran patrol ships do you see?" Derek asked.

She pointed at a blip on her display screen. "Looks like only the one. The others are all trade vessels and mercenary ships. No Drokaran battlecruisers in the region either."

"Good to know."

"They don't need much with that defense network in place, though. Theoretically, no one's coming in who shouldn't be."

"Just us," Derek muttered under his breath.

CAELI

CHAPTER 7

"Why didn't you bring Navi to the hospital?" Caeli asked.

Two days had passed since Karan had dragged her from her cell to his home. When they finally returned to the lab, Caeli was clean, well-fed, and clear-headed. Even locked in the spacious facility with armed guards outside the door, she felt less threatened, less vulnerable than when she'd been held alone in her cell. Karan needed her, at least for now.

"Sick children are admitted into a research program," Karan replied, avoiding her gaze. "They're kept institutionalized and receive experimental treatments. Many die. Navi will likely die with or without treatment, but I'd rather he do so at home." Karan tapped at a screen, new data scrolling up. "This is your genome, completely sequenced, and this is mine," he continued, as if she'd never asked the question at all.

Caeli could feel his emotions churning beneath his hard, expressionless features, but she didn't let on as she looked over his shoulder at the screen.

"Here," he pointed. "This marker is present in both our DNA, but in mine, it's corrupted."

Moving next to him and sitting in a chair, she leaned in to

view the sequences. "Look. There's another," she said.

Within moments, the analytic program identified three more key nucleotides that were corrupted in Karan's DNA but not Caeli's. Caeli manipulated the touch screen so three-dimensional images of the biomolecules rotated on the screen. "These corrupted nucleotides may be causing the genetic diseases afflicting the population," she said, her professional curiosity piqued.

"They are. Our scientists have identified the problem. But, thus far, they have not found a permanent solution."

Caeli's eyes darted between Karan's hard features and the spinning models in front of her, between his corrupted DNA and her healthy DNA. She heard his thought just as her own mind churned over a similar hypothesis. Her body might hold the key to a cure for the Drokarans.

"You will keep my son alive. When you are not with him, you will be here. If you don't wish to be the subject of my research, you will do your own."

When he left, the metal door slammed, locking her in.

Karan needed her, she repeated to herself.

Alone in the silence, Caeli scanned the room. She stood and wandered from one corner to another, assessing the equipment, opening cabinets and drawers. At the far end of the room, metal sliding doors led to a climate-controlled room filled with cold storage units. She pulled one open to find tissue samples and tiny vials of blood, coded and arranged in some kind of sequential pattern.

Karan may have given her unfettered access to all the science, but she had no idea what research had already been done, what percentage of the population was impacted by disease, or what current treatments were already in place. She sat back down in front of the screen and began sifting through files.

Hours later, her vision swam and her head ached from squinting at figures and formulas. From the information she'd seen so far, she concluded that the impact of the mutations amplified in each successive generation. Drokaran children born now faced over a fifty percent chance of carrying the defective genes, and the carriers had a devastating ninety percent fatality rate before they reached adulthood.

Maybe they'll just die out. The thought should have horrified her, and yet at first, it didn't. If no cure were found, Almagest would be safe. The Alliance would be safe. Entire worlds would be free from the looming shadow of a Drokaran invasion fleet. She could go home.

Then she pictured Navi's sweet face, the fractures in his tiny bones, the tears slipping down his cheeks, and squeezed her eyes shut. She couldn't let that baby die if there was any way to help save him. Swiping at the tears that slid down her own cheeks, she opened another file.

***

For the next several days, Caeli worked. The Drokarans kept an enormous database of sequenced DNA from their own population. From it, she definitively traced most of the genetic diseases to the malformed nucleotides carried by the afflicted.

She studied the different types of drugs the Drokarans had already tested and familiarized herself with others that were still in the trial phase. As she scanned through the mind-numbing series of catalogues and lists, a compound name caught her attention: Parahippocampal Stimulus-A #220.

This had to be one of the drugs they'd been testing on her. Laina, the scientist she'd accidentally killed, had referenced this region of her brain during the experiment. Caeli's fingers darted over the keyboard, eyes flowing over the trail of data. Vital signs, dosage amounts, and medical notes, clearly unfinished, filled the screen. The patient, referred to as Beta-1, had to be her.

Sweat prickled her forehead as she relived the horror of those moments, the onslaught of unfiltered emotions slamming into her brain, the amplified rage spewing from her own mind into another person's body. She'd killed a woman. Not an innocent woman, and not on purpose, but she'd still done it. Her stomach roiled, her breakfast threatening to reappear.

She rested her head on the cold desktop, the edges of her vision tunneling to blackness. After the Amathi had invaded her home and massacred most of her people, Caeli had struggled with panic attacks for years. She recognized the symptoms. Forcing herself to take long, deep breaths and count her own heartbeats, her mind finally quieted.

When she could sit up again, her shirt stuck to her body with sweat and she shivered in the temperate room, but she brushed a damp curl off her face and turned her attention back to the report on the screen. Her thoughts circled as she tried to imagine why Karan would be testing this kind of drug on her. If he thought their shared ancestry held a cure for the disease afflicting his people, why had he experimented with numbing and then amplifying her empathic and telepathic abilities?

Her stomach lurched again when she thought about Marcus, the fallen dictator on Almagest, selling gifted Novali children on the black market. Derek and his team believed those children would be used as weapons. They could steal secrets from the minds of military and government officials, be trained as assassins, or any number of other unthinkable things.

If the Drokarans thought using her gifted people might help

win their war with the Alliance, Caeli had no doubt they'd do it. If Karan thought he could use *her*, she knew he wouldn't hesitate.

As she sat in stunned silence, an idea began to take shape. Her hands shook, and she felt ill when she considered it, but her resolve strengthened. She had to escape, whatever it took.

DEREK

CHAPTER 8

Once they'd landed and been assigned a dock space, Derek and Kat exited the ship, leaving the rest of the crew behind temporarily. A kiosk directly outside his bay prompted Derek to log in his ship's identification and swipe the keycode from his cargo manifest.

The port bustled and buzzed like any trading post. Around them, conveyors and carts ferried cargo toward a central facility, and crews from a myriad of worlds accompanied their goods. The atmosphere was one of calm efficiency. Only the armed guards, in full combat gear prowling around the loading docks, gave Derek pause, hinting that this particular trading post might be filled with less-than-scrupulous characters.

"Let's do this," he said to Kat.

Their cases were light and easily slid onto the cart. Once loaded, Derek and Kat followed the rest of the crowd into the expansive main warehouse. They found an open receiving gate easily and approached the agent.

"He's Miran," Kat whispered to Derek, who nodded his agreement.

"Ship identifier and manifest, please," the gate agent requested. Worry lines creased his brow, and bluish circles rimmed his eyes. He looked overworked and underfed, his shirt hanging from his bony shoulders.

Derek gave him his tablet to scan.

"Please confirm your ship is designated the *Kairos*," the agent asked perfunctorily.

"It is," Derek answered.

"I am taking delivery of therapeutic pharmaceuticals. They will be inspected and catalogued by the ranking medical official. When it is confirmed that this merchandise matches the cargo manifest you've submitted, an automatic deposit will be made to the account you've indicated here. Once payment has been rendered, you will have twenty-four hours to depart Drokar Protectorate airspace. Otherwise, your ship will be confiscated. I need confirmation that you understand these terms." The instructions were delivered in a monotone while the Miran scanned the containers, entering data into a tablet.

"Twenty-four hours and your ship will be confiscated. How very *Drokaran*," Kat mumbled under her breath.

Clearing his throat, Derek agreed to the terms. "Where can my crew rent rooms and get some food?" he asked.

The agent squinted up at Derek. "First time here?"

"First time in a long time," he said, holding the Miran's eyes. "Any help would be appreciated."

The man gave a small, knowing nod. "You're in the Arad district. You'll find lodging on the south side. Take the underground to Cluj and get off there."

"Thanks," Derek said, giving the agent a quick wave.

He and Kat walked back toward the ship, surveying the

controlled chaos around them. "Let's get the team and head out," he said.

***

"I don't know how long before the payment's transferred, but we've got a tight timeline to gather intel," Derek said. His team sat around a table in a quiet corner of a small tavern, eating and planning.

They'd had an uneventful ride on the underground from the docking port to the Cluj district and easily found lodging in a newly reconstructed building. Derek had surreptitiously watched Drew during the brief walk from the underground. If the younger man was feeling anything about being back on his war-torn home world, he was hiding it well.

"There's a few hours of daylight left," he continued, "so let's split up. Talk to the locals. See if we can learn anything useful." He turned to Drew. "I know this isn't where you grew up, but have you ever been to Arad before?"

Drew nodded. "Arad was a commercial center, and the neighboring areas supported visitors and tourism. It's probably why the Drokarans chose to make it the trade port. The infrastructure was already in place. What they didn't destroy, they could repurpose and rebuild. I'll see if anything I remember is still standing. Or anyone," he added, staring down at his plate.

"Take Kat with you. Sean, you're with me. Alaric, stay with Kade. Make sure you're all back here by curfew," Derek said.

He paid the tab and left the tavern with Sean at his heels. In the afternoon sunshine, the tight row of buildings cast long shadows onto the street. This region of Mira was temperate nearly all year long, and Derek only needed a light jacket to feel comfortable.

As they wandered the neighborhood, crumbling structures stood as stark reminders of the war that had altered this planet's destiny. Construction projects, scattered about in various phases of completion, would eventually erase the physical damage, but the damage to the human psyche would take longer. There was a palpable tension in the air that Derek could feel but not quantify.

"Not many Drokarans around," Sean observed.

"Almost feels like business as usual, but not quite," replied Derek.

"I guess a hostile occupation force will keep a damper on things."

At the end of the block, a large outdoor park met the edge of a riverbank. Across the river, the residential feel of the neighborhood gave way to industrial sprawl. Even from this side of the river, Derek recognized a Drokaran military base tucked among the factories and access roads.

"There they are. At least some of them," Derek said, leaning against the railing at the river's edge.

Shielding his eyes from sun glare, Sean nodded. "I'd like to get a closer look at that."

Derek was about to answer when one of the hangars on the opposite side of the riverbank erupted into flame.

The explosion shook the ground beneath them and sent a plume of black smoke billowing into the sky. "Shit," Derek said, instinctively raising his hands to shield his head.

"I think that was a bomb," Sean said, eyes narrowing as he watched the smoke rise.

People ran from the park to the edge of the river, crowding

the rails next to Derek and Sean. Alarms blared from the base, and within moments three small aerial craft lifted off and circled the area from above.

"Surveillance," Derek said, watching them.

A young mother peeled a squirming child off the fence. "You'll fall into the water," she scolded, trying to juggle another toddler on her hip.

The young boy climbed again, this time looping a leg over the top rail. Derek caught him by the scruff of his collar just before he careened over the side. On solid ground again, the boy grabbed onto his mother's leg and looked wide-eyed at Derek.

"Thank you," the mother said, sighing and shaking her head.

"No problem," Derek answered. "I have nephews." He turned back to the activity across the water and asked, "This kind of thing happen a lot?"

The woman gave him a sideways glance. "Not from here?"

He gave a noncommittal shrug.

"It's happening regularly now," she answered. "I suppose this could be an accident, but it's probably the MLA. We'd better get off the streets. The Draks will be out in force. Thank you again," she added as she walked away, shifting the baby to the other hip and pulling her son along behind her.

Sean looked at Derek and raised his eyebrows. "Interesting."

"Very," Derek agreed. They stood watching for another few minutes. As the crowd cleared away from the bridge, so did they. Shadowing a small group of locals, they headed away from the park, down an alley, and into a bar.

Dive bars were pretty much the same on any planet, Derek thought as the sour smell of spilled booze and sweaty bodies assaulted him. The place buzzed. He and Sean found empty seats at the end of the counter, where they could see and hear a good bit of the surrounding conversation.

They ordered drinks. A few seats down, a quiet argument became loud enough for Derek to take notice.

"That was a joint base. The bomb probably killed as many Mirans as Draks," the man closest to Derek said, shaking his head and taking a long swig from his cup.

"Good. Fuck those collaborators. The MLA's taking a stand," a younger, angrier voice argued.

This man raised his glass, receiving cheers all around, except from the person who'd spoken first. He put his head down and kept drinking. "They're only going to make it worse for everyone else," he muttered under his breath so that Derek could barely make out his words.

Before the energy in the room turned violent, the bartender banged a bottle on the counter. "Shut up or get out!" she yelled over the noise.

Her sharp reprimand quieted the crowd. Most patrons went back to their private conversations, and Derek motioned for a refill. When the bartender leaned over to pour, he asked quietly, "What's the MLA?"

Narrowing her eyes at him, the woman stopped pouring midway. "This place is for locals only."

Derek held his hands up in a position of surrender. "Sorry. We're just trying to get off the streets and stay out of the way."

Behind them, on the screens hung over the bar, a message from the Drokaran authorities played repeatedly, advising citizens to comply with Drokaran interrogators and come forward with any useful information on the destructive incident that had killed both Miran citizens and Drokaran troops.

The bartender's expression didn't soften, but she topped off his drink and left him alone. In that moment, Derek wished he had Caeli's empathic skill. Even without invading this woman's mind, Caeli would still have been able to get a clear read on her.

Once he started thinking about Caeli, the ache of missing her slammed into his gut. He stared down at his glass, swirling the amber liquid.

Sean's quiet voice spoke. "You okay?"

Derek opened his mouth to answer, then clamped it shut again. He wasn't okay and he knew it. But he had to keep his shit together.

"She could be here somewhere," he said, still staring into his drink.

CAELI

CHAPTER 9

Caeli had filled the vial with only a quarter of the dose Laina had previously injected her with. Still, she hesitated as she held the pneumatic syringe against her carotid. Taking a deep breath, she depressed the plunger. A quick, hot sting followed, then a warm tingle as the drug spread through her body.

Slowly, like the volume of a radio being dialed up, the noise in her mind increased. She focused her attention on the area immediately surrounding the lab. The inner thoughts of Drokaran security personnel, researchers, and staff tickled in the background. Sifting through them, she focused on one Drokaran, just to see if she could.

The clarity of his thought was like a voice speaking in her ear. Quickly, she let go of the connection, sat in her chair, and opened a file. A spinning model of a damaged chromosome materialized on the workspace in front of her.

Two guards stood posted outside the door. Their thoughts rang through Caeli's brain, her head pounding. Focusing her attention, she visualized an explosion here in the lab and then flung the image from her mind to theirs.

Within seconds, they burst through the door. Caeli jumped

out of her chair, feigning surprise but not fear.

"What's wrong?" she asked, her eyes on their drawn weapons.

The first guard scanned the room. "Was there an accident?"

"In here? No. I'm working on the molecular modeling for nucleotide sequence 234A . . ."

He interrupted her. "It sounded like an explosion."

"No, of course not. There aren't any flammable materials around. At least, I don't think there are," she added.

His cold stare froze her in place. "There was an explosion," he said, taking a step toward her.

"No," she protested.

She could feel his growing suspicion. He knew what he'd heard, and he knew his companion had heard it too.

"There's nothing here. Maybe it came from somewhere else," Caeli whispered directly into his mind. Her thoughts brushed against his so gently that he believed the idea to be his own.

His expression softened and he looked around the room again. "I don't see anything," he said to the other guard. Then he turned to Caeli. "Let me know if you have a problem."

"I will. Thank you," she said as they left her to her work.

A quarter dose of the neurostimulant seemed to be the sweet spot for efficacy without loss of control. Caeli didn't dare record the results of her personal experiments, but she committed everything to memory.

Sinking back into the chair, she rubbed her temples. Excess noise still hummed in her brain, grating against her already frayed nerves, but she could tolerate it.

***

When Karan came for her that night, two armed guards followed him into the room. Caeli stood wide-eyed as he strode toward her.

"There was an incident today."

Shaking her head, she backed away from him. "An alarm went off, but it wasn't in here. The guards came to check. Everything was fine."

He stood in absolute stillness, his eyes boring into hers. She resisted the urge to nudge his thoughts with hers and force him to believe her words, afraid he might sense even the smallest encroachment into his mind.

"Bring her," he ordered. The guards trained their weapons on her and motioned for her to move.

Her mouth went dry when they stopped at the entrance to the medical lab.

"No. Please, no." She staggered backward, only to feel a gun pressed between her shoulder blades.

When the door slid open, the guards shoved her through. Karan gripped her by the throat and pushed her onto the metal table. One of the guards secured her wrists and ankles.

Without a word, they left. When the door slid closed and locked, the room plunged into absolute darkness.

Caeli didn't know if she screamed out loud or only in her mind, if her eyes were open or closed, if she was in the throes of a nightmare or wide awake.

Eventually, her bladder let go. The warm wetness turned cold, and then dried. Her stomach ached with hunger. Her lips dried and cracked, and her tongue stuck to the roof of her mouth.

She dreamed of Derek, of his crash. Instead of pulling him from the wreckage and saving him, she found herself trapped on the other side of a river. When she tried to cross, the current dragged her farther and farther away from him.

When the door to the lab finally opened again, the light blinded Caeli. Rough hands loosened her restraints and pulled her from the table. Her legs collapsed, and someone gripped her under the armpits, hauling her to her feet. She blinked. It was Karan, dragging her from the room out to his waiting vehicle.

Once inside, she leaned against the side door, letting her head rest on the cool metal as they sped away from the facility. When they arrived at Karan's home, he led her inside. She swayed as the world spun around her.

When Marta caught sight of Caeli hovering in the doorway, she rushed to her side.

"Caeli? Are you all right?"

Caeli didn't answer, but she allowed Marta to help her inside, leaning on the older woman so she wouldn't stumble.

Karan left without speaking to either of them.

"Come with me," Marta said, leading Caeli to the bathroom. The other woman ran a bath and helped Caeli strip off her soiled clothes. "What can I do?" she asked.

Caeli eased her aching body into the warm water, her bottom lip trembling. "Water. Please."

Marta nodded. She returned moments later with a cup.

Caeli's entire body shook. She had to hold the cup with both hands to keep it from dropping into the bath. Marta knelt on the floor and smoothed Caeli's hair back from her forehead.

"Marta," she said, choking back a sob, "I have to find a way out of here. I have to go home." She knew her voice sounded pleading, desperate.

"He hurt you."

The older woman's eyes locked onto Caeli's wrists, rubbed

raw and bruised from trying to escape her restraints. Caeli's chest heaved.

"I want to help," Marta whispered.

For the rest of the day, Marta took care of Caeli. She tucked her onto the couch under layers of blankets and fed her bowls of soup and warm tea. Caeli dozed while Navi played quietly on the floor nearby.

Karan didn't appear until the next morning, when he collected Caeli and brought her back to the research lab. For the next several days, two armed guards remained inside with her, watching her every move.

***

"If you can get away, I might know someone who could hide you," Marta whispered, leaning over the table as she and Caeli shared breakfast. Karan had gone, leaving them alone in the house to watch over Navi. Caeli had spent the previous night repairing another of the little boy's broken bones.

Caeli stilled and held Marta's gaze. "Who?"

"There's a former student of mine named Luka who had some difficulties as a boy. I advocated on his behalf for many years, and he grew into a very decent young man. He survived the war and took it upon himself to check in on me afterward. I still maintain contact with him. I think he would help you if I asked him to."

"Will that put you in danger?" Caeli asked, her forehead furrowed. She held her steaming mug of tea in her hands and blew on the contents.

Marta shook her head. "I don't think so. I see Luka when I go shopping in town with Navi. The guards are with us, but they don't pay close attention to me after all this time. Let me speak to him."

"Thank you," Caeli said, covering the other woman's hand with her own.

The next day, as she prepared to leave the lab for the evening, Caeli tidied her workspace. The guards had become used to her routine. While she replaced tissue cultures and slides into the cold storage unit, they stood waiting by the exit door.

Out of their line of sight, Caeli carefully slipped three vials of neurostimulant into her pocket.

***

A few days later, over another cup of tea, Marta told Caeli that she'd contacted Luka. "If you can get to him, he will help you," Marta said.

Caeli blinked, her pulse suddenly racing. "How do I find him?"

"Get to the underground system before curfew, stop at Solivat. Head toward the center of town, where you'll see a large obelisk tower. It was built when this colony was founded. Somehow, it's still standing. Luka will wait there every night for the next week, half an hour before curfew. Will you be able to get away by then?"

Caeli's heart pounded in her chest. The idea of running terrified her, but she had to escape. If there were someone willing to help her, she had to at least try. She took slow, steady breaths until she could speak again. "Yes."

"I've told him what you look like, so he will approach you by name."

"Will you be okay?"

Marta placed a reassuring hand on her shoulder. "Don't worry about me."

That night Caeli lay awake, staring up at the ceiling. Alone in the dark, she allowed herself to think about Derek, to imagine him beside her, to feel his breath on her cheek while he slept.

***

Marta and Caeli didn't speak about escape, curfews, or clandestine meetings again, but on a night when Karan left the house after dropping her off, Caeli waited until Marta went to bed. She stuffed the few articles of clothing Marta had procured for her into a backpack, carefully wrapping the extra drug vials in a shirt before tucking them inside.

Sitting on the edge of the bed, she rolled one vial back and forth in her sweating palm. Her stomach churned. Around her, the house was silent. Finally, she injected herself with a quarter dose of the stinging liquid.

When she felt it rush through her body, she stood and tiptoed through the dark house to the rear door. The security panel blinked a muted red, indicating it was armed. Her biometrics wouldn't disable it, and she didn't know the override code.

Reaching out with her mind, she located the nearest security guard. She imagined a crashing sound and directed the noise into his brain. Within seconds, the security panel chirped quietly and flashed green. The door swung open, and Caeli found herself face to face with a Drokaran soldier in full tactical gear.

Before he could utter a word, she used her mind to compress the vessels leading to his brain, choking off the blood flow. He grabbed at his throat and promptly passed out, collapsing in a heap on the ground. Caeli hurried to him and dragged his heavy body out the door by his feet, the door clicking closed behind them.

She could hear others approaching, feel the hum of their minds vibrating against hers. Stepping over the body, she released her mental grip on his carotid and ran through the yard. With the enhanced strength of her gift, she hid herself from the soldiers who were fast approaching their fallen companion, imagining herself as only a wisp of darkness in the already murky night. They passed her, and she slipped unnoticed into the street.

Marta had given her detailed instructions on how to get to the nearest subway entrance. Mira's infrastructure included a vast network of underground tunnels. Before the war, they'd been used mostly for cargo transport, but when huge chunks of the above-ground, multi-leveled highway system had been damaged during the invasion, the trains became the primary form of transportation for the majority of the population. The Drokarans, according to Marta, repaired the highway routes that served their needs, prohibiting most other traffic. The civilian population used the subway.

A brisk night breeze sent a chill up Caeli's spine. Her feet falling lightly on the empty streets, she ran until her chest ached and her lungs heaved.

She skidded to a stop when she came upon the entryway for the underground. Turning the corner, she pressed herself up against the building, away from the mass of people still coming and going before curfew, and tucked her blonde curls under a light hat. Shifting the backpack to her other shoulder, she released the shadow image held in her mind and stepped into the crowd.

DEREK

CHAPTER 10

"I just received the confirmation code. We've got to get our ship off this planet in twenty-four hours," Derek said.

The team sat crammed into the small rented quarters an hour after curfew. Everyone had returned before the Drokaran aerial drones began their nightly patrol of the streets.

"We can't leave," Drew said.

"No, we can't," Derek agreed. "Alaric and Kade, you're going to take the *Kairos* off-planet and rendezvous with *Horizon*. Sean, Kat, and I will stay. We'll make contact when we find Caeli."

"Got it," Alaric said.

"What's our plan?" Drew asked.

Glancing at Sean, Derek said, "I want to try to track down the MLA."

"They're the ones who blew up the military base, right? The Miran Liberation Army?" Kat asked.

"I think so," Derek answered. "From what I heard, they're aggressively attacking Drokarans every chance they get. They must be collecting intel. If we can hook up with them, maybe they can help us find Caeli."

Kat crossed her arms and nodded. "They must be pretty well

organized at this point to go after a military base."

"At the very least, we know they have explosives. Maybe weapons too," Drew said.

Leaning forward, Derek asked, "Did you make any useful contacts?"

"I may have," Drew replied. "Kat and I went back to the port. *Kairos* is docked at the interplanetary port, but there's a local transit authority that deals with continent-to-continent trade and travel. It isn't as well-regulated as the off-world section. I got the impression there's an underground network that operates outside Drokaran authority."

Derek raised an eyebrow. "They might have access to the MLA."

"They might be *supplying* the MLA," Drew said.

Leaning back in his chair, Derek rubbed his hands over his face. He trusted Drew's gut, and following up with this lead seemed like a solid option. "This is a good start. There's nothing more we can do tonight, and we all need to sleep. Tomorrow we'll get *Kairos* out of here and keep digging."

***

In the stillness of night, Derek stared up at the ceiling, remembering the last time he'd been on Mira. The Drokarans had blockaded the planet with their battlecruisers, and their ground assault had overrun both continents. If the Alliance had continued to fight, the planet's population would have been annihilated.

Derek and his team had spent the final days of the war making last-ditch efforts to evacuate civilians. Their small shuttlecrafts could maneuver between Drokaran patrols and evade detection. Until they couldn't anymore. Eventually, the Drokarans knew where to look for them.

He squeezed his eyes shut, trying and failing to shut out the memories.

***

The next morning, when Alaric and Kade lifted off on the *Kairos*, Derek was apprehensive. He hoped the two wouldn't run into any trouble on their way out of the system. As he looked around at Kat, Sean, and Drew, it hit him fully that they were now trapped on Mira with no leads on Caeli and no real plan to get themselves off-planet.

Derek stared at *Kairos* until the ship disappeared into the clouds.

Kat put a hand on his shoulder. "We've been in worse shit," she said.

"Yeah," Derek agreed.

It was true. Even when a mission started out solid, Derek could always count on something going sideways. Part of what made his team so effective in the field was their ability to adapt, to think on their feet. Still, as far as mission plans went, this one felt pretty thin.

***

It took Drew three days before he was able to arrange for them to meet someone who might be willing to talk to them. "My contact is skittish," he warned the team as they sat around a table in their rented room.

Derek shrugged. "I would be too. You've essentially been

off-world for over a decade, and we're a complete unknown. Mercenaries don't usually hide out on occupied planets. Our cover is thin, and they can sense it."

"How do you want to play this?" Drew asked.

"Let's stick to the story that we're looking for intel on our crewmate who was taken into Drokaran custody," Derek answered. He sat back in his chair and looked around at the small group. "Drew and I will go to the meeting. If they don't believe us and feel threatened, I don't want all four of us jammed up."

He could tell by Kat's scowl that she didn't like being left behind, but she nodded. "Makes sense."

They'd managed to smuggle some communication equipment off the *Kairos* before the ship left port and had hidden it among Derek's personal effects. Crammed into his small quarters, they each placed a tiny device next to their ears. As soon as the thin adhesive stuck to their temples, it changed color, blending seamlessly with their varied skin tones.

"Stay close, but don't compromise yourselves," Derek warned. He and Sean wandered out ahead of Kat and Drew to give them a few moments of privacy.

"If we find them, I'll probably have to tell the MLA the truth about us eventually," he said, mostly thinking out loud, but also wanting Sean's gut reaction to the idea.

"They might not have a very high opinion of the Alliance," replied the other man.

"Can't say I blame them."

Exhaling slowly, Sean said, "Telling them might be our only option, though. If she's here, Caeli would be considered a high-value prisoner, not just some mercenary who got herself into trouble over a transaction gone wrong. They'll probably need that information in order to help us find her."

"I hope they're willing to help," said Derek. "Otherwise, I'm out of ideas."

Drew and Kat emerged from the doorway and joined Derek and Sean on the crumbling sidewalk. Kat shaded her eyes against the bright morning sunlight.

"Good luck. We'll be listening," she said, squinting at Derek and tapping her com.

He and Drew headed toward the subway entrance without looking over their shoulders. When they emerged at the transportation center, Derek followed Drew through the busy market toward the waterfront.

"My contact runs a high-speed ferry service up and down the river. I know he can get us to people higher up in the MLA. We just have to convince him to do it," Drew said.

"And not get caught by the Drokarans," Derek added.

"That too."

They found the man they were looking for in a messy office, piles of schedules and cargo manifests littering his desk. More were pinned to the walls. The remnants of breakfast sat abandoned, pushed to one corner of a table.

When they entered, the man looked up. At first, his face wrinkled with annoyance at being disturbed, but recognition followed, then a sigh of resignation. "I was hoping not to see you again," he said to Drew.

Drew shrugged. "We need help."

"Who's this?" the man asked, jutting his chin at Derek.

"My boss," Drew answered.

"And what happened to your girlfriend?"

Drew shrugged again, noncommittally.

"Sit. My name's Keegan," the man said, addressing Derek

and motioning to a couple of mismatched chairs shoved under the table. "Sorry for the mess. The communication and wireless infrastructure were destroyed during the war. We have to keep track of everything the old way."

Derek and Drew dragged two chairs over and sat. "Simple to keep a separate set of logs. Unhackable records. Easy to forge or destroy," Derek commented, gesturing at the piles.

Keegan lifted an eyebrow.

"I'm Derek. My crew and I just started making deliveries to Mira from the Baishan system. There was a misunderstanding, and one of my people was taken into custody by the Drokarans."

Tapping his fleshy, callused fingers on the desktop, Keegan leaned forward in his chair, his dark eyes boring into Derek's. "Let me be clear, the only reason I am speaking to you at all is that your friend was born here, and he convinced me you aren't Drokaran agents. But I won't put any of our people at risk."

Derek held the older man's gaze for several heartbeats. He could feel Drew tense beside him. "I promise you, we have no love for the Drokarans. We need to find out where they hold prisoners."

Keegan sat back, squinting at Derek. Finally, he nodded. "I can put you in touch with someone."

"Thank you," Derek said.

"Don't thank me. They might just as easily shoot you as listen to you."

CAELI

CHAPTER 11

Caeli didn't make eye contact with anyone. Holding a handrail, she focused on keeping her balance as the train accelerated. The humming thoughts of the other passengers battered against her overactive brain. She felt her pulse quicken in response to someone else's anxiety, her stomach churn with someone else's dread, her limbs weaken with someone else's exhaustion.

It would wear off soon. She'd have control of her own mind. Turning her focus inward, she counted one breath at a time and waited for the train to stop.

Following the rush of bodies out and up, she stepped back into the night. Once the crowd cleared, she turned in a circle, searching her surroundings. There it was, a few blocks in the distance, the towering obelisk, with rotating lights at the top, calling attention to itself. A beacon, or a warning.

She approached the monument and purposefully stretched her mind out. There was someone nearby, a figure in the shadows. "Luka?" Caeli sent the question from her mind to his.

"Caeli?" The figure stepped toward her.

"Yes," she answered, relief flowing through her body like a warm wave.

"Follow me," he said. They wound through deserted alleyways, emerging into a cluster of residential homes. Luka led her through backyards overgrown with bushes and grass. Even in the dark, the neighborhood had an abandoned, unkempt feel to it. They stopped at a house with dim light escaping its shuttered windows, and Luka tapped softly before opening the door and ushering Caeli inside.

An older woman looked up from the table, startled. Dark, greasy hair hung to her shoulders, and her skin glowed with an unhealthy, yellowish undertone.

"My friend is staying here tonight," Luka told her.

"You're going to get us in trouble, bringing home every stray you find," the woman complained. Caeli caught the slight slurring of her words.

"Leave it alone, Mom," Luka answered, gesturing for Caeli to follow. "Don't worry about her. She'll pass out and forget you were ever here." He pointed to a small bedroom. "You can sleep there."

"Thank you, Luka."

"Are you hungry? I can probably find something for you to eat."

"No, I'm all right." Her stomach still hadn't settled from the night's activities. She sat on the edge of the bed and let her pack fall to the floor at her feet.

Luka leaned in the doorway, stuffing his hands in his pockets. He bore a slight resemblance to the woman in the kitchen with his dark hair, piercing brown eyes, and the angular shape of his cheekbones, but the similarity ended there. Thin as he was, his skin was clear and his expression alert.

"I appreciate your help," Caeli said.

"You can't stay here long. If you're in trouble, which I guess you must be, I know people who can hide you. I'll get you to them tomorrow."

Caeli could feel his curiosity, but also the self-protective instinct warning him not ask. "I appreciate that very much."

"Let me know if you need anything. Washroom is just there on the left, and I'm right down the hall," he said, backing into the hallway and pulling the door closed behind him.

Caeli exhaled and lay back on the bed. As the adrenaline and drugs wore off, she could feel her body crashing. Her eyelids fluttered closed, and she gave in to the darkness.

***

She woke to kitchen sounds—clanking pans, sliding drawers, cupboards opening and shutting, and the smell of toasted bread. Although the window was shuttered, warm morning light made its way into the room, flecks of dust floating in the narrow streams.

Venturing out, Caeli found Luka moving efficiently around in the small space. When she rounded the corner, he gave her a cautious smile and said, "You must be hungry by now."

At that, her stomach growled noisily and they both laughed. "Can I do anything to help?" Caeli asked.

"I've got it under control," he said, placing a jar of jam on the table.

There was no sign of Luka's mother. Caeli could feel another presence in the house, but she suspected the woman was asleep. "Marta speaks very highly of you," she said.

"She was a great teacher and a really good person. I owe her a lot," Luka admitted, taking a seat across from Caeli.

"Thank you again for helping me. I hope I'm not putting you and your family at risk."

"No more than usual," he assured her between mouthfuls.

"This world has been occupied for a while. It must be hard," she said, wanting information, but not wanting to pry or make Luka uncomfortable. He seemed nonplussed.

"Some people adapt. Some never will. The Draks invaded my home, bombed my neighbors. I was only a kid when it happened, but my choice has always been clear to me," he said, matter-of-fact.

"My world was at war not so long ago. One side didn't think the other had a right to exist. We fought, and we won. But it cost us a lot," she said quietly.

He held her gaze. "We understand each other, then."

"I think we do."

They finished their breakfast in companionable silence. Caeli helped tidy the kitchen, watching as Luka carefully put aside a plate for his mother. Her heart broke a little for him. He was still so young. Too young for the wariness in his eyes.

When they left the house, Caeli tucked her hair under her hat again. In the bright morning sun, she got a better look at the neighborhood. Debris, partially covered with weeds and dirt, littered the abandoned yards. Several homes had been reduced to rubble and never rebuilt. Nature continued its relentless encroachment, vines and moss pulling the remnants back into the earth.

"The bombs missed my house, but they weren't so lucky," Luka said, following Caeli's gaze.

As she stood staring, the memory of her own home, reduced to ashes, slammed into her brain.

"Are you okay?" Luka's soft, concerned voice pulled her back to the present.

She blinked and shook her head, willing the images to disappear. "I'm sorry."

Luka shrugged and quickened his pace, Caeli trotting after him. They hurried through the neighborhood, back behind alleyways, and into a part of the city that hadn't been rebuilt.

"Aren't you afraid the whole thing will come down on top of you?" Caeli asked as Luka led her into a building with half the roof missing.

"It's safe enough. We've done a little work on the interior," he answered.

"What was this? Before?"

"An industrial complex," Luka answered. "I think too much was destroyed for it to be worth rebuilding. Because of that, the Draks don't come around here much, which is good for us."

Caeli was about to ask who he meant by "us" when they came to a heavy steel door. Luka knocked, his fists beating out a particular rhythm. In seconds, the door slid open. Two heavily armed guards ushered them inside and slammed the door shut behind them.

"Who's this?" one asked, interested but not overly concerned.

"A runner," Luka answered. The guard nodded and waved them on.

As they wound through dimly lit corridors, the sound of voices grew louder. The corridor emptied into a large space that looked like it had once been a warehouse. Now, it resembled a camp.

Small areas were partitioned off for privacy and sleeping, a common cooking space buzzed with activity, drying clothes hung from makeshift lines, and supplies lined shelves and formed neat stacks around the perimeter. The sounds and smells of humanity living in close quarters assaulted Caeli's senses. The collective hum of their minds against hers felt oddly comforting. There was little fear among them. Caeli mostly sensed purpose and determination, with an undercurrent of impatience. It felt like they were preparing for something. A few people looked at her curiously as Luka led her further inside, but most were occupied and paid no attention.

At the far side of the compound, Luka knocked on another door. This time a voice answered, "Come in!"

Luka pushed the door open and ushered Caeli inside. The room looked like a command center, with charts and maps pinned to the walls, equipment piled on tables and in corners, and weapons leaning against walls.

A tall, solidly built man looked up from a screen. He stood when she entered, his piercing, dark eyes holding her gaze.

"Ezra, this is Caeli. She needs help," Luka said.

"Caeli, welcome." Ezra extended his hand. Caeli took it, her skin pale against his and her hand tiny in his large grasp.

"I'll leave you to talk." Luka closed the door behind himself.

"Please have a seat," Ezra said, his voice deep and soothing. "People often find their way to us when they're in trouble." He opened his arms, inviting Caeli to speak.

She let out a breath and sank down into a chair across from him. "Thank you." Reaching out with her mind, she brushed against his, not to steal his thoughts, only to confirm her initial impression that she was safe here. She felt honesty in his intent, but still she hesitated, fearing what he might do if he knew the whole truth.

"I escaped from the Drokarans. It took me a long time, but a friend of Luka's helped me," she offered.

"Marta. The boy speaks highly of his former teacher."

"She's become a friend to me as well."

Ezra squinted at her. "Who are you, Caeli?" His tone was nonthreatening, but it was clear he wanted more information.

She opened her mouth to speak and then shut it again, a lump forming in her throat. Taking a deep breath, she tried again. "I'm not from Mira," she began.

Ezra lifted his eyebrows and leaned back in his chair.

"My home world was recently at war too. But in our case, one civilization tried to destroy the other. I was part of a resistance movement. We won. Once our government stabilized, we petitioned the Inter-Planetary Alliance for membership. I was on my way to formally accept our full member status when the Drokarans attacked my ship, killed my crew, and brought me here."

"You're a diplomat, then?"

Caeli smiled at that. "A doctor, actually. But we do what we have to."

Ezra smiled back. "Indeed we do. War is an ugly, ugly thing."

He stood and poured her a glass of water. She took the cup with shaking hands, and he waited for her to continue.

"They're sick. The Drokarans," Caeli said.

"We know. When they established control of the planet, one of the first things they did was take blood and tissue samples from a large portion of the population. They experimented on us."

"They experimented on me too, Ezra."

She wasn't willing to tell him anything more. But as much as she kept hidden, real fear and desperation filled her voice.

"Is there some way off this planet?" she asked.

Ezra shook his head. "We haven't found one yet. After the war, the Drokarans kept Mira isolated. No off-world contact. They've recently opened us up to limited, highly regulated trade with unaffiliated organizations. My group has tried to make some initial connections outside Drokaran authority, but the people we're dealing with are questionable characters at best. They have no interest in jeopardizing their business without serious incentive, and they certainly aren't interested in our cause."

Eyes widening, Caeli tapped her fingers lightly against the cup in her hand. Off-world trade. The people involved were mercenaries, or worse, but they had ships that regularly left Mira.

"It's a possibility, but these people are dangerous," Ezra cautioned, reading Caeli's hopeful expression correctly.

Nodding, she put her cup down, shut her eyes, and rubbed her temples. When she looked up again, Ezra gave her a gentle smile.

"You're welcome to stay with us. We could certainly use another doctor, and all intel filters through here, so if anything does sound promising, I'll let you know."

"Thank you, Ezra. You have no idea how much this means to me." Her voice hitched when she spoke. She could rest here, recover, and try to come up with a plan.

DEREK

CHAPTER 12

Derek leaned his head against the damp cement wall, grateful that so far that the interrogations had been half-hearted at best. His body ached, mostly from sleeping on the hard floor.

When Drew and Derek had met Keegan's contact a few days ago, they were greeted with open suspicion, blindfolded, and dragged off. Derek knew his captors wanted to keep their location hidden, and they'd done a good job disorienting him. They'd also separated him from Drew, but he wasn't all that worried yet. He'd kept to the story that the Drokarans had detained one of his crewmates and he and Drew had stayed behind to figure things out.

He'd communicated once with Kat when he was sure he was alone in the locked cell, convincing her to lie low with Sean and not to come looking for them. The lack of action went against both their natures, but he wanted to align himself with this group, and having Kat and Sean try to break them out of a hidden MLA safe house wouldn't help his cause.

When the door to the cell opened, Derek pulled himself to his feet.

"Move." An armed guard motioned at him with a gun,

cuffed his hands behind his back, and marched him down the hallway. He shoved Derek into what looked like a supply closet turned interrogation room, forced him into a chair, and left.

A few moments later, a woman entered, flanked by two armed Mirans. Derek recognized her immediately. She squinted at him. "You're the off-worlder from the bar," she said.

He didn't respond.

She stepped closer. "Who are you?"

"My crew and I were doing a little business here, and one of us was detained. I heard you might be able to help." Even as he said it, he knew she didn't believe him.

"You're trying to infiltrate my group," she hissed.

"I'm just trying to help my friend."

"You found me in that bar, and now you've managed to track me down here. Are you collaborating with the Draks?" she asked.

"No. I had no idea who you were in the bar," he answered truthfully.

She looked at the man to her left. In one quick motion, he hit Derek in the face with the butt of his gun.

Derek knew his nose was broken from the sickening crack that rang in his ears and the warm, wet gush of blood splashing onto his shirt. It took a few seconds for the pain to register.

The woman squatted down, her face only a few inches from his. "Let's try again. What are you doing here?"

He choked on his own salty blood. When he could finally speak, his voice carried all the pent-up rage and desperation he'd been holding in check. "The Drokarans took someone I love, and I will tear this fucking planet apart to get her back."

She sat back on her heels. "Now *that* I believe."

He closed his eyes and let his head hang.

"What information can you give me?" she asked.

"She's an off-worlder too. A doctor. Her ship was attacked by the Drokarans, and I believe they brought her to Mira."

"I'll make inquiries. If I find out you've done anything to put my people in danger, or that you are collaborating with the Draks in any way," she said, pointing an accusatory finger, "I will kill you."

He didn't doubt her.

She stood and brushed off her pants. "I don't have time to continue our conversation right now, but you will tell me the rest of your story. I'll get it from you, or I'll get it from your friend. Lock him back up."

One of the men hauled him to his feet, and he stumbled back to his cell.

***

Kat's tense voice echoed in his ear. "That's it. We're coming to get you."

"No, we're okay," Derek answered back, slouched in the corner of the dark, empty cell. In truth, he was miserable. His face hurt, his chest ached from breathing in the persistent dampness, and his shirt was plastered to his body with dried sweat and crusted blood. He tried to keep the discomfort out of his voice, but Kat wasn't fooled.

"You don't sound okay," she said.

"I find it relaxing in here. Thanks for asking," Drew said.

"Damn it, Drew. You know I want you guys out of there. It's been two days since you've seen that bitch of a bartender. We'll go back to the bar. Follow her," Kat said.

Derek imagined her pacing, her face tight with a scowl he knew so well.

"We have to give it a little more time," he insisted. "We have no idea what their network is like or how fast they can gather intel."

"But we don't even know if she's really following up. She thinks you're a potential threat. She may be happy to keep you locked up and out of the way."

"I know," he agreed. "Believe me, I want to get out of here too, but let's give it a little longer. If there's a chance they can find out anything about Caeli, it will be worth it."

"Okay," Kat sighed reluctantly.

He tapped off his com, leaned back, and closed his eyes.

***

It may have been minutes or several hours later when the door opened again. He'd lost track of time in his windowless prison. When one of the guards gestured, he stood and turned around, accepting the metal cuffs again. This time, they led him in the opposite direction, through a dimly lit tunnel.

He felt her mind touch his even before the guard shoved him through the door.

Suddenly Caeli was there in front of him, throwing her arms around him, burying her face in his chest. When she pulled away, she gently cupped his face in her hands. "Oh, Derek," she whispered.

He wanted so badly to hold her, but all he could do was touch his forehead to hers. Relief flooded through every atom of his being. "How are you here?" he asked, searching her face, barely believing that she stood before him.

"I made some friends," she said.

He couldn't help the short laugh that escaped. "Of course you did."

She gently ran her hand down his cheek before turning away. "Ezra, please, let him go."

Derek followed her gaze to the large man standing across the room. "That's Rayna's call. This is her unit," the man said.

Rayna moved toward Derek. "I found what you were looking for. Now I want some real answers."

He hesitated, but knew it was time to risk the truth, or at least part of it. "I'm Captain Derek Markham. My mission here was to find and recover Dr. Caeli Crys."

Her eyebrows lifted in surprise. "You're an Alliance soldier?"

Derek gave a curt nod, his expression guarded.

When Rayna opened her mouth to speak again, Caeli stepped protectively in front of Derek and said in a clipped tone, "How about we talk more when you've uncuffed him and let me treat his injuries?"

Rayna gave Caeli a measured look. "Fair enough."

As soon as his hands were free, Derek pulled Caeli against him. He felt her body trembling.

"Take them to the infirmary," Rayna ordered the guard. Then, to Derek, "Get cleaned up. We'll talk more in a few hours."

"Let Lieutenant Chase go as well," Derek demanded. Rayna nodded.

He followed the guard out with Caeli at his side. She gripped his hand so hard his fingers hurt, but otherwise she held her composure as they wandered through tunnels.

"In here," the guard said, motioning them into a large office space that had been converted to a clinic. Medical supplies filled shelves, and a few empty cots acted as hospital beds. A young man sat on the ground, sorting through a box of bandages. He looked up in surprise when they entered, his eyes darting back and forth between the guard and Derek's battered face.

"Can I help you?" he asked, getting to his feet.

"Get them what they need," the guard ordered and left.

Stepping forward, the young man said, "I'm the medic here. What can I do?"

"I'm Dr. Crys," Caeli said, smiling. "I'll take care of him. Could I get some water? And maybe a clean shirt?"

The young man nodded vigorously. "We've got water here," he said, pointing to an industrial sink in the corner. "And I'll see what I can find for extra clothes." He rushed off to do Caeli's bidding.

Caeli led Derek to a cot and gently pushed him down onto it. He grabbed her by the hand and pulled her next to him. "I thought I'd lost you. I knew the Drokarans took you alive, but I was so afraid I'd be too late." He brushed a wisp of blonde hair off her face.

She put her head on his chest, and he held her.

"I knew you would try to find me, but I didn't think you would, especially when I realized I was on Mira," she said, her voice catching.

"I would never have stopped looking."

She held his gaze. "I know."

"Are you okay?" he asked.

When the Novali made a deep empathic connection with someone, like Caeli had with him, it was intimate and permanent. He *felt* her. And he knew she wasn't okay.

She touched his face and avoided the question. "You're a mess."

"It probably looks worse than it feels," he said. She got up, filled a basin with water, and deftly gathered supplies. He watched her graceful movements as she familiarized herself with the space, at home anywhere healing took place. "Where are we? Do you know?"

"Underground," she replied. "The subway system on Mira is extensive, but the Drokarans don't use it. This branch of the MLA hides down here, and Ezra's unit is in a blown-out factory complex."

"How coordinated are the groups?" Derek asked.

"They communicate and know how to find one another, but they have their own objectives. Rayna's group is more aggressive. I think they've actually attacked the Drokarans. Ezra gathers information and hides people on the run."

"You've become quite the intelligence agent."

"I learned from the best," Caeli said, giving him a small smile as she sat back down and gently dabbed his face with a wet cloth. "How did you find this group?"

"We heard about the MLA too, and thought they might be our best chance for gathering intel about you. We followed a contact of Drew's and ended up here."

When Caeli had finished washing away the dried blood, she put her hands on his cheeks and closed her eyes. He felt the warm, familiar tingling of her mind working to heal his body.

"The bruising will fade on its own," she said once she'd finished.

He took her hands in his and kissed them. "I feel better already."

At that moment, the medic returned with a clean pile of clothing. He glanced between the two of them, placed the clothes on the cot next to Derek, and scurried off again.

"I'd kill for a shower," Derek said under his breath as he pulled his filthy shirt over his head.

"How long have you been here?" Caeli asked, handing him the clean one.

"We've been on Mira for about three weeks, but I've only been locked up down here for a couple of days."

"Drew's with you?"

"And Kat, and Sean Asher, the agent we worked with on Elista. Speaking of Kat, she's probably climbing the walls right now." He smiled as he tapped his com.

CAELI

CHAPTER 13

When Drew joined Caeli and Derek in the infirmary, Caeli threw her arms around him in a fierce embrace.

"I've missed you too," he said, smiling. He didn't look any worse for wear, but Caeli insisted on giving him a quick exam.

Rayna made an appearance and invited the three of them to share a meal in her private quarters. Although the gesture seemed friendly enough, Caeli could feel the tension and suspicion still radiating from the woman. Ezra accompanied them, his calm presence reassuring.

"Ezra, thank you," Caeli said.

Through his communication networks, Ezra had learned that Rayna's MLA unit was looking for intel on an off-world prisoner—a doctor. He'd come to Caeli with the information, and, with Ezra's assurance of protection, Caeli had agreed to meet with the other group.

"I'm glad you found each other," he answered, placing a gentle hand on her shoulder and nodding toward Derek.

From the way Derek and Drew attacked their food, Caeli knew they hadn't had much to eat in the last couple of days. She glared at Rayna, who shifted uncomfortably in her chair.

"Why didn't you tell me who you were right away?" Rayna asked Derek.

He paused and carefully lowered his fork. "Because the Alliance surrendered this world to the Drokarans. I had no idea if my real identity as an Alliance soldier would get me shot. If anyone has the right to be angry, it's the people still fighting here. But I also knew you'd be my best chance at obtaining useful information."

"To find Dr. Crys?"

"Yes."

"Why did the Drokarans take her?"

Derek glanced at Caeli, who put a gentle hand on his leg under the table and sent a thought to him. "My world recently fought a bloody civil war. It's still vulnerable, but we've sorted ourselves out enough to petition the Alliance for full membership and protection. I was on my way to Cor Leon to formally accept when my ship was attacked by the Drokarans."

"Caeli was co-leader of the transitional government," Derek took over, "and before that, a major player in the resistance movement that overthrew the dictatorship. She has sensitive, tactical information about her world that the Drokarans could use to their advantage. They're going after vulnerable planets in their territory grab."

"The Alliance is still fighting, then?"

"Staying ahead of the Drokarans and protecting our member worlds has become our primary focus," Derek answered.

Caeli felt Rayna's curiosity when she turned to her and asked, "How did you escape Drokaran custody?"

Caeli stiffened, and Derek reached for her hand. "Not easily. But I am a medical doctor by training, and you know the Drokarans are sick," Caeli said, choosing her words carefully.

Rayna nodded.

"I offered to help one of them. Over time, he lowered his guard enough for me to escape."

From Rayna's expression, Caeli knew she'd hoped for more detail, but the other woman read Caeli's tone and didn't pursue the subject.

Rayna turned back to Derek. "You've found Dr. Crys. Now what?"

"I'd like my other two teammates to meet us here tomorrow."

Even without her empathic sensitivity, Caeli knew Rayna bristled at Derek's authoritative tone. She felt the other woman struggling with the discomfort, but in the end, Rayna nodded in agreement.

"Of course. We'll arrange their safe passage. I'm sure you're tired. I'll have someone show you around. It's a bit of a maze down here," Rayna said, standing.

Derek politely thanked her for dinner. Caeli, glancing at Derek's bruised face, offered only a frosty goodnight.

***

Caeli curled her body around Derek's, needing to be as close to him as possible. They'd been given a cot in a relatively private corner of the room. The extensive underground facilities included the rail lines themselves, but also storage areas, warehouses, offices, and recreational space for the workers who spent large chunks of time underground. The MLA had divided the space up as functionally as they could to accommodate their ranks.

Derek had, in fact, gotten to take a shower. Caeli inhaled his soapy smell, burying her head in his neck. They both wanted more, but desperate as they were, neither could ignore the bodies sleeping on the other side of the storage shelf.

Careful of his still-healing face, Caeli leaned up on her elbow and kissed him. In the dark, she couldn't see his expression, but her mind was open to his, and she felt his angst.

"What did they do to you, Caeli?" he asked. She knew the question had been on his mind since the moment he saw her.

"There's so much I need to tell you, but . . ." Her voice faltered. She couldn't speak some of the things aloud.

"Show me," he said gently, pulling her against his chest.

"Are you sure?" she whispered.

"If I could take away your pain, or suffer it myself instead, I would. But I can't do that, so at least let me carry this with you. Please," he urged.

She didn't want him to endure any more of her trauma, but she understood his need to.

"I woke up in a cell, disoriented. They ran tests . . ." Her words trailed off as she linked her mind to his in the most intimate way possible. She remembered her panic at being cut off from her gift entirely, and the absolute terror and near madness she felt when it was amplified.

"I killed someone, Derek," she whispered.

She felt his concern rush outward in a wave. "Oh, Caeli."

"I was so scared. I had to get away."

"It wasn't your fault," he whispered, soothing her with his own mind.

"She's still dead."

"I know," he said, and Caeli knew he understood, firsthand, the terrible weight of taking a life.

"They turned you into a weapon. It wasn't your fault," he repeated.

She felt herself spiraling inward, her entire body responding to the memory.

"Breathe, Caeli," he said. So many times, he'd pulled her back from the darkness lurking in her own mind. She held onto him now, linking her breath to his, her heartbeat to his, until she fought her way back.

She kept her hand on his warm chest, and he stroked her hair. "There's something else."

"Tell me," he coaxed.

"The Drokarans . . ." She stopped. The thought sickened her to her very core. She didn't want to say it.

"Caeli, whatever it is, we'll deal with it," he said.

Taking a breath, she spoke. "The Drokarans are dying, we were right about that. They invade worlds for both resources and people, trying to cure themselves. But when I questioned Daksha Karan on Tharsis, he *knew* who I was, because the Drokarans never lost their history. They knew they were the coveted result of a genetic experiment. They knew they'd fought a war and lost. They knew they had to flee their home world and rebuild themselves."

Derek's embrace tightened around her.

"The Drokarans are the original Novali, the ones designed to be the next step in human evolution." She fell silent, allowing Derek to process the information. As her mind lingered next to his, she was surprised by his lack of surprise.

"When we found those old records on Almagest, it crossed my mind that their modified traits sounded a lot like the Drokarans. High intelligence, ruthlessness, physical prowess. I didn't give it much thought, though, because it was such ancient history." He paused, rubbing a thumb across her wet cheek. "It doesn't make a difference who they are or where they came from. They have no claim to your world anymore. And your people are nothing like them."

"Derek, my DNA has the same genetic biomarkers as Karan's, only mine are healthy. My people may have been an undesirable side effect of that experiment, but I think we hold the key to saving the Drokarans. They don't just want us as weapons. They need us to heal them." Her panic began to rise. "Derek, we have to get off this planet and warn Almagest."

He ran a hand soothingly over her back. "They're already on alert. As soon as I saw the cockpit video feed from the *Carina*, I knew it was the Drokarans who'd taken you, and I assumed they'd targeted you specifically because Karan knew about your gift."

Some of the tension in Caeli's body eased. Her people knew there was a threat. They'd be paying attention, even if they didn't understand the full measure of that threat. The Alliance would help protect them now too.

She allowed herself a moment's relief before linking her mind with Derek's again. "I need to show you something else," she said, and shared an image of Navi, first pale and in pain with his arm broken, and later as a serious but sweet little boy arranging his blocks on the kitchen floor. "I lived with this boy, took care of him, rocked him to sleep. He's Karan's son."

Derek leaned his head back on the pillow. Caeli felt his emotions churning, and it was several moments before he spoke again. "They invaded this planet. Took what didn't belong to them. Started a war that's lasted a generation. We've had to do things . . . *I've* had to do things, because of this war . . ." His voice trailed off.

"I know," she whispered.

She had nothing to offer him as they held each other in the dark.

DEREK

CHAPTER 14

The next morning, Derek sent Drew off with a small group of Rayna's men to meet up with Kat and Sean and lead them back to the hideout. When Kat arrived, she went straight to Caeli and pulled her into an enthusiastic hug.

"Are you okay?" she asked.

"As okay as everyone else," Caeli answered.

Kat looked over at Derek, whose face still displayed a colorful array of purple bruises, and raised her eyebrows. "That doesn't reassure me."

"I've missed you, Kat," Caeli said.

"Back at you. What's on the agenda for today?"

"We're meeting with Rayna and Ezra to talk."

"Good," Kat said.

"Caeli, this is Sean Asher," Derek said, gesturing at the agent. "We worked together on Elista, and he's been on mission with us here."

Caeli smiled at Sean, and Derek caught him staring at her just a fraction of a second too long before he composed himself and smiled back. When Derek had first met Caeli, he'd been enchanted by her too. It was more than just the physical attraction, although that had been there from the start. People were naturally drawn to her. The Novali had a compelling quality about them, one Derek suspected was related to their empathic nature. When Caeli focused on someone, she listened to them with her whole being.

"Thank you for trying to bring Nysa home," Caeli said.

Derek had hated telling Caeli about Nysa. It was one more loss to add to her heartbreakingly long list.

"I'm sorry it ended so badly," Sean answered, looking away.

A puzzled look passed over Caeli's face, but before Derek was even sure he'd seen it, it had disappeared.

Derek rescued Sean from his obvious discomfort by ushering the group into Rayna's meeting room. He made introductions and they all sat.

Tension simmered again between Derek and Rayna. Mindful of Rayna's command position, he aimed for a respectful tone when he spoke, acutely aware that his team was inside *her* compound, surrounded by *her* armed resistance fighters.

"Thank you for helping us find Caeli." He meant that, at least.

Rayna glanced at Caeli and gave a curt nod. "You've found her. Now I assume you'll sneak out of here the same way you got in."

"No. Not yet."

She squinted at him. "Why not?"

"You have a coordinated resistance movement on the ground. Intel. Weapons. It seems like the Drokaran hold on Mira is slipping," Derek said, watching Rayna's expression carefully. She looked as if she were trying to work out a puzzle. When she hit on the solution, she looked between Derek and the rest of the team, then pinned him with a cold stare.

"You're Alliance Intelligence, aren't you?" she said.

"Technically, I'm still in charge of the brand-new space fleet on Almagest, Caeli's home world."

"Technically," Rayna repeated.

Derek blew out a breath and caught Sean's eye. The other man gave him a nearly imperceptible nod. Time for more truth-telling.

"*My* primary mission was to find Dr. Crys. At the same time, Lieutenant Commander Asher was assigned to assess the strength of the Drokaran occupation force here on Mira. He'd learned the Drokarans were allowing limited off-world trade and saw an opening to infiltrate. He'd also received separate intel suggesting the Drokarans brought Dr. Crys here. Our two operations coincided, and we were ordered to work together."

"So, you're going to stay to gather intel on behalf of the Alliance?"

"Yes."

"And you expect me to cooperate with you?"

"Why wouldn't you?"

She glared at him. "The MLA has been fighting this war for over ten years without the Alliance, without contact from other worlds. The Draks slaughtered us, experimented on us, wore our people down. But the MLA didn't give up. We kept moving and reinventing ourselves, and when our fighters died for the cause, more would take their place. We never gave up. But you did. The Alliance left us here to fight this battle alone."

She stood, her chair clattering over behind her. Derek watched her pace, his own body tense and still. The whole room froze in stunned silence.

Finally, she stopped moving and leaned forward on the table as if the energy had leeched out of her. "But if there's a chance

the Alliance will help us now, what kind of leader would I be if
I didn't take it?"

***

Rayna introduced Derek to her second-in-command,
Harlan Gage, formerly Miran military. A tall, wiry man, older
than Derek, he had both a wariness about him and a quiet
appreciation for Derek's combat experience. Rayna instructed
Gage to give Derek whatever information he wanted.

While they explored the weapons cache, Derek questioned
Gage on everything from the number of MLA groups active on
the planet, to the location of Drokaran bases, to the illicit trade
operation both locally and with off-world mercenaries.

"You've been in the military a long time, yeah?" Gage asked
when Derek had run out of logistical questions.

Derek nodded. "I started as a pilot, first on Erithos, and then
for the Alliance."

"How'd you get into intelligence?"

Leaning against the wall, Derek shoved his hands into his
pockets.

"My first assignment with the Alliance was mostly flying
fighter escorts for high-level diplomatic missions and leading
their protection details. Back before the Drokaran threat,
animosity among Alliance worlds ran high and the political
landscape was complicated. My job required some intelligence
work, and I was good at it."

Derek paused, staring blankly over Gage's shoulder. "Then the
Drokarans changed the game. They caught us totally off guard,
and we lost Arendal and Delphis without a shot fired. After that,
the Alliance went from mainly a peacekeeping organization to

the largest military force ever created. Intelligence skills became an asset, and I was assigned to *Horizon*. The first time I ever saw real combat was here on Mira," Derek finished.

They fell silent. Derek ran his hand over the hard metal casing of a laser-guided rifle, his mind wandering back in time.

Horizon had arrived late to the fight. The Alliance battlecruiser Freedom *was already fully engaged, outnumbered and outgunned by the Drokaran warships orbiting the planet.* Horizon *deployed her entire fighter squadron, with Derek as a newly commissioned lieutenant commander. They'd done some damage. Taken out one of the big Drokaran ships. But it hadn't been nearly enough. He'd watched in horror as the* Freedom *and her crew of two hundred and fifty-nine souls disintegrated in Mira's upper atmosphere.*

Gage planted a solid hand on Derek's shoulder, and Derek shook off the memory.

***

Within a couple of days, Derek had gathered enough information to contact *Horizon*, give the Alliance a report, and start planning a way off Mira, but an idea had taken shape in his mind that he wanted to work through with his team. He glanced at Caeli, who gave him a questioning look.

"From what we've seen, Mira has the potential to launch an effective offensive against the Drokarans. They aren't fully coordinated in their efforts, but the MLA is well armed and has a reliable communication network. They've already caused significant damage to Drokaran bases and troops, and they're becoming more strategic in their approach."

"I agree. We need to pass along that intel," Sean said.

Derek's knee bounced under the table.

"What are you thinking?" Kat asked.

"I'm thinking that aside from the shield array, the planetary defense is almost nonexistent. There's no sign of Drokaran battleships or cruisers in this system. *Horizon* is out there waiting. If we can locate the operational control for that shield and bring it down, *Horizon* could take advantage of the opportunity, punch through the perimeter, and provide air support for a ground assault."

"You want to stay and fight with the Mirans," Caeli said quietly.

He gave a quick nod.

"The Drak occupation force is still dangerous," Sean said.

Derek agreed. "It's a risk. The MLA would need to engage them in a coordinated ground effort and hold on for reinforcements, but we've all seen committed groups do more with less."

He could see the thoughts spinning in his teammates' minds.

"What are the chances Alliance Command will authorize *Horizon* to engage?" Kat asked.

"I don't know. We'd have to convince them there's a real possibility for success. But if the MLA backs the plan, I'm willing to make that case." Derek looked around the room and then rubbed his hands over his face. "I'm not sure I trust my judgment on this one, though," he admitted.

A decade ago, when the order had been given to leave Mira, Derek had followed it. He knew the Drokarans had blockaded the planet, he understood that Alliance soldiers and pilots were being slaughtered, and he'd seen the Drokarans callously sacrifice civilians when it served them. Surrendering Mira had probably saved lives, but Derek had never been able to reconcile the decision.

"I may not be objective either, but with our team and the

MLA on the ground and *Horizon* in the game, I think we've got a shot at taking this planet back," Kat said.

"I probably shouldn't even offer an opinion," Drew said. "You know what I want."

Derek looked to Sean, who he thought might be the only relatively impartial person in the room when it came to Mira. "Tactically, it's a sound plan. Everything could go to shit, but everything can always go to shit. I'd rather stay and fight than abandon them. This is what we do."

Finally, Derek looked at Caeli. Guilt ate at him. He knew what she'd already endured, and now he was asking her to stay and fight instead of trying to get her to safety. But they were at war, and he was a soldier.

"We're here. They need us," she said simply.

Looking around the room one more time, Derek found resolute faces staring back at him. He stood. "Okay, let's go talk to Rayna."

He found her in the operations center and asked for a sit-down. She studied Derek curiously, and then cleared the room except for Ezra and Gage.

"My team has enough intel to make our report to Alliance Command. They'll either use the information or not. But we have another idea," Derek said.

All eyes fixed on him in tense anticipation. Rayna tilted her head. "Let's hear it."

When he laid out the plan in detail, Derek could see hope battle with caution on Rayna's face. He looked between Rayna and Ezra before finishing, "Mira will become a battleground again. Only you know if your people have the stomach for this."

Ezra spoke first. "There are Miran children who have known only Drokaran rule. The Drokarans invaded our home, killed tens of thousands of people, experimented on us. We have no freedom, no voice. Fear is our constant companion. This is no life."

Rayna leaned forward in her chair, palms flat on the table. "This could be a real chance."

"I think so too," Derek said.

CHAPTER 15

When Captain Donovan backed his plan, Derek knew Alliance Command would follow suit. A few days later, he received official word that if the shield array came down, *Horizon* would provide tactical support for the Miran ground forces, and the Alliance would send reinforcements.

In Rayna's operations center, the energy in the room buzzed as plans took shape.

"Derek, you and your team will be in charge of taking the shield offline," Rayna said.

Derek nodded. "We need good intel on the location of the ground operations and the power source."

Rayna started to answer him when Caeli interrupted. "I can get that information."

Derek turned to her, his body tensing.

"The Drokaran who took me, the one I escaped from. He'll know. And I know where to find him," she said.

Rayna looked at Derek, her expression softer than he'd ever seen it. He closed his eyes and ran a hand over his face.

"Okay," Derek said.

He motioned for his team to follow, and they exited the noisy ops center in favor of a quiet corner in the mess hall.

"Any idea on how to get to Karan?" Derek asked Caeli.

"I think questioning him at his home is the only option," she replied.

Nodding his agreement, he asked, "Can you get us back there?"

"Probably not, but I met someone I think could help."

"I want to keep our group small and tight. Caeli, you've been hiding your gift, and I agree with your instinct, but we may need to use it," he said.

"If I had to pick someone to trust, it would be Luka," she said, her voice firm.

"Okay, talk to Ezra about borrowing him." Derek continued, "Once we have more information, we'll have to plan as we go, but we'll definitely need arms and explosives."

"I'll check in with Gage and take care of it," Drew said, shoveling food into his mouth.

Derek sat back, poking his own food around his plate.

"You okay?" Kat asked him.

Dropping his fork, he sat back. "We're about to start a fight. People are going to die. I hope this is the right call."

"We did *not* start this fight," Kat corrected emphatically. "But we can finally help finish it."

Derek appreciated Kat's righteous clarity, but every battle came with a body count, and he felt the weight of those lives squarely on his shoulders, right next to the bodies he'd put in the ground himself.

"The Mirans are ready," Sean said.

Shaking his head, Derek replied, "Maybe."

"This is the right thing to do," Drew added, pushing his plate away and crossing his arms. "I wouldn't want to live like this."

"No, me neither," Derek agreed, sighing.

Caeli searched his face, her silent concern brushing his mind.

He knew this was the wrong time for self-doubt and second guesses. He'd helped put something in motion, and he needed to focus on making it work.

He shook off his dark thoughts and stood, nodding at his friends. "Get some rest. See you back here in eight hours."

***

Derek took Caeli back to their semi-private cot and stretched out next to her. She rested her head on his chest, and he breathed in the familiar scent of her hair.

"Are we going to have to kill Karan?" she asked.

He stiffened, knowing she was thinking about another interrogation, on another world. When they'd finished with the man, maybe Derek could have handed him off to the local authorities, or found some other option that would have spared his life. But in those few seconds, he'd had to make a decision, and only one option had guaranteed that his prisoner wouldn't blow their cover and put the entire operation at risk.

"I hope not," Derek answered. But he knew if it came down to saving his team or his mission, he would pull the trigger. Again.

"Derek," she said in a tight, quiet voice.

"What is it?" he asked, gently stroking her cheek.

"I stole some of their experimental drugs. I used them. I turned myself into a weapon, on purpose, so that I could escape."

Derek could feel her body beside his, tense and still.

"I have more of it," she confessed.

"Caeli, no. You won't need to use it."

She leaned up on her arm, her eyes feverish and panicked. "We can't fail."

He didn't know what to say. She was right. If they failed, they'd be dead, or worse.

She settled back down, resting her head on his chest. "Who will we be when this is over?"

Derek stared silently at the ceiling for a long moment. "If we're alive, we'll figure it out."

***

While Rayna, Ezra, Gage, and leaders of the other MLA factions met and planned for a couple of days, Derek's team prepared as much as they could for their part of the mission.

Drew found what he needed in the form of small pellets. The explosive materials were easily transported and wouldn't become reactive until triggered by a specially designed chemical detonator. He'd worn the ghost of a smile when distributing bits and pieces of his wares into their separate travel bags. They'd also been given free rein in the weapons locker and now carried a diverse assortment of guns.

When the MLA finished finalizing their plans, Derek's group followed Ezra back to his base of operations in the factory complex. They used the underground tunnels and subway system to travel those miles, and when they emerged above ground they kept to back alleys and abandoned, decimated parts of the landscape until they made it to safety. Once they'd temporarily settled into Ezra's compound, Caeli introduced Derek to Luka.

Not built like a teenager, but not fully grown into his body yet, Luka reminded Derek of Noah, a Novali boy he'd gotten to know during his time on Almagest. But Luka had a wariness and an edge that came from growing up in a war zone, rather than having the conflict thrust upon him unexpectedly.

They found a private place to talk on an upper floor of the factory building. The windows had been blown out, and a warm breeze circulated through the musty room. Breathing in the fresh air, Derek appreciated the fact that he wasn't underground anymore, or locked in a damp cell.

"Luka, thank you for bringing Caeli to safety," he said, his voice filling with more emotion than he'd intended.

"It's what I do for the MLA," Luka answered. "Find people in trouble. Bring them to Ezra."

"That's what Caeli tells me. Luka, we need your help. Are you up for joining us on a mission?" he asked.

"What did you have in mind?" Luka asked.

"We need to get into Daksha Karan's home to question him. He's the man who was holding Caeli."

"He's the one who took my teacher. Made her take care of his kid."

"That's him," Derek confirmed.

"Why do you want to question him?"

"He's a high-ranking Drak official, and he has information we need."

"Something's going on, isn't it?"

Derek nodded. "Hopefully something big. But it all depends on whether we can get this information."

"What do you need me to do?" Luka asked.

"Lead us to his house."

"That's it?"

Before answering, Derek looked at Caeli. "Once we're in, we'll need you to get Marta and the little boy to safety."

"I can do that," Luka said.

"Luka, I need to tell you a few things before this mission," Caeli said. Luka looked at her expectantly.

"On my world, some of the people can do things with their minds, like heal, or feel other's emotions."

Luka raised his eyebrows. Derek saw interest wrestle with doubt in the look he gave her.

Caeli smiled. "I know it sounds unbelievable, but I can do those things and more."

"Why are you telling me this?" Luka asked.

"Because I may have to use my skills on this mission. But Luka, aside from Derek's team and Marta, no one else knows." She held his gaze, her smile fading. "And I don't want anyone else to."

"That's why the Drokarans took you, isn't it?" he asked. Derek was impressed by his insight.

"That's one of the reasons, yes," she admitted.

"Why do you want to keep it a secret from the MLA? You're on the same side."

"When people are desperate, they do desperate things. During the war on my world, I was forced to do things with my gift against my will," she said.

That memory lived in Derek's mind, next to so many of Caeli's, deeply embedded and almost as real to him as his own. She'd violated the mind of a young soldier, stolen his thoughts. The alternative had been a bullet to the young man's brain by their mutual captor, which in the end was what he'd gotten anyway. Caeli had never really forgiven herself, and Derek knew some of her nightmares were from that moment of violence and her unwilling part in it.

"I'm sorry. The people I know would never do that to you." Luka paused and looked at Derek. "But I guess I don't know all of them."

Once again, Derek appreciated the young man's intuition.

"Let's go introduce you to the rest of the team," he said.

CAELI

CHAPTER 16

They took the last train before curfew from Solivat to Karan's district. Dressed as locals, with weapons tucked under their clothing and bags slung over their shoulders, they boarded separate sections and didn't speak to one another.

When the train stopped, they blended in with a crowd of travelers and met up behind the building.

"Luka, we need to stay out of the drones' path," Derek said. "Caeli will be able to hide us from people, but her gift works on the human mind. We don't think we'll be invisible to a drone."

Luka nodded. "I know their routines. Follow me. I'll keep us out of sight."

Before they moved from the shadow of the building, Caeli took a vial from her bag. "I'm not taking any chances tonight," she said. Stopping Derek mid-protest with a gentle hand on his arm, she assured him, "It's just a small amount, and it wears off quickly."

Pressing the syringe to her neck, she administered the partial dose. A now-familiar, hyper-alert feeling swept through her, and the background noise from surrounding minds near and far amplified in her brain. Ignoring the sound as best she could,

Caeli created an image and projected it outward. Anyone looking in their direction would see only a dark shadow instead of this small group sneaking through back alleys and abandoned buildings.

As they grew closer to Karan's, the landscape became more familiar, until finally they stood at the edge of his backyard. Crouched behind a patch of overgrown bushes, Caeli could see the house, mostly dark at this late hour except for one room. Light glowed from the window in Karan's study.

She sat back on her heels and stretched her mind out over the entire property, listening. "There are three guards. One on the roof, one at the front entryway, and one patrolling the grounds. He's rounding the front west corner now. Only Karan is awake inside the house," she whispered.

"Kat, you take the one on the roof. Drew, front of the house," Derek ordered. "I'll take the moving target." Squatting next to Caeli, he dropped his bag on the ground, shrugged out of his overcoat, and pulled his sidearm from his waistband.

"Caeli, can you keep us all hidden?" he asked.

"Yes," she answered.

"Okay, you three stay here. As soon as the guards are down, move to the entryway. Coms on. Everyone find a position, report when ready, and wait for my mark."

The three set off, Derek to the left, Kat and Drew to the right. With little effort, Caeli simultaneously shrouded the three and kept a delicate connection with the guards.

Within moments, Drew and Kat checked in.

Derek's voice counted down over the com, and all three took out their targets on his mark.

With her mind still linked to the guards, Caeli experienced a split second of sheer terror and blinding pain before the numbing silence. She gasped and fell forward onto her hands and knees.

Sean knelt down next to her. "What's wrong?"

"The guards are dead. Let's get to the entryway. I'm okay," she lied, stumbling to her feet.

She felt his concern, but couldn't begin to explain what it felt like to experience another person's death as if it were her own.

Luka and Sean stayed out of sight when Caeli pressed the call button on the security panel at the back door. She turned her face toward the tiny camera mounted in the upper corner of the entryway.

When the door opened, Karan stood pointing a gun at her. "You've come back."

A moment of blinding panic immobilized Caeli. Memories of her time as Karan's prisoner flooded her brain, and she stood rooted to the spot, her body quaking. In the background, the hum of Derek's familiar mind tugged at her consciousness. She reached for him and held on tightly.

Karan hadn't moved. Caeli imagined pinching the vessels that carried oxygen to his brain. His eyes widened before he crumpled to the ground. Caeli caught the door as it swung closed.

"He's down," she said into her com.

Sean and Luka rushed inside first, followed quickly by the others. Sean secured Karan's weapon, and Derek went straight for Caeli. "You okay?"

She nodded. "It's already wearing off, but I'll be able to question him."

"Good." He turned to Drew. "Get him secured."

Kat hauled a kitchen chair over, and Drew and Sean lifted Karan's unconscious body into it. They held him upright while securing his ankles and wrists. A few seconds later, Karan took a startled breath and opened his eyes. Drew moved behind him and held his gun to the base of his skull. Wisely, Karan sat perfectly still.

At that moment, a startled Marta came rushing from her room, throwing her hand over her mouth when she saw the well-armed group who'd invaded the living room.

"Marta," Caeli said, stepping toward her.

"Caeli? What's happening?"

"It's all right. Luka's going to take you and Navi somewhere safe."

Marta's eyes darted from Caeli to Luka, who still hovered by the door.

"Let's pack some things for Navi. Clothes, his medicines," Caeli said, touching the older woman's arm.

"What are you doing with my son?" Karan didn't even try to hide the fear in his voice.

Caeli froze. "We're taking him somewhere safe. We'd never hurt him."

She hurried into Navi's room. "Pack your own essentials as well," she said, folding Navi's favorite blanket.

"What's happening?" Marta asked again.

Caeli hesitated. She wanted to tell Marta everything, but she couldn't risk it. She hoped with all her being that Luka would get Marta and Navi to safety, but if they were captured, they couldn't know the plan. That was why Derek hadn't shared any details with Luka, and it was why she couldn't share them with Marta now.

"When you've made it to the safe house, you'll understand, but I can't tell you now. Luka is a smart young man, very capable. He loves you. Just follow him and you'll both be all right," Caeli said.

Marta still wore a stunned expression, but she nodded and continued efficiently packing. Caeli found Navi's painkilling medication, the one she had used to keep him asleep while repairing his broken arm. She measured out a dose in the dropper and gently pinched his nose until his mouth opened. As he looked up at her, startled, she quickly squeezed the liquid into his mouth. Stroking his hair, she hummed a lullaby until his eyes fluttered shut again.

When Marta was finished packing, Caeli carefully wrapped Navi in a blanket and scooped him into her arms. His small body felt warm against her chest, and she felt his rapid heartbeat against her own.

They walked back into the living room, and Caeli knelt in front of Karan. She maneuvered the boy's sleeping form so that Karan could lean forward and press his forehead to his son's.

"Keep them safe," she said to Luka, forcing herself to stand and hand the sleeping boy off to Marta.

He gave her a solemn-faced nod, and the small group disappeared into the darkness.

DEREK
CHAPTER 17

When they were gone, Caeli turned to Derek. He was sure her pained expression mirrored his own. Running a hand over his face, he said, "Let's get this over with."

Drew, who had wordlessly stepped back from Karan while Caeli held Navi, now lifted the gun and held it to their prisoner's head again.

Derek moved in front of the captive. "I need some information."

Karan's expression hardened. Derek didn't have to be empathic to know the man would kill him with his bare hands if he got the chance.

Caeli dragged another chair in from the kitchen and placed it so she sat eye-level in front of Karan. She stared at him, and he flinched.

"How are you doing that?" he asked.

"I've been able to freely access you since that day in the lab. It's like I found the code to your mind," she said.

His eyes widened briefly and then narrowed. "You kept that hidden from me. Shrewd. You and I are not so different."

Derek watched Caeli's face. She didn't flinch, but he knew

the words cut her. "Shut up unless you're answering my questions," he ordered.

Karan lifted his eyes to Derek's. "Here we are again."

The urge to shoot Karan made Derek's finger twitch. "There's a defensive shield network protecting this planet. Where is the operational command and power source?"

Karan didn't hesitate. "It's across from the laboratory facility. The ground source powers the initial beam. Orbital satellites are part of the network, but they're controlled from the ground. Take out the ground and everything goes down."

He stared past Caeli, expression blank. "But you'll never access it. The security system is biometrically coded."

"You can do it," Derek said. He paced, tapping his thumb against his thigh, and then turned to Kat. "We'll have to take him with us. We'll need plans for the building. All entry points, location of personnel, security cameras, drones. We're going to have to account for every variable."

"I don't like this. One wrong move from him and we're screwed," Kat said, gesturing at Karan.

"I know," Derek said, running a hand over his head.

"Help us."

Caeli's words stopped Derek in his tracks.

She sat staring at Karan. "Help us because I'll make you a promise. If we take down the shield and make it out alive, I will save your son. I will do *everything* in my power to find a cure for him. You have my word."

Uncertainty played over Karan's features. Caeli put a hand on his leg and leaned in. "I promise," she repeated.

Derek had interrogated his fair share of prisoners. He knew they'd broken him.

Karan closed his eyes and sank back in the chair. "I have

duplicate files of your research here. Take it all. I'll do whatever you want."

Derek should have felt relief that Karan was going to cooperate, but instead, he was unsettled by this sudden humanity his captive had revealed. Motioning for Caeli to switch places, he sat down in the chair staring at Karan, this enemy he'd been at war with for almost his entire adult life, and felt as wrung out as the other man looked.

"Why?" Derek whispered, his question so much more complicated than just the single word.

In the heavy silence, he felt the attention of everyone in the room riveted on the two of them.

Karan kept his face expressionless. He looked beyond Derek, at some distant memory. "Twenty years ago, a star fewer than thirty light years from our world went supernova. The stratospheric ozone on our planet diminished by half and allowed damaging radiation to reach the planet's surface. Finding a new home became imperative," he answered.

"There were other habitable planets out there, but you invaded sovereign worlds," Derek said, eyes narrowing.

"The radiation had already made many of us sick."

"Then why didn't you reach out? The Alliance would have helped your people."

"Are you sure?" Karan asked.

Derek stared at him. If the Alliance had figured out who the Drokarans were and where they'd come from originally, they may not have been willing to help. Most of that information had long since been lost and forgotten, but the Drokarans would have had no way of knowing that.

Karan continued speaking. "A few in our leadership felt we should make our presence known to outsiders and ask for help. But most believed we should take a healthy planet with infrastructure already in place and assimilate its people. We targeted two remote worlds with small populations."

"Delphis and Arendal," Derek said.

Karan gave a curt nod. "I participated in the planning and invasion, believing it was the correct course of action."

"That decision cost hundreds of thousands of lives."

"The instances of disease in our population were growing exponentially. We've been genetically altered to pass along modified traits to our offspring, and our bodies didn't distinguish between the originally designed mutations and the new harmful anomalies. We were desperate," Karan said.

"In your desperation, you turned Arendal into a biological wasteland," Kat said, her voice low and deadly.

"No," Karan answered.

"What do you mean, no?" Derek demanded.

Karan locked his gaze onto Derek's own. "I mean, we did not turn that world into a biological wasteland. We made a mistake, yes. We tested a gene therapy protocol on the colonists, and most of the test subjects died. It was unfortunate and unintended, but there was no contamination."

"That world is under a level one quarantine. If you didn't turn it into a biohazard, what the hell happened?"

Karan stared straight ahead. A muscle in his cheek twitched. "When the first attempt to find a cure failed, we discontinued that line of research. By then, the Alliance had received word of the invasions and sent a fleet. We met them with our own, and a standoff ensued. Our commanding officer was authorized to negotiate a peace treaty."

"The Alliance never negotiated with Drokaran leadership," Derek said.

"An Alliance admiral met with ours, and we came to an agreement," Karan insisted.

This wasn't a version of history Derek had ever heard. He glanced at Kat, who looked similarly confused. "What agreement?"

"We would surrender Delphis and move our people to Arendal, and the Alliance would assist with medical care and research. We agreed to every term, including reparations for the loss of life on Arendal. We were past the point of thinking about anything but our children's survival."

Derek's stomach churned. "But that's not what happened."

"No," Karan agreed.

Drew and Kat looked stunned, and Caeli stood wide-eyed. Derek got up from the chair and paced. Only Sean seemed unsurprised by the direction of the conversation.

"When we'd moved our civilian population from Delphis to Arendal, the Alliance fired on our ships, destroying the fleet, and then bombed Arendal until the planet was, in fact, a wasteland."

A stunned silence filled the room. Derek stopped moving. He didn't want to believe Karan, but even without Caeli's horrified look of confirmation, he knew the man was telling the truth.

When Karan spoke again, his face was devoid of emotion. "We sent only the first wave of our colonists to Delphis and Arendal. Once the Alliance betrayed us, we were united in a new strategy."

***

Derek felt like he'd been kicked in the gut. From the shocked silence filling the room, he knew everyone else was struggling to process the implication of Karan's words.

"That's not the story we've all been told," he said to Karan.

"It is the truth."

Kat shook her head in denial. "No way. We're missing something."

The color drained from Drew's face, and he dropped his weapon to his side.

Derek knew he had to pull his shit together quickly. He looked around the room at his stunned team. "We will find answers. I promise you. But whatever happened on Arendal, it doesn't change what we have to do here. We have to finish our mission."

Drew still hadn't moved. Derek watched the emotions play over his friend's normally impassive face. Disbelief morphed into an icy rage. "This was my *home*."

Derek knew what the younger man was thinking. If the Alliance had the opportunity to negotiate for peace over a decade ago and didn't take it, the Mirans had been the first to pay the price for that decision. Derek couldn't allow his own thoughts to circle down that dark path.

Shaking his head, he stepped toward Drew. "I swear to you, we'll do whatever it takes to find the truth, but right now we're going to fight beside the Mirans because we owe it to them. We have to lock this shit away right now. Can you do that?" he asked.

Drew stood silent and still, working to compose himself. Finally, he answered, "Yes, sir."

Kat hesitantly reached for Drew's hand. Derek vaguely noticed Sean taking in the scene. Something was going on in the agent's head. Now wasn't the time to ask, but he had to know if Sean could do his job. He had to know that everyone could.

"Can you all do that?"

Kat and Sean gave him tight nods. When he turned to Caeli, she still looked stunned, but she nodded too.

CAELI

CHAPTER 18

Caeli knew Derek wasn't in a good place. She was still reeling from Karan's words as well, but they had to move. The MLA, strategically placed outside targets all over the continent, were waiting for them to initiate the offensive.

Drew wore Karan's clothing, a version of the Drokaran standard military uniform that would hopefully help him blend in with the staff at the base. Caeli, her worn clothes covered with a lab coat, tucked her last vial of neurostimulant into her pocket.

Her stomach lurched as their vehicle picked up speed to enter the highway system. She'd been with this group on other occasions at the start of an operation. The tense silence felt familiar as each person mentally prepared for the coming mission, but this time there was an undercurrent of distraction, an inner disquiet they all shared.

When they were within half a mile of the command center, Karan disengaged the auto-drive and maneuvered onto a deserted side road. Derek, Sean, and Kat grabbed their gear and jumped out into the darkness.

"Stay safe," Derek said.

"You too," Caeli answered.

He stared at Caeli as if trying to memorize every detail of her face before he turned and jogged off the road with the others. She sat back and squeezed her eyes shut as Drew slid the door closed.

Karan, seated in the front of the vehicle, sealed off the back compartment to shield Drew and Caeli from view. Explaining their presence at the security gates of the command center would create too much of a risk. They'd stay hidden until the vehicle was well inside the facility.

In the quiet compartment, Drew said, "Every time we leave each other, I wonder if this is the last time I'm going to see her, either because I'm dead or she is."

Caeli reached for his hand and squeezed. Drew leaned his head against the seat back and stared at the ceiling.

A few moments later, the vehicle slowed and came to a stop. Drew reached into his bag and pulled out a gun. Caeli held her breath and listened to Karan's muffled voice. She could feel his tumultuous thoughts, the tension and sharp pain of emotional trauma lurking just beneath the surface.

The only reason Derek had allowed Caeli, instead of Kat or Sean, to accompany Drew inside the facility was that Caeli would know instantly if the Drokaran tried to expose them. But Karan kept his outward composure and followed the plan. Within seconds, they were moving again.

When the vehicle stopped a final time, Karan opened the rear compartment. Drew and Caeli gathered their gear and followed his lead. Winding through the underbelly of the facility, they were able to avoid contact with anyone until they reached the main operational level. There, Karan nodded brusquely at the staff, most of whom yielded a wide berth when he passed.

There were no Drokaran guards keeping watch outside the locked control room. The biometric security panel played that role instead, denying unauthorized access and initiating a facility-wide lockdown if it suspected any kind of breach. In fact, this was the mission's biggest complication. Karan had warned them they'd trigger a lockdown sooner or later, even with his cooperation.

Karan placed a hand over the sensor. A second panel opened at his eye level and initiated a retinal scan. When both were complete, a heavy metal door slid open.

Drew already had his weapon drawn when all three hurried into the room. Met by startled looks, Karan spoke. "I am initiating a command override. Step away from the terminals," he ordered.

"Yes, sir." An officer stood and backed away from his post.

The second occupant, a woman, also stood, but eyed Drew and Caeli with open suspicion. "Sir, this is highly irregular," she said.

"It is," Karan agreed, settling himself at the vacated control terminal and otherwise ignoring the woman.

Watching her, Caeli felt her wariness and knew she was poised to act. As the woman's hand inched toward her weapon, Caeli shouted, "Drew!"

He fired. The Drokaran woman slammed backward into the wall, eyes wide with shock. Her body slid to the ground, a crimson pool spreading beneath her.

Drew turned to the other Drokaran and fired again, hitting the man before he could make sense of the situation and draw his own weapon.

The sudden violence gave way to stillness. Drew gave Caeli a pained look and squatted down to open his bag. "We have to set the charges."

He surveyed the room. Caeli felt his mind calculating and planning. Gently, he removed six pellets from a container and placed them on the ground, then unscrewed the lid of another container and rolled bits of a claylike substance between his fingers. After folding a pellet into each of the soft balls, he pressed a detonator into each. When he'd finished, he stood and began strategically placing the small bombs around the room.

Karan watched Drew for a moment and then turned back to his workstation. "I'm initiating a system-wide shutdown and locking out remote control access. The only way to override the command will be from this room," he said.

As soon as Karan finished, an alarm blared, and Caeli jumped. "Unscheduled shutdown detected. Security breach. Level one alert." The message repeated itself.

Karan stood. "You have less than three minutes before a security team arrives."

Drew hurried to place the final charge and then gestured to Caeli and Karan. "Done. Let's go."

Karan sat back in his chair. "Remember your promise," he said to Caeli.

She froze.

"We don't have time for this. Move," Drew ordered, pointing his gun at Karan.

"I'm not leaving. Once you're out, I'll secure the room from inside. This is the only way to guarantee the security team won't breach and reactivate the shield."

Drew hesitated. "They won't be able to disarm all the devices."

"No, but they can easily transfer command of the network to a remote site."

Caeli knew Karan was lying. The security detail would never be able to undo what he'd done in time. She held his gaze.

"I am not leaving this room. I have betrayed my people. I am a traitor to my cause, but *we* are not allies. My son's survival is what matters to me now. Nothing else."

"Leave him," Caeli said to Drew.

"Are you sure?"

"Yes. Let's go."

Drew punched the control panel, and the door opened.

"Caeli," Karan called. She turned.

"The ground forces here will fight, but you'll likely prevail. Our fleet isn't going to come to reinforce Mira." He spoke slowly, deliberately, his eyes holding hers. "It's on its way to Almagest. They're going home to take back what's ours."

DEREK

CHAPTER 19

"Detonating now." Drew's voice sounded in Derek's ear. Activity around the facility had already increased, and Derek knew once the control room blew, things would get messier.

From his vantage point atop a hill, he watched through night vision glasses as a cloud of debris erupted from one side of the building. The vibration shook his whole body.

"That was thorough," he said under his breath.

Confusion reigned. Soldiers ran from the security checkpoint toward the destruction. Alarms blared. People staggered from the rubble.

Reaching into his pack, Derek removed a long-range transmitter. He sent a brief, coded message to Rayna on the frequency she'd given him, letting her know the shield was down.

As he replaced the radio in the bag, Drew's voice spoke in his ear again. "We're in a little trouble."

"What's wrong?" Derek asked.

"A firewall just blocked our path to the exit, and since we didn't have time to learn the layout, I'm running blind here."

"Can't Karan find an alternate route?"

There was silence on the other end of his com.

"Drew?"

"He didn't make it," Drew answered.

Derek took a moment to process this. "Shit."

"Yeah."

"Can you still move around without being recognized?" Derek asked, his mind working to formulate a plan.

"Yeah, so far," answered Drew. "I'm backtracking. The facility's locked down, but people have to get away from the blast zone. We'll try to follow the crowd outside."

Derek could hear alarms blaring and voices shouting through the open com. "It looks like they're evacuating from the south exit. See if you can get out on that side."

Bodies streamed from the doorway and congregated in the yard, still locked within the perimeter gates but outside the building. Huge stadium lights flared on, bathing the courtyard in an artificial glow as bright as the midday sun.

"Drones coming in from the west," Kat alerted them. "I'm sure troops will follow. We have to do something quick, otherwise Caeli and Drew are going to be trapped in there."

"Agreed." Shouldering his gun, Derek slid down the dirt embankment. The back side of the facility abutted a hilly forest of old growth trees, offering good cover as he circled around to meet Kat and Sean.

The others had taken positions across from the main security checkpoint and were hidden in a lot full of metal storage containers. Watching the sky for drones, Derek ducked in next to them.

"Think we can blow a hole in the perimeter wall?" he asked, slightly out of breath.

"I've got enough explosives to do it," replied Sean. "We

should hit the south side. It'll cause some collateral damage, but Drew and Caeli will be able to use the chaos to their advantage."

Derek didn't like the idea, but Sean was right. "Drew? Are you out of the building yet?"

"Almost," Drew answered. His voice sounded strained.

"Follow the crowd, but stay tight to the building."

"Roger that."

"One charge should be enough," Derek said, turning to Sean. "Set it up here. Make a run for the wall, and Kat and I will cover you while you place it."

Sean squatted down and opened his pack. They'd known they'd have to improvise at some point in the operation, so they'd divided a few of the explosive devices between them. Before leaving Karan's, Drew had given them all a quick lesson on arming the bombs.

Derek held a small flashlight while Sean worked. With steady hands, Sean placed the detonator into the sticky ball and stood up. "Ready when you are."

"Go," Derek ordered.

Sean took off at a run, Derek and Kat following him out from behind the container and through the lot. He passed the security gate unchallenged and rounded the corner to the south side. Derek and Kat flanked him, watching their backs and keeping an eye on the sky.

The moment Sean approached the wall, a drone screamed by. Derek dropped to one knee and tried to track it in the scope of his gun, but it was in and out of his line of sight before he could get a shot off.

"Did it see us?" Kat asked.

Before Derek could answer, the drone circled back and

slowed directly over their heads. Small pinpricks of light targeted Sean's back.

"Sean!" Derek yelled, firing at the drone.

It exploded in a bright flash. Pieces of metal rained down, littering the ground.

"Another one!" Kat yelled. She fired, and it went down in a heap.

"Charge is set," Sean said.

"Get clear," Derek ordered, shooting another drone out of the sky as Sean raced toward them.

Derek's heart pounded in his chest, adrenaline coursing through his body as they ran, full speed, back toward the shipping containers. As he dove under cover, Derek shouted, "Drew, Caeli, fire in the hole."

Sean pressed the remote trigger.

The blast rattled Derek's teeth. Through the open com, he heard screams. Glancing at Kat, he caught her tense look.

After the seconds had stretched to a minute, Drew finally said, "We're okay." Derek exhaled the breath he'd been holding. "We have to keep moving. Meet you at the access road."

"See you there," Drew promised.

Tapping off his com, Derek turned in time to watch Sean slide down the side of the container, leaving a dark smear on the wall behind him.

"Shit," Kat said, squatting beside him.

"How bad is it?" Derek asked.

Sean coughed, and a trickle of blood ran from the corner of his mouth. "It doesn't hurt. But I don't think that's a good sign," he said, leaning his head back as his eyes drifted closed.

"Stay with me," Derek ordered, an edge of panic in his voice.

"We need Caeli," Kat said.

"I know, but we can't stay here."

Kat gave him a tight nod. "You move him. I'll cover us."

"Sean, we've got to go," Derek said, looping an arm around the man's waist and hauling him to his feet.

Sean groaned, leaning heavily on Derek. They stayed tight to the container walls and stumbled through the yard.

"There's a lot of activity outside the perimeter now. People running. Chaos. Looks like the rest of the drones are circling the blast site for now," Kat reported.

"Good," Derek said, breathing heavily and sweating under Sean's weight. "Drew and Caeli should be able to get out. If we can get back behind the hill, the trees and rock formations will give us cover." Otherwise, he didn't add, they'd be easy targets once the drones expanded their search grid.

Fifteen minutes later, he carefully laid Sean on the dusty ground under a rocky outcropping. Sean struggled to breathe.

"Derek. I need to tell you something," the wounded man said, but a wet, rasping sound accompanied his every inhalation. Small, bloody bubbles leaked from the corner of his mouth.

"Save your breath. You can tell me later." Derek tapped his com. "Drew. Where are you two?"

"Heading to the access road now. Caeli's hiding us, and the drones are sticking close to the building."

Sean's head lolled to the side. Alarmed, Derek used his pack to prop him up. "I'm sending Kat to meet you. Sean's in bad shape."

Kat hurried out, her form quickly disappearing in the shadows.

Derek sat back on his heels, frustrated by his helplessness. Without medical supplies, there was almost nothing he could do but apply pressure to the wound.

Time crawled by. Derek spoke to Sean, urging him to hold

on, willing him to survive. As pale dawn light bathed the shallow cave, the blood smeared across Sean's cheek stood in sharp contrast to his pale, grayish skin and blue-tinged lips.

"Kat!" Derek yelled into his com.

"We're here," she said, emerging from the shadows in a full sprint. Caeli was right behind her, Drew taking up the rear.

Derek backed out of the way, and Caeli dropped to her knees beside Sean. Placing her hands on his chest, she closed her eyes.

"His lung is shredded. Several ribs are splintered," she said softly, almost to herself.

Derek watched her silent healing, as he had so many times before. Kat leaned back into Drew, who put his arms around her. All three stared, tense and transfixed, while Caeli worked.

A little color crept back into Sean's face, but drained from Caeli's. Her body shook from exertion, and sweat beaded on her forehead. When Sean's chest began to rise and fall rhythmically, Caeli sat back on her heels, swaying with exhaustion.

"I've repaired the damage, but he's in shock. We have to replace his blood volume, and I can't do that here," she said, looking up anxiously at Derek.

Derek ran a hand through his hair. "Let's get to the access road."

Drew and Kat carried Sean's limp body between them, and Derek helped Caeli to her feet. He held her around her waist as the ragged group made their way toward the road.

They stopped a few yards from the edge of the street, and Derek left Caeli sitting against the thick trunk of a tree. The other two deposited Sean next to her, his head on her lap.

Derek checked his weapon, positioning himself in the middle of the road. "We don't have time to ask nicely," he said.

The warm morning breeze promised a hot, dry Miran day.

Drew and Kat stood off to the side, their weapons drawn. Derek heard the first vehicle approach and prayed it wasn't a Drokaran patrol. Squinting against the rising sun, he made out only one person inside a vehicle that looked too worn to be military issue. He allowed himself a moment's relief.

The vehicle stopped a few feet in front of him. Derek pointed his gun at the windshield and circled to the driver's door. Kat and Drew joined him. As he gestured with his weapon, the driver got out, holding his shaking arms in the air.

"Where are you going?" Derek demanded.

The man nervously lifted an identification badge from a lanyard around his neck and held it out to Derek. "To the hydro-purification plant. I work maintenance there."

"Not today," Derek said. "Drew, Kat, get Sean and Caeli. We can all fit in here."

The pair jogged back toward the woods.

"I can't be late . . ."

"There's some trouble in the city. You don't want to be there right now. What's your name?" Derek asked.

The man hesitated for a second, then answered, "Garret. Garret Colson. Who are you?"

Derek could only imagine how he looked, covered in Sean's blood and carrying a high-powered assault weapon, but he ignored the man's question. "We need a clinic. One without Draks. Can you get us to one?"

Garret licked his lip and ran a hand over his sweaty brow, eyeing the gun trained on his chest. "Don't imagine I have a choice, do I?"

"Not really, no."

Garret glanced toward the woods, where Kat and Drew reemerged, supporting Sean between them. He looked back at

Derek, frowning. "What happened?"

"Help them," Derek barked.

Garret hurried to slide open the rear compartment door. Kat and Drew maneuvered themselves and Sean inside, Caeli climbing in beside them. Circling around to the front, Derek got in next to Garret.

"Go," he said.

Garret turned the vehicle around and drove back down the access road, his hands shaking. "The district where I live has a small clinic. No Draks. They don't come around much."

"Good. We aren't going to hurt you. Just take us to that clinic," Derek said.

The wooded area gave way to desert-like terrain. Red dirt and brown canyons stretched out on all sides. After several miles, they arrived at their destination—a compact town nestled into a low-lying valley.

"We're pretty self-sufficient out here," Garret explained, nervously rambling as he drove slowly through the streets. "That's our water supply in the tank. We use condenser technology. I work with the hydro plant in the city and use my skills to keep ours running. Most people have to work somewhere else to get enough food credits, but we manage to keep the Draks out of here."

"There's probably nothing they need from these small border towns except workers," Drew said from the back.

Garret raised his eyebrows and glanced quickly over his shoulder. "That's true."

"How much longer?" Caeli asked, her voice tight.

"We're here," their driver said as they pulled up in front of a small, dusty building. "No one's in yet. I'll go around the back."

While Kat and Drew carried Sean from the vehicle, Derek

strode toward the front door of the ramshackle building.
Flipping his gun in his hand, he brought the butt down on the
lock and then kicked the door open.

CAELI

CHAPTER 20

Caeli scanned the area. "Put him there," she said, pointing to a gurney in a room that looked like it was set up for emergencies.

Kat and Drew carefully lifted Sean onto the bed and backed away to give Caeli room. Derek shoved Garret into a chair in the opposite corner.

Rummaging through drawers and cabinets, Caeli quickly found what she was looking for. Even in the middle of a desert town on a foreign world, there were only so many ways to get fluids into an injured body. She pulled a stool up to Sean's bedside and went to work. Bone-deep fatigue made her sluggish, but her hands were steady even as she had to fight to keep her eyes open.

Once the artificial plasma flowed steadily into Sean's veins, Caeli allowed herself a moment to breathe. She put one hand on his chest so she could feel his body respond and let her head rest on the edge of the bed.

"How is he?" Derek asked softly.

"He's lost so much blood," she answered. Derek gave her shoulder a gentle squeeze.

"What's going on in here?" a woman shouted.

Caeli jumped. All at once, Drew, Kat, and Derek turned, raising their weapons at the new arrival.

She froze. Caeli felt her fear like a blast of heat from a furnace.

"Guess we should've had a guard at the front door," Drew said.

"Garret?" the woman asked, stumbling backward a step. "What are you doing? Who are these people?"

"Are you the doctor here?" Derek asked.

She swallowed and nodded.

"Our friend needed help," he told her. "We couldn't wait."

"Why the guns?"

Derek carefully lowered his weapon so it pointed at the woman's feet, but Caeli noticed his finger still hovered over the trigger. "There's been some activity in the city overnight," he said.

"Emergency alerts just started going out," the doctor replied.

Suddenly, Garret stood. "I need to get to my family," he said, his voice quaking with nerves.

Derek pointed the gun at him.

"Please," he begged.

"You told me the Draks wouldn't bother us out here," Derek said.

"They usually don't, but something's happening. You're here with guns. These alerts. Please. I only want to get my family out of harm's way."

"He's telling the truth," Caeli said softly.

"Everyone has a place to hide, just in case," the doctor added.

After a moment's hesitation, Derek gestured at Garret. "Go."

"Thank you," the other man replied, and hurried out the back door.

"You sure that was a good idea?" Kat asked.

Derek sighed. "If things go to shit, we're *all* in trouble."

Kat raised her eyebrows and nodded her silent agreement.

"What about you? Do you have family you want to be with?" Derek asked the doctor, whose fear seemed to have transformed itself into resolve.

"Yes, but he knows the drill. He's already in the shelter. Now tell me who you really are," she demanded.

Derek shouldered his weapon and leaned wearily against the wall. "Alliance military."

Caeli watched the emotions play over the woman's face. "Did you start whatever's going on out there?" she asked.

Derek looked at Kat and shrugged. "We're trying to help finish it."

The doctor stared past Derek, at a memory so vivid Caeli could almost touch it.

"I'm Shea Maher. My husband was Major Quinn Maher, Miran Air Defense. He was killed in the first wave."

Derek closed his eyes. "I'm sorry for your loss," he said. The words were formal, but Caeli felt the depth of Derek's own losses echoed in them.

"I wanted to fight, but I was pregnant," Shea said, as if needing to explain herself. "When it was clear the Drokarans had won and the occupation force was here to stay, things got ugly for a while. The Draks still keep a tight grip on the cities. Out here, though, they leave us alone. I stayed to keep my son safe, and because I'm the only doctor."

The room fell silent for several moments. Caeli could feel the indecision in Derek's mind. Finally, he nodded at Shea. "Go. Be with your son."

"I came over to grab a few things. With the alerts, no one will be out today." Shea paused and looked at each of them. "I can hide you in our shelter," she offered.

"We can't move him." Derek gestured at Sean.

"Is there anything I can do to help?"

Derek looked to Caeli. She shook her head. "He nearly bled out. The plasma replacement is what he needs. I just hope it was in time."

"I hope so too. There are some supplies, food, and water in the staff room. I'll keep the shutters closed and lock the front door. Good luck," Shea said, turning to leave.

"You too," Derek answered.

When the door clicked shut behind Shea a few moments later, Caeli let her head drop back onto the bed. Her body shook with fatigue, but her mind raced, playing back the events of the last few hours.

***

They ran from the control room, Karan's words echoing in Caeli's mind. "Our fleet isn't going to come to reinforce Mira. It's on its way to Almagest."

Everything she'd fought for, everything they'd all sacrificed, would be for nothing if the Drokarans sank their teeth into Almagest.

She stumbled, Drew pulling her along. When they were far enough away from the control room, she heard him speaking with Derek over the com. Their words barely registered.

With her mind still linked to Karan's, she felt the explosion in her whole body, a moment of blinding pain followed by an emptiness so complete she collapsed onto the ground.

Drew knelt next to her, brows furrowed in concern. Caeli shook her head and staggered to her feet, following him again, until a dead end blocked their path. Backtracking, they turned a corner and ran straight into a Drokaran security unit.

Six guns trained on them. Drew held his own weapon up in a position of surrender. With his other arm, he pushed Caeli behind him.

She felt the patrol leader's suspicion immediately. "Who are you?" he demanded.

"What's happening?" Drew countered, stalling for time with his own question. Tension radiated off him and slammed into Caeli's body like a wave.

Partially hidden from Drokaran view, Caeli's hand crept into the pocket of her lab coat and removed the last vial of neurostimulant. She didn't have time to adjust the syringe to administer a lower dosage. When she depressed the plunger into her upper thigh, the entire vial emptied into her body.

The noise in her mind grew to an unbearable pitch. She gripped Drew's arm. Six Drokaran heartbeats drummed discordantly against her own. In her mind, she squeezed. The first Drokaran dropped his gun and clawed at his chest. One by one the others followed, their faces contorted, unable to push breath out of their opened mouths.

Caeli screamed. She screamed as the agony of each bursting heart filled her own chest. She screamed until the darkness dragged her under.

When she opened her eyes again, she was curled in the fetal position, face pressed to the floor. The sound of Drew's voice, the gentle touch of his hand on her shoulder, pulled her back to consciousness.

"We have to move."

Around them, bodies lay strewn on the ground, their expressions frozen in terror. "No, no, no . . ." Caeli mumbled.

"I've got you. We have to go," Drew coaxed. He lifted her to her feet and held on.

Within moments they were in another corridor, joining a crowd of people, heading toward an exit.

"Drew, are you out of the building yet?" she heard Derek ask.

"Almost," Drew answered.

"Follow the crowd, but stay tight to the building."

"Roger that."

Caeli squinted at the bright stadium lights as they emerged into the courtyard. "Get down," Drew ordered, yanking her toward the ground. Moments later, the ground rocked beneath them.

As the south wall blew, Drew's body covered hers. For a few seconds, they stayed curled on the ground amidst the turmoil. Finally, Drew moved.

Caeli's ears rang. She sat up, blinking in confusion.

The wide, bloody gash on the side of Drew's head snapped her disoriented mind back into the moment. "You're hurt," she said.

"I'm okay," he said, but when he tried to get up, he collapsed onto his hands and knees and vomited into the dirt.

"Stay down," Caeli said, putting a shaking hand over the wound. In moments, she'd stopped the bleeding and sealed the hairline fracture in his skull. "Better?"

"Much." He searched her face. "Are you alright?"

Her momentary surge of clear-headedness began slipping.

"I killed them," she said.

"You saved us."

She wrapped her arms around herself, body trembling.

"We have to keep moving, Caeli. Lock it away," Drew urged.

She tried to drive the image of dead Drokarans from her mind.

"You can do this. You're one of the strongest people I know."

He staggered to his feet, pulling her up with him. Dust swirled. Bodies, and parts of bodies, lay scattered among the rubble. The living crawled around the dead in panic. Caeli threw a hand over her mouth and stared.

Drew grabbed her by the other hand and dragged her past the carnage. She wanted to stop, to help, to undo some of the horror of her own actions, but he wouldn't let go. "We can't, Caeli. We'll be trapped in here when more troops arrive. They'll figure out who we are." When they finally cleared the blast zone, they began to run.

***

Sean shivered, his weakened body unable to regulate its own temperature. Blinking, Caeli forced herself back into the present. She jumped off her stool and pulled open drawers and cabinets until she found a pile of blankets. Derek, standing on the other side of the gurney, caught the end she tossed to him.

Replacing Sean's empty IV bag with a full one, she listened to his heart, the beat growing steadier and more rhythmic. "He's getting stronger," she said, allowing hope to creep into her voice for the first time since she'd touched Sean's ravaged body in the cave.

Derek's shoulders relaxed and he let out a deep exhalation. Kat, who'd been sitting in tense silence next to Drew in one corner of the room, stretched and got to her feet. "I'm going to go check out those supplies Shea said were here." Drew followed her.

Caeli lingered over Sean, touching his forehead, scanning his body with her mind. He stirred, and his eyes fluttered open.

"Hey there," she said, relieved.

Shivers still wracked him under the heavy blanket, and dark circles rimmed his eyes, but he looked back at her lucidly. "I feel like someone's sitting on my chest," he whispered.

"I know. One lung was torn to shreds, and your ribs on that side were shattered. It was a bit of a challenge putting you back together again. Once I've had a little more rest, I can help speed up the healing. For now, though, I'm sure I can find you a good pain-killer."

"That would be outstanding," he said, wincing when he spoke.

Derek sat with Sean while Caeli searched through the supply of medications. "I should be dead," she heard Sean say.

"I'm glad you aren't," Derek answered.

"Thanks for getting me out of there."

"This should do it," Caeli said, returning to Sean's bedside and drawing up a syringe.

As she injected him, Kat and Drew trailed back into the room, arms full of bottled water and energy bars. Drew tossed a bottle to Derek, who unscrewed the top and drank it down.

"Welcome back to the land of the living," Kat said to Sean. "You had us worried for a while there."

"Thanks for having my back," Sean answered.

Drew held a bottle out to Caeli, who took it and helped Sean take a few careful sips. His eyelids were already growing heavy again.

"This feels nice," Sean said, smiling as the powerful drug flowed into his system. Caeli gently lowered his head back onto the pillow.

The rest of them drank down the water and split the food. Caeli didn't realize how hungry she was until she found herself licking crumbs off her fingers.

"It feels strange to sit this one out," Kat said.

Derek ran a hand over his face. "We're in no condition to fight."

"I know," she agreed, sighing. She leaned back into Drew and closed her eyes.

Caeli could barely keep herself upright. Sean was out cold

from the cocktail she'd just given him. Drew still had a nasty concussion, despite her work to heal his fractured skull and bleeding brain. And none of them had slept in almost three days.

"We've done our part. Hopefully it will be enough," Derek said.

DEREK

CHAPTER 21

Derek wheeled another gurney next to Sean, and Caeli gratefully collapsed onto it. Kat and Drew found another bed in the adjacent room. Now sitting alone by the front window for first watch, Derek adjusted the shutter for a clear view of the street.

Not a single person appeared. The whole town was eerily quiet, as if it had been abandoned. Really, they'd learned to adapt. They'd found ways to survive, to take care of one another, to *live* in this occupied state. Derek wondered if any of them would still be alive by nightfall.

When Kat came to relieve him a few hours later, they stood together in silence. Finally, Kat sighed. "They're still the enemy. We've seen what they can do, what they're willing to do."

"I know. But what if they're not the only enemy?"

"Get some rest, Derek," she said, nudging his elbow.

Venturing back inside, he climbed into the hospital bed next to Caeli and wrapped himself around her, too exhausted to think anymore.

Several hours later, Kat shook him awake. He sat up, disoriented. Caeli stirred beside him.

"Fighter squadrons," she said, and he jumped out of the bed.

The pair of them raced out the door. Shading their eyes from the glare of the setting sun, they looked toward the horizon. Hundreds of dark specks filled the sky. As the fighters approached, the ground vibrated under Derek's feet, and a roaring hum echoed through the entire valley.

Drew and Caeli appeared. Sean followed, holding up his own IV bag and leaning precariously in the doorway.

"Alliance fighters," he said, grinning.

The squadron passed over them, heading toward the city.

"You think a Drokaran force is close behind?" Kat asked.

"No," Caeli answered, and all eyes turned to her.

"Karan said they won't send reinforcements to Mira." She paused and wrapped her arms around herself. "The Drokaran fleet is on its way to Almagest."

Drew nodded his solemn confirmation, and Derek swore.

"They're going home," Caeli finished.

Derek could see realization dawning in Kat's eyes. "The Drokarans are from Almagest. Those old lab records we found in the bunker . . . They started the war on your home world a millennium ago."

Caeli stared vacantly at the sky. "We were all created in some hideous experiment. They were the desired outcome. We were an unintended mistake."

Derek could see Caeli's whole body trembling. He felt the despair and horror spill from her unguarded mind into his.

"But now they're sick, and my DNA, *Novali* DNA, can cure them."

"Ah, Caeli," Kat said, putting a hand on her shoulder.

"And they want to turn us into weapons. They'll use us . . ." Her voice trailed off, and she wrapped her arms protectively around herself.

"Caeli," Derek said cautiously, as if talking to a skittish animal.

She blinked at him, shaking her head. "They want to save their children, but they'll destroy us to do it. I want to go home and fight, and I want to save those children too. Everything is different. Everything I thought I knew, the things I believed, they're all different."

"Not everything is different," Kat said. "Your home and your people are worth saving. You've worked so hard, sacrificed so much, to build a future for Almagest. The Drokarans, no matter where they came from, invaded and enslaved sovereign worlds. Almagest doesn't belong to them." She paused and looked at Drew. "If the Alliance deceived us in some way, we will find out and we will deal with it. But saving Mira, saving Almagest, that's *right*."

She stepped toward Caeli and put a hand on her arm. "We fight for principles, sure. None of us would be here if we didn't believe in something bigger than ourselves. But at the end of the day, we fight for each other."

Caeli's face softened, Kat's words seeming to reach her.

As they stood outside the clinic, Derek noticed movement around various buildings. A few cautious observers had surfaced, presumably to investigate the noise.

"It's time to go," he said. "Kat, stay here with Caeli and Sean. Drew, let's see if we can find a way out of here."

***

Two hours later, they were back in Garret Colson's vehicle. It had taken a little coercion, but they'd managed to locate him and convince him to take them as far as the nearest underground train terminal.

Caeli had done a little work on Sean and Drew before they left the clinic, and both were in better shape than they had been a few hours ago. Derek had an arm around Caeli as they sped along, her head resting on his shoulder.

"We need to get back to the command center," he said. "Before we left, Rayna said they'd be staging the operations from the old factory complex above ground. Ezra has a better communications array there. She was ready to make contact with the Alliance as soon as they had a ship in range."

"We have no idea where they're engaged on the ground, though," Kat said.

"I know. We have to be careful where we stick our heads up."

The subway was nearly deserted, and the few people they did see stayed clear of them. They exited the train at the stop closest to Ezra's compound and cautiously emerged into the evening.

A distant rumble shook the ground, missiles detonating on targets not far from their position. Derek recognized the sound. Ships filled the night sky, and, unlike the border town they'd just left, the city buzzed with frenetic energy.

When they arrived at the run-down factory complex, an armed guard escorted them to the command center. Ezra embraced Caeli.

"Are you all right?" he asked, looking with concern at the dirty, bloody group that stood before him.

"We'll live," Derek answered. "How about you?"

"It's been rough on the ground, but now that we've got air support, it's already turning around. We're providing the Alliance with target coordinates," Ezra answered.

"I need to make contact with *Horizon* as soon as possible," Derek said.

"Rayna's in here." Ezra gestured for Derek to follow.

Placing a hand on his arm, Caeli said, "I'm going to take Sean down to the infirmary and see if they need a hand down there."

"I'll come find you soon," Derek said.

Sean, still pale and shaky on his feet, didn't argue.

Derek, Kat, and Drew followed Ezra into the communications room. Rayna, her back to them, stood in front of a large map, talking with Gage and marking coordinates. When she looked up, her eyes widened.

"Glad you made it back. What happened?" she asked.

"After we took down the shield, Caeli and Drew were caught inside. We had to improvise to get them out, and Sean was badly injured. We holed up in a border town clinic so Caeli could treat him."

"He'll be okay?" she asked.

"I think so."

She nodded sharply. "Good. Your ship, *Horizon*, and two other Alliance vessels sent fighter squadrons to provide aid. I've given them every military target the MLA knows about. We're in the middle of a massive coordinated strike right now."

"I need to contact *Horizon* immediately," Derek told her.

Rayna gave him a questioning look, but didn't argue. She offered him a seat and pointed to the transmitter.

"*Horizon* control, this is Captain Derek Markham, authentication code 758959 Delta."

A familiar voice answered. "Authentication verified. Captain, it's good to hear your voice."

"Back at you, Riley. My team needs immediate extraction."

"Roger that, sir. I'll pass along the message and get back to you on this channel ASAP. Send coordinates."

"Stand by one."

He looked to Rayna, who turned to the map and tapped a spot with her finger. "They could safely land here, away from the action."

Derek passed the information to Riley, who confirmed a few minutes later that a ship would be coming for them.

Leaning back in the chair, Derek closed his eyes. "I have credible intel that the Drokarans won't be sending reinforcements."

Rayna stopped moving and ran a hand over her face. "How do you know that? Never mind. It doesn't matter," she said, shaking her head and clearing her throat. "By tomorrow morning, we could be free of the Draks. I never thought I'd see this day. Thank you. For everything."

Derek met her gaze. "I'm sorry it took so long."

CAELI

CHAPTER 22

The injured poured into the understaffed infirmary. Several medics worked triage while the doctors dealt with the most critical cases.

Caeli had brought Sean with her to continue treating him, but he looked the picture of health compared to the bodies piled on stretchers and slumped against walls. She turned to one of the medics. "I'm Dr. Crys. Give me the next patient," she ordered.

The frazzled medic pointed at a gurney. "Chest cavity's a mess. Heart's still beating, but if you want to call it, I'll black tag him."

"Let me have a look first," she replied, gesturing for Sean to help push the stretcher into a trauma room. Already filled with another team, the space was cramped and loud, and no one paid them any attention.

Placing her hands on the young man's chest, Caeli used her inner vision. "This is what your chest looked like, practically shredded inside."

"Can I help?" Sean asked.

"Find me a large-caliber needle and syringe. Try those

drawers," she said. Sean dug through them until he held up something.

She nodded. "I'm going to remove blood from the sac around his heart. That should relieve some pressure."

Closing her eyes, Caeli positioned the needle. "There," she said, and depressed the plunger. When she drew it back up, bright red blood filled the syringe.

"Now, I'm going to remove the bone fragments from his lungs." She placed her hands back on her patient's torn chest, envisioning each piece connecting back where it belonged, like fitting the pieces of a puzzle together.

When she finished, she searched the supplies for an IV set-up and started a line. "If I do much more with my gift, I'll be too tired to help anyone else. This should be good enough for now."

She and Sean returned to the triage area to find Derek looking for them. "We have to go," he said.

"They need help here," she said.

"I know, but we have to get back to *Horizon*."

Torn between her need to alleviate the suffering around her and her urgent desire to help the people on her own world, she stood staring at the carnage.

"The Alliance will send support, medical teams," Derek said.

"Not in time for them," she whispered.

Derek didn't try to convince her otherwise. He simply waited for her to make the only choice she could.

They left the chaos of the infirmary for the slightly more controlled chaos of the operations center.

"Where are Navi and Marta?" Caeli asked.

She could tell by the way Derek looked at her that he'd all but forgotten about the little boy.

"I made a promise, Derek," she said.

"I know you did. I haven't seen Luka around."

Just as Derek mentioned his name, the boy appeared, his face splitting into a wide grin when he saw Caeli.

"I heard you were back."

Caeli pulled him into a tight embrace. "You're okay?" she asked.

"Better than you guys, I think," he answered, looking them up and down.

"We're a little banged up, but we'll be fine. Luka, where are Navi and Marta?" she asked softly.

His expression turned somber. "I didn't want to bring a Drak here, even a baby one. I thought about what you said before. How people do things when they're desperate. I just had a bad feeling."

Luka turned to Derek and said, "My orders were to keep them safe. They're safe."

"Good call," Derek said. The young man glowed under the praise. "We have to leave soon, and Navi's coming with us. Can you bring him and Marta to a meeting point?"

"Yes, sir," Luka answered.

***

Mira's lack of cloud cover allowed the heat of the day to dissipate quickly once the sun set. Caeli shivered in the evening breeze. Derek put an arm around her, and she leaned into his warmth.

Overhead, a patch of stars winked out and a stronger gust of wind blew her hair back from her forehead. Caeli recognized the *Solstice* even before she saw the ship's familiar insignia.

When the ship touched down and Kieran Kade emerged, Derek greeted him affectionately. "Good to see you, Kade."

"Same, sir. Let's get you guys aboard."

"We're waiting for someone."

"Extra guests?" Kade asked.

Derek nodded.

"They're coming," Caeli said, feeling Luka's energy before she heard him call her name.

"You're okay?" Kade asked, turning to her. She reached out and squeezed his hand.

"I am. Thank you for coming." Kade had been with the covert Alliance unit on Almagest for the worst of the fighting, and he'd gone from a teammate to Caeli's friend in a very short amount of time.

"Wouldn't have missed the chance," he said, smiling.

Two figures walked cautiously toward them, illuminated by the glow of the ship's lights. Marta carried Navi, with Luka trotting beside her.

Caeli rushed to them. The little boy lifted his head from Marta's shoulder and, recognizing Caeli, put his arms out. She scooped him from Marta and held his warm little body against hers.

"Karan's dead," Caeli whispered to Marta. "I don't really have a plan for Navi yet, but I don't think he's safe here."

"I don't think he is either," Marta replied.

"We can take you with us, Marta," Caeli urged. "Mira will be liberated in a matter of days, but I know you love Navi, and you're all he has left."

The other woman looked wistfully at the little boy. "I want to be with him."

Marta turned to Luka, and he stepped into her open arms.

"Take care of yourself, Luka. You are a fine young man, and I couldn't be prouder if you were my own son."

"You be safe, ma'am," he answered softly.

Caeli returned Navi to Marta, and Kade ushered them forward. "Let's get you settled," he said.

When Marta and Navi disappeared onto the ship, Caeli hugged Luka hard. "Fighting isn't always the hardest part of a war. Sometimes it's finding a way to live with things afterward. Remember who you are and be true to yourself. Have a *good* life, Luka. You deserve it."

"Thank you, Caeli," he whispered in her ear.

Luka said goodbye to the rest of the group and, with a wave over his shoulder, disappeared into the dark.

Kat and Drew stepped onto *Solstice*, and Caeli started to follow.

"Caeli," Sean said. She stopped and turned around.

"I need to tell you and Derek something," he said.

"What is it?" she asked. She could feel the tension rippling off him. An icicle of dread crept up her spine. Derek stopped beside her.

"Nysa, the Novali girl." Sean paused and held Caeli's gaze. "She's alive."

"What?" Caeli gasped. "How?"

He took a deep breath and gazed out over Derek's shoulder, his face blank and his voice deadpan. "After our mission ended on Elista, my cover was blown and I was reassigned. My orders were to track the Novali girl, fake her death, and turn her over to Admiral Reyes."

Caeli stood in stunned silence. "Admiral Reyes? What did he want with her?" she asked when she found her voice again.

Sean ran a hand over his face. "What everyone else wanted, I imagine."

Video footage of Nysa first healing and then killing a small animal with her mind had created a frenzy among human traffickers on the black market. They'd realized the girl's gift could be a deadly weapon.

"So, Reyes has her now?" Derek asked. Caeli heard a dangerous undertone in his voice.

"No. I have her. Well, my wife does."

Caeli's eyes widened, and she felt Derek shift beside her.

"I've done a lot of questionable shit, but I couldn't do this. She's just a little girl."

Caeli felt Derek's mind churning at Sean's words. "Did you know about Arendal?"

They both stood in tense silence, waiting for Sean's answer.

"No. I swear. But Derek, I don't always get my orders the same way you do."

DEREK

CHAPTER 23

Derek's whole team was getting a thorough work-up by the *Horizon* medical staff. As he waited to be cleared for duty, his mind raced. Instead of forming a plan, though, his thoughts ran in circles.

Captain Donovan had met them as soon as they'd stepped off the *Solstice*. Surveying the condition of Derek's team and eyeing the extra passengers who'd exited with them, he'd said, "I think we have a lot to talk about."

"An invasion fleet is heading to Almagest," Derek told him.

A look of alarm had passed over Donovan's face. "Are you certain?"

Derek had nodded firmly.

"I'll let command know immediately. We'll debrief when you've been cleared."

"Yes, sir."

Before turning away, Donovan had narrowed his eyes at Derek. "This mission was rougher than usual."

"It got complicated."

Now, lying on his bed and staring at the ceiling in sick bay, his stomach churned. Their war was far from over, and something dangerous and corrupt lurked in their midst.

Caeli joined him, tugging the curtain closed and climbing onto the bed with him. Derek pulled her next to him. He knew she was exhausted, but instead of sinking into sleep, he felt her breathing speed up and her heart rate spike.

"What is it, Caeli?" he asked, his alarm growing as her body began to shake.

"I did something, Derek."

"Talk to me. I'm right here."

"I killed them."

"Killed who, Caeli?"

"Six Drokaran soldiers. The whole detail. I didn't knock them unconscious. I killed them. I didn't mean to, but I took too much."

"Of the neurostimulant?" he asked softly.

She nodded as the horror in her mind poured unchecked into his. "They cornered us. We had to get out."

The scene unfolded in his head. The security detail stopping Caeli and Drew in the corridor. Drew stalling for time, knowing they were caught. Caeli injecting herself with the stimulant and, in a moment of uncontrolled panic, taking out all the soldiers with the power of her mind.

He felt her mind spiraling into darkness and tried to grab hold of her thoughts, but this time he couldn't.

She pushed away from him and off the bed, backing into the wall. Sliding onto the ground, she wrapped her arms around her knees. As she rocked back and forth, the scene played over and over in her mind and in his. Her hair stuck to her forehead with sweat and her cheeks flushed pink. He sank to his knees in front of her, watching helplessly.

When her mind finally ran itself out and he felt the frenzy recede, he brushed the back of his hand over her wet cheeks.

She blinked at him with recognition. As he wrapped his arms around her, she leaned into him, shivering. Scooping her into his arms, he carried her limp, exhausted body back onto the bed.

"I can't do this anymore. Derek, I'm losing myself," she whispered.

"You're still you, Caeli. You've had to do things to survive that you'd never do in ordinary circumstances. We all have. You had to make a choice, and you chose to live. You saved Drew's life." He held her closer. "I am so, so sorry for all the things that have happened to you. But you're a survivor, and a leader, and a healer. You were those things before the war, and you're still those things."

She didn't answer.

***

When the ship alarm sounded a few hours later, they'd both fallen asleep. Despite the weight of anxiety Derek carried, his physical exhaustion had won out. Startled awake from his deep, dreamless state, his eyes flew open. Caeli sat up beside him.

"What's happening?"

"We're leaving the system."

A few seconds later, a voice spoke over the ship's com. "This is Captain Donovan. We've been reassigned. Prepare to jump at 15:30."

"We're going to Almagest," Caeli said.

"Looks like."

"How long have we been asleep?"

Before Derek could answer her question, Dr. Gates appeared,

pushing back the curtain. "Four hours. I'd hoped to buy you a few more, but I know you're needed elsewhere. Consider yourself cleared for duty. Kat and Drew as well, but I'm keeping Lieutenant Commander Asher for a few more hours."

"Thanks, doc," Derek said, sliding off the bed.

"How is Sean?" Caeli asked.

"Per your usual thorough work, he'll be fine. We're just building up his fluid volume some more."

Caeli gave Gates a small smile. "I know he's in good hands."

"Caeli," Gates called as she turned to leave. "Very soon, we need to talk about our smallest patient."

"Yes, we do," she agreed.

Derek took her hand, and they left sick bay for the captain's briefing room.

Kat and Drew met them outside, and all four entered together. Donovan stood waiting for them at the head of a long conference table.

"We're heading to Almagest," he said. "Alliance Command is tasking all available ships to the region as soon as possible."

Derek frowned. "My intel was clear that no Drokaran reinforcements are being sent to Mira, but we don't want to leave their defenses too thin."

"As soon as you left for Mira, we dropped sensors around the region so we could track traffic in and out of the system. We'll know if anyone else comes calling, and the *Atlas* and *Phoenix* are staying behind. Their squadron size and firepower are double ours."

"Good," Derek said, satisfied the planet wouldn't be left out in the cold again.

"What happens next on Mira?" Drew asked.

"Based on current reports, we expect full surrender by the

Drokarans on the ground in the next few hours. Diplomatic and humanitarian ships are already on the way. The Alliance will install a temporary government until Mira can get back on her feet," Donovan replied.

Drew closed his eyes, and Kat touched him gently on his shoulder.

"Now, do you want to tell me what else is going on?" Donovan demanded.

Derek's hesitation lasted only a fraction of a second. He'd served under Malcolm Donovan for most of his military career. He'd never questioned the man's honor or integrity, and he didn't now. Whatever had happened on Arendal, Derek was convinced Donovan wasn't involved.

Once he started speaking, he didn't stop until he'd spilled everything, from Sean's orders to fake Nysa's death, to Karan's revelation about the Alliance bombing Arendal, to the fact that the Drokarans were the original Novali. When Derek finally fell silent, Caeli took his hand and squeezed. He leaned back heavily in his chair.

Donovan sat stone-faced, finally moving to pour himself a glass of water. "When the Drokarans first appeared on our radar, Reyes was rear admiral of Delta Fleet. He was the first to arrive in the Lyrid system, where Delphis and Arendal had come under attack. As far as I know, no one ever questioned his report of the situation. A level one quarantine isn't something to take lightly. All travel to that region was immediately halted."

"Why would he have done it?" Kat asked, incredulous.

"I hope we get to ask him at a war crimes tribunal," Donovan said, slamming his glass on the table.

Next to Derek, Caeli started at Donovan's uncharacteristic display of emotion.

"This could go all the way to the top. What if the minister was complicit?" Derek asked.

Donovan shook his head. "I've known Celeste Bonnaire for a very long time, and I was there when she got the news about Arendal. She was newly elected when conflict broke out. She almost stepped aside then and there, uncertain if she could lead us in a time of war. She's never been in this for power, only ever to serve."

"Then we have to get this information to her," Derek said.

Folding his hands together on the table, Donovan leaned forward. "I agree. But right now, we have the immediate Drokaran threat to deal with. The *Aquila* is on alert, and the Almagest fleet has been mobilized. Derek, we need to get you back there to take command of their air defense."

"Yes, sir," he said.

"Stealth shielding has been fully integrated on *Horizon,* and we're prepared to test the newly developed field detection technology. If it works, we'll be able to pick up distortion patterns from any ship using the shield," Donovan said.

Derek whistled softly. "That could give us a huge advantage."

"It could," Donovan agreed.

The room fell into pensive silence.

Finally, Donovan spoke again. "Caeli, before we leave the system, I'd like to meet our guests."

"Of course," she answered.

"I'll follow you to sick bay."

CAELI

CHAPTER 24

Marta sat in a chair by Navi's cot. The little boy quietly played with empty cups and boxes, stacking them intricately on a tray table. When he saw Caeli, a whisper of a smile passed over his face. Sean dozed in the bed next to Navi's.

"Hi, Navi. Can I sit with you?" Caeli asked.

He nodded enthusiastically.

"This is my friend, Captain Donovan," she said, crouching down at his side. "You're on his spaceship."

Navi looked back and forth between Donovan and Caeli, and then went back to his makeshift construction project. Caeli touched his baby-fine hair and helped him build for a few moments. Derek and Dr. Gates joined them, hovering near the edge of the room.

"Navi's bones are extremely fragile," she explained to them. "They're prone to breakage and take a long time to heal. He has a drug therapy regimen that helps a little, but ultimately it doesn't affect the underlying genetic disease."

"When we guessed that the Drokarans were sick, we were right," Gates said.

"Daksha Karan told me that when their sun went supernova, they had to find a new home, but the damage was already done to their DNA. Because of the way they've been engineered, the mutations are passed down generation to generation." Caeli paused, knowing she had to tell Gates the rest, but dreading it nonetheless.

Donovan recognized her hesitation. "It's all right, Caeli."

She took a deep breath. "The Drokarans are from Almagest. A millennium ago, my world conducted an illicit genetic experiment. The Drokarans were the desired outcome, and my people, the Novali, were an unintended side effect. The Drokarans started the war on my world that destroyed our civilization, and now they're coming home."

Gates stared at her, wide-eyed. "Caeli, I'm so sorry."

"You and your people have suffered enough, and I'm sorry that your battle isn't over yet, but we are beside you this time. All of us," Donovan added.

"I know you will be. Thank you," she said. "There's more. Karan took me because he knew who I was. He experimented on me."

"If the Drokarans are originally from Almagest, and you both are the product of the same genetic modification program, your DNA might hold the key to a curative therapy for the Drokarans," Gates said.

"I believe it does. Karan gave me access to all the available data and resources the Drokarans had on Mira. He wanted me to find a cure." Caeli put a gentle hand on Navi's back. "A cure for his son."

Both Donovan and Gates turned to look at Navi.

"It's always complicated, isn't it?" Donovan sighed.

"I have the research from Mira. Karan gave it all to me in exchange for attempting to save Navi. I've identified the damaged nucleotides, and I've located their healthy counterparts in my own DNA. With the right facility, I don't think it will be all that complicated to manufacture the gene therapy."

"We could get the research to Telouros," Gates suggested.

Looking pointedly at Donovan, Caeli replied, "I'm not willing to turn anything over to the Alliance."

Gates looked confused, but Donovan answered, "Nor would I expect you to, at least not until we have some answers."

Caeli nodded. "But we have to do something. There are innocent people suffering."

Donovan rubbed his temples. "Ideas?" he asked.

"Actually, I do have an idea," Derek answered. "When we were looking for a way onto Mira, I found someone on Baishan who'd been producing therapeutic drugs for the Drokarans. She has the facility and the expertise. It's a risk. No one working on Baishan has much of a moral compass, but they understand profit and opportunity."

"How would we get the research there and set up the deal?" Caeli asked.

"I'll do it," Sean answered, and all eyes turned to him. "I'll leave before we jump out of this system. Derek can give me his contact's information, and I'll take it from there."

"This would be an unauthorized action," Donovan said. "I can't access Alliance funds, or even acknowledge your mission, not while we're still in a combat situation, and not until I understand fully what's happened." Looking between Derek and Sean, he sighed. "But I think it's the right thing to do."

Sean nodded. "I understand. I have my own network of contacts and resources."

"Well, we're jumping in four hours," Donovan said.

Sean caught Caeli's eye. "I'll get this done," he promised.

***

Caeli stayed behind in the infirmary when Derek and Donovan left to begin working on tactical strategies. She helped Sean get ready, checking him one last time.

A part of her wished she could go with him and help complete the development of the drug therapy. But, as much as she wanted to see the project through, she needed to go home to Almagest. Her place was with her people.

"I've thanked everyone else for saving me, but I haven't had a chance to thank you, Caeli," Sean said.

"I'm so relieved you're all right. It's one thing to work in a hospital or clinic when there's equipment and other people backing you up, and quite another in the middle of nowhere. How are you feeling now?"

"Good as new," he said.

She put a hand on his arm. "I never had the chance to thank *you* for saving Nysa."

"It was the right thing to do," he answered.

"It couldn't have been easy, going against your orders."

"Nothing about this war has been easy. Sometimes I have to do the wrong thing for the right reason. Reyes didn't want to save that little girl. He wanted to use her. I knew it in my gut. Wrong thing, wrong reason."

"She's okay?"

"She is. She knows we're hiding her from bad people who want to make her do things with her gift. I just didn't tell her who all the bad people were."

"You're married?" Caeli asked, casting a sideways glance at him.

He raised his eyebrows at her, and she laughed. "Sorry. I'm just curious."

"I am. I didn't intend to be, not while I was still so deep undercover, but when we met, I just knew." He shrugged.

"I understand completely. Derek literally crashed in my backyard. Well, outside my cave, in the forest, where I was hiding out from a genocidal maniac. But when you know, you know."

They both laughed.

As the lighthearted moment passed, she held his gaze. "Be careful, Sean."

"You too, Caeli. If I don't make it, this is where they are. You'll know if and when it's safe to contact them," he said, giving her the name and coordinates of a small non-Alliance world. "It's a relatively stable colony, but no one asks questions the way they do on member worlds."

"You'd better make it back to them. I didn't work this hard saving you only to have you go and get killed delivering medical data," she said.

"I'll do my best," he promised.

When Sean left, Caeli went into Gates's empty office, sat heavily on his chair, and dropped her face into her hands.

DEREK

CHAPTER 25

Horizon detected five Drokaran battlecruisers just outside Almagest's perimeter alert network. To Derek's relief, the ship's stealth shield and its untested counter-stealth technology performed flawlessly. *Horizon* passed into low orbit without attracting unwanted attention.

He and Caeli stood together in the operations center of Almagest's military compound with Finn and the newly elected president, Ben Glas. An Amathi civilian engineer before the war, Ben had married Caeli's childhood friend Lia. In addition to their son Jamie, who was now a precocious three-year-old, they were raising the orphaned nephews of Jon, one of the martyred resistance leaders.

In Derek's experience, the first officials elected after a conflict tended to be people who had somehow been involved in the struggle. Ben had been captured and tortured by Marcus during the tail end of the civil war, and he still wore scars from that trauma. The public felt grateful, sympathetic even, toward those who had sacrificed for the cause, but the qualities that made successful resistance members often didn't translate into good political leaders.

In this case, though, Ben might actually make a solid president, Derek thought, if Almagest survived long enough to give him the chance. He'd grown to appreciate the man as intelligent, diplomatic, and well spoken. Derek valued Ben's quiet strength now more than ever as they prepared for yet another conflict on this war-torn world.

"We have an advantage for a limited amount of time," Derek explained. "We know the Drokaran positions. If we hit them now, with a coordinated strike, we'll catch them by surprise."

"What's the downside?" Ben asked.

"It's a big one," Derek admitted. "We've got *Horizon* and her fighter squadron, the *Aquila*, and the Almagest fleet, which consists of two cruisers and six squadrons of very new pilots. More Alliance vessels are on the way, but if we do this, the fight will be well underway when they get here."

"If we wait, we lose the element of surprise," Ben said.

"Yes, and we have no idea when they're planning to engage. It could be at any moment. They may be waiting for more ships to arrive or just gathering intel on our defenses."

"What's your recommendation?"

"I think we should hit them hard, as soon as possible. With five battlecruisers, they have the advantage. If they engage before our reinforcements arrive, we're in trouble. If we can hurt them first, we'll even things out a bit."

"Alliance Command agrees?" Ben asked.

Derek felt for Ben. His first major decision as president was going to plunge his planet back into war.

"They've given the green light to support any tactical decisions you make. They know we're here and they're not."

Ben closed his eyes and ran a hand over his face. "Do it. You have my authorization to engage."

"Yes, sir," Derek said.

"I thought my first big project was going to be overhauling the education system," Ben muttered to himself. Caeli put a hand on his shoulder.

"Typically, the Drokarans don't send ground forces until they've established control over the airspace, but they're out of time and desperate," Derek said, turning to Finn. "You need to be ready."

"We will be," Finn answered.

Derek blew out a deep breath. "Okay, let's do this. Lieutenant Verone, I need visual on all ships. Mattis, give me coms," he ordered.

Over the table in front of him, a three-dimensional real-time rendering of Almagest, her moons, and the ships in orbit appeared. On several large, flat screens around the room, each command ship had its own monitor with enhanced details.

"*Horizon*, this is Almagest control. Transmit coordinates for all Drokaran ships."

"Roger that. Coordinates streaming now." Derek recognized Riley on the other end of the com and felt nostalgically reassured by her familiar voice.

"Okay, here they are," he said, watching new forms blink to life on the model. "The Drokarans can't see *Horizon* because of her stealth shielding, but they'll be able to track everyone else's movements. We need to get into position before they realize what's happening."

Seconds after he input all the data, Derek had targeting positions for the ships. Opening his com link, he said, "Attention, all ships. Proceed to new coordinates and hold for my order."

While the ships moved, tense silence enveloped the room. Next to him, Caeli brushed her hand over his. He felt her body stiffen.

Seconds turned into minutes. Derek paced back and forth in

front of the monitors.

Finally, Verone spoke. "Sir, they're in position."

Derek looked at Ben, who gave a solemn nod.

"All ships, engage targets. Repeat, engage targets," Derek ordered.

The monitors lit up with a brilliant display of flashing colors.

***

Derek wasn't used to being on the ground while a battle raged above him. He paced between the screens and the central display. Sweat trickled down his neck, and his damp shirt clung to his back. He knew Caeli was worried about him, but her own tension and angst kept her preoccupied.

Almagest's fighter squadrons were taking heavy casualties, but they'd still managed to cripple the Drokaran ship they were attacking. As frustrating as it was not to be flying his own fighter, Derek was able to see the whole picture and feed tactical information to all the ships.

When one Drokaran cruiser began inching its way closer to orbit, Derek leaned over Verone's shoulder. "Project their course," he ordered.

The young lieutenant ran the calculations and turned to Derek. "They're heading for low orbital insertion."

"Damn it."

"What's wrong?" Ben asked.

"They're going to try to land troops on the ground," Derek answered. "Alpha Squadron, pursue and engage that battlecruiser. Verone, send them the new course heading."

"Sir, you want us to change our target?" the Alpha Squadron leader asked.

"Affirmative. Watch for landing craft and fighter escorts."

"Derek, what do you see?" Donovan's voice interrupted.

"They've got a ship on course for low orbit. They're trying to get troops on the ground."

"Kat, follow Alpha," Donovan ordered. "*Horizon* can finish off this target."

"Yes, sir," Kat answered.

Derek watched the fighters alter course to intercept the largest Drokaran battleship, but not before twelve transport ships and dozens of Drokaran fighters had launched from the cruiser.

"Mattis, get me Major Braden," Derek said.

"Finn," Derek shouted into the com. "We're not going to be able to take them all out."

"Copy that. We'll move ground forces to intercept," Finn answered.

"Verone, keep track of any ship that breaks through and send that information to Major Braden."

"Yes, sir."

Derek turned his attention back to Kat's team and Alpha Squadron, now engaged in a fast-moving firefight with the Drokarans.

"Derek, we can't target the transport ships yet," Kat warned him. "These fighters are keeping us too busy."

"I can't divert anyone else. Stay in it," he said.

Caeli, who had been standing beside a very ashen-faced Ben, moved next to Derek and took his hand.

"We just have to buy a little more time," he said to her.

"They can do a lot of damage in a little time," Caeli replied.

"I know."

***

For eighteen months, Derek had worked to build Almagest's fleet. His job wasn't only to oversee the physical construction of ships, but also to help build the human element, to work with Finn and essentially turn a ruthless dictator's former army into a group of soldiers committed to protecting and defending *all* Almagest's people.

Most of the commanders who'd been devoted to Marcus's extremist vision were killed in the war. Derek was left with mainly bewildered young men and women, or actual members of the resistance movement itself. Together with the civilian government, they'd worked to give Almagest a new vision for itself. He trained his group of pilots hard and demanded excellence, but also cared deeply for them.

Now, relatively safe in the underground bunker he'd repurposed as a command center, Derek watched, and listened, as those same pilots were torn apart by the Drokarans.

On the ground, Finn's forces engaged the heavily armed, well-trained Drokaran troops. While Almagest's soldiers outnumbered the Drokarans, enemy drones cut into them with deadly results.

Caeli trembled beside Derek. He knew she could feel their terror and suffering viscerally.

"I have to do something," she whispered.

"You can't. Not yet," he said.

When the battleship *Endeavor*, the first of its kind in the Almagest fleet, disappeared from the grid, Derek slammed his fist onto the table.

In the stunned seconds that followed, another voice cut in over the com. "This is Captain Morgan Amari of the Alliance battleship *Libertas*. How can we help?"

Relief poured through Derek. He ran a hand through his

damp hair. "Captain, glad to have you. The *Aquila* could use a hand finishing off her target, and we need air support on the ground. All our squadrons are engaged, and we are taking heavy casualties down here."

"Roger that, Almagest control. We're coming."

CAELI

CHAPTER 26

Six hours later, it was over. Another Alliance cruiser joined the fight shortly after the *Libertas*, and by the end, only one Drokaran warship survived to surrender. As soon as she could leave the bunker, Caeli raced to the newly constructed military hospital, well equipped for trauma, but soon to be overrun with casualties.

Before she left, Derek pulled her into a fierce embrace, burying his head in her neck, as physically and emotionally exhausted as Caeli had ever seen him. She held his face in her hands.

"We lost so many," he said.

"You can't do anything for the dead, but the living need you," she said.

"I know."

He held her a moment longer. She could feel his mind working hard to bury his emotions, to lock them away so he could do what he had to do.

When she entered the chaos of the hospital, she had to do the same. The smell of blood and death assaulted her. Bodies writhed on stretchers as the staff worked furiously to triage and treat the worst of the injured.

A familiar face caught her eye. "Jana?" she called over the noise.

When Caeli had first come to Alamath after the attack on her home, she'd been allowed to work in the civilian hospital. Jana, a doctor herself and later a resistance member, had befriended Caeli.

"Caeli?" The young woman rushed over. "I heard they'd found you. Are you all right?"

"I am," she said, hugging her friend.

"This is a disaster," Jana said, tears filling her eyes.

Caeli could only nod in acknowledgment. "Where do you need me?"

"They're coming in through the trauma center. Take the next critical case," Jana said. Before heading back into the swirl of activity, she turned back to Caeli. "I'm so glad you're safe."

As she went to work on her first patient, Caeli recognized the devastating damage caused by the Drokaran drones. The soldier's abdomen was shredded, his intestines spilling out in a wet, bloody mess. Another young soldier had his hands clamped over the wound. The panic on the young man's face and the ashen color of his skin told Caeli he was in shock himself.

"Keep pressure and stay with me. I'm going to need your help," she instructed him, her voice gentle but firm.

Wide-eyed, he nodded.

With her inner vision, Caeli scanned her patient. The rest of his body was untouched, but the drone's firepower had nearly cut him in half.

"He's in bad shape and bleeding out. First thing, we're going to transfuse him," Caeli said, knowing her voice kept the other soldier from slipping into a darkness she knew all too well.

"What's your name?" she asked while quickly setting up the

plasma infuser. A steady flow of artificial blood pumped into her patient's arm.

"Cole. Nathan Cole," he answered.

"Nathan, I'm Caeli," she said.

"I know, ma'am."

Caeli glanced at him. Everyone on the planet knew who she was, but the reality of that fact still surprised her.

"Okay, Nathan, I'm going to work on his internal injuries now. You can stay right where you are."

She repaired his spleen first, and then moved on to his stomach and intestines. By some miracle, his spinal column had been spared. The work left her sweaty and fatigued, but using her gift was faster than surgery, and there wasn't time to spare.

Once she'd repaired his critical injuries, she used tissue glue to knit his torn skin together. Satisfied she hadn't missed anything, she allowed herself a moment to breathe.

"It's amazing what you can do," Nathan said, stepping back and wiping his bloody, shaking hands on his pants.

"I'm glad I was here for him," she answered.

"Me too."

"Nathan, I have to go take care of more patients, but you should stay." Caeli touched his arm gently.

"I will," he promised. Some color had returned to his face, and his expression was no longer as dazed and horrified as it had been a few moments ago.

"We'll get through this," she said.

Eyes bright with unshed tears, Nathan looked between his still-unconscious friend and Caeli. Clearing his throat, he said, "Thank you, ma'am."

***

Hours later, the steady flow of injured slowed to a trickle. Caeli's body was ready to shut down. Sluggish, she tended to one last patient whose injuries she could manage without using her gift. When she turned around, Finn stood leaning against the wall.

They stared at one another for a brief second. Their friendship and shared history made words unnecessary. When he pulled her into an embrace, the flood of emotions she'd carefully walled off broke through, and she collapsed, sobbing, onto his chest. Waves of his grief and exhaustion melded with hers as they clung to each other.

"Anya and Sari are safe?" she asked when she could speak again. Finn's wife and new baby daughter had taken shelter with Ben's family in a separate underground bunker.

"Yes," he answered.

"And Jason?" Finn's second-in-command, Jason, had been a resistance fighter from the start.

"He's okay too."

Caeli breathed a sigh of relief. "Maybe this is the last time we have to do this, Finn."

"It has to be, Caeli," he answered, as if his intentions could will it to be so.

They both wiped their faces and tried to compose themselves. "You're exhausted. Go home and get some rest. This will all be here tomorrow."

"You too, Finn."

"Soon," he promised.

***

Home. She entered the kitchen and closed her eyes. Empty silence greeted her. A coating of dust covered the counters, and a vaguely stale smell hung in the air. It seemed like a lifetime ago that she and Derek had stood here making dinner and talking about their day.

They'd settled into a life together. He'd loved working with the young pilots. His enthusiasm for flying matched theirs, and he'd come home each day tired and satisfied.

For Caeli, her work rebuilding Almagest's infrastructure, integrating the Novali into the mainstream life in Alamath, and helping her planet heal from the trauma of war had been exhausting and frustrating, but always rewarding. Cautiously, her people had been becoming whole again. Now, they had to endure another devastating blow.

Not much damage had been done within the city proper. The Drokaran ships needed open space to drop their troops, and the bloody fighting had mostly occurred on the outskirts of town. The price of this battle had been paid with precious human lives.

The world felt like it had shifted under her feet again, just like the morning Novalis was attacked. Disoriented and numb, Caeli wandered through the small apartment. She found herself in the bedroom, sank onto the bed, and buried her face in Derek's pillow.

She woke to his body pressed against hers, his mouth on hers, his emotions pouring into her mind unfiltered. Potent anger and a deep, cavernous grief washed through her. Beneath those, urgent desire. He wanted to lose himself in her, and she let him.

The heat built between them, and with their thoughts linked, his need amplified her own. When release came, it felt as if her body had shattered. Spent and shivering, he held her, one hand tangled in her hair, the other tracing gentle circles on the damp skin of her back.

His frenetic, intense thoughts had tempered, but the darkness still lingered there, brushing against Caeli's mind.

"The day the *Carina* was attacked was the worst day of my life," he murmured to her. "I thought you were dead, and nothing mattered if you were gone."

Caeli listened. Intimately connected to Derek, she felt most of what he kept walled off in his mind, but those were broad feelings, not specifics. Even with Derek, she was careful not to violate the privacy of his thoughts.

He fell silent, but Caeli knew he was struggling to put words to his emotions.

"After all I've seen and done throughout this war, today might be the second worst day. We lost so much in the blink of an eye. I know we can rebuild the ships, but those kids . . ." His voice broke and trailed off. Caeli listened to his heartbeat and held him.

"I lost three quarters of my pilots and all hands on the *Endeavor.* They were under my command. I sent them out there. Their lives were my responsibility."

Leaning up on one elbow, Caeli put her other hand on Derek's cheek. "The Drokarans were coming to invade this world. All of us, pilots, soldiers, civilians, we all would have defended our home, whether you were here or not."

He squeezed his eyes shut. "But I made the call to take the first shot. What if the right thing was to wait? Maybe we wouldn't have lost so many."

Caeli understood the danger in his thinking. She knew the exercise only led to more agony and self-doubt. "What if the

Drokarans attacked before reinforcements arrived and they were at full strength? We would have lost even more, maybe the whole planet. You can't ever know what might have happened. It's hard, but try not to go there, Derek. It leads to a dark place."

"I know," he said.

She brushed her lips over his. "Let me do something for you, something you've done for me so many times."

Forcing the recent images of trauma and death from her mind, she focused on something else.

They'd spent the better part of the year working with hardly any downtime. Derek urged her to take a few days off. When she finally acquiesced, she knew just where she wanted to go.

Instead of hiking for a month through the pristine forest, Derek flew her there in just under three hours. Commanding the fleet had its perks, he'd told her. She knew the exact section of the beach on sight, and he'd landed there.

It was just how she remembered it. White sand meeting frothy waves. Blue-green water blending with sky on the horizon. Sunlight sparkling off the surface.

They'd stood for a moment, lost in their own memories of the place. This was where they'd first met, where Caeli had pulled Derek from his wrecked ship and risked herself to save him. Now, scrub brush and other wild vegetation covered the scar in the earth made by Derek's ship when it crashed.

They hiked to her hidden cave deeper in the woods. Caeli knew the path. Some of her supplies, the things she'd gathered over weeks in hiding, were still there. Standing at the mouth of the cave, Derek kissed her long and hard.

"When I opened my eyes, and you were looking back at me, with your hands on me, healing me, I knew everything would be okay." He

had been so badly injured that she'd been terrified she wouldn't be able to save him.

While he'd recovered, they'd been alone here, away from the turmoil of both their worlds. It felt like stolen time. She'd shared her memories with him, forming a bond between them that was intimate and enduring.

When they'd finally made love, it was in this cave, and then again on the beach, and then in as many places as they could, knowing time would run out for them long before they were ready to let go of each other.

The beach had been their favorite. The warmth of the sun against their skin. Hot sand between their toes. The water, lapping against the shoreline with a rhythm almost like a heartbeat.

"Sleep, Derek," Caeli whispered, trailing her fingertips along the line of his jaw. The sound of waves echoed in their minds, and they inhaled the tangy scent of seawater, as real as if they were standing on the shore.

DEREK

CHAPTER 27

Over the next few days, Derek sat with every grieving family, listened to countless stories, held sobbing mothers. Because there were so many dead, one memorial service was held to honor them all. Derek spoke, along with Ben Glas. The lost soldiers and pilots were hailed as heroes. They had saved the planet and helped to end a decades-long interplanetary war. But at the end of the day, they were still gone, and no amount of ceremony could ease that loss.

Derek barely saw Caeli. She spent most nights at the hospital, working herself to exhaustion and grabbing a few hours of sleep in the staff room. If she wasn't at the hospital, she was with Marta and Navi, healing the accumulating damage in the boy's fragile body. Derek understood her need to keep moving, to work until her body simply shut down. Falling into bed utterly exhausted each night kept his own grief at bay.

His days ran long into the evenings, anyway. While the loss of life had been devastating, all the infrastructure on the planet remained intact. Plans for rebuilding the ships and hardware, and even recruiting new pilots, began immediately. *Horizon* had suffered significant damage during the battle and had to land on Almagest for several weeks of repairs. On the rare evenings Derek found himself free, he'd meet up with Kat and Drew and they'd drink themselves numb.

With all his attention focused on Almagest's recovery, Derek paid little attention to the greater political climate, until one evening Captain Donovan asked to meet him privately.

Donovan brought an expensive bottle of ale to the apartment. "Caeli's not here?" he asked.

"At the hospital," Derek answered, procuring two glasses. They sat across from one another at the kitchen table.

"How are you, Derek?" Donovan asked.

From his tone, Derek suspected Donovan knew the answer already. Although technically they were now equal in rank, the older man had been Derek's commanding officer for over a decade. At this point in Derek's life, Donovan knew him better than his own father.

Derek swirled his glass, staring into the amber liquid.

"It never gets easier to lose people under your command, and it never should. The day it does is the day we get out," Donovan said. He took a long drink and leaned back heavily in the chair. "If it helps, I would have made the same call, to hit them first."

Derek looked up with more relief than he probably should have felt. He'd had to make impossible decisions before, involving himself, his team, even Caeli. But sending all those young men and women into combat, when he knew most of them wouldn't come back, that was a new experience.

"I asked them to sacrifice themselves. It might feel different if I'd been out there with them."

"That's the real burden of leadership, Derek, the part most people don't understand. We'll put ourselves in harm's way, but asking others to do it is something else entirely."

There wasn't anything more to say about the subject. Derek tossed back his drink and poured himself another. He knew Donovan hadn't requested this meeting only to talk about his questionable mental health. "What's going on?" he asked.

Donovan ran a hand over his face. "Something's happening on Cor Leon. There's serious political unrest."

"Already? That didn't take them long."

"The information I have suggests that Reyes and Minister Bonnaire are at odds. Reyes wants to go after the remainder of the Drokarans and wipe them out."

Raising his eyebrows, Derek shrugged. "Not sure I entirely disagree with him." Even with what he knew about the Alliance's deception early in the war, Derek couldn't deny how ruthless an enemy the Drokarans had been, and would likely be again if they were allowed time to disappear and regroup. The thought had the potential to keep him up at night.

"The Drokarans who surrendered are being interrogated. They're saying they're the last of their military fleet, and the only survivors now are sick civilians, most of whom are children."

"Do you believe them?" Derek asked.

Donovan sighed. "They're on Dorscha."

Derek winced. Dorscha was one of the Alliance's dirty secrets, a black hole of a prison facility. The advanced interrogation techniques used there could squeeze the truth from a stone.

"The Minister wants to offer asylum to the noncombatants," Donovan said.

"And Reyes doesn't," Derek finished for him.

"No. He's trying to convince the Assembly that the Drokarans are somehow lying, and he's making a vehement case that we should finish the job or live to regret it."

"How is the Assembly reacting?"

"So far, they're standing behind the minister, but I think they're shaky."

"Shaky about committing genocide? What the fuck? The Drokarans surrendered. They want asylum for their sick civilians. How is this even a discussion?"

But he knew why it was a discussion. The Alliance had been at war with the Drokarans for a long time, sacrificed hundreds of thousands of people. As admiral of the Alliance fleet, Reyes was the commanding officer who'd finally served up victory. If he said the Drokarans still posed a threat, people would be inclined to believe him.

Derek went still. "What are you planning to do?"

"I'm not sure yet. *Horizon* still isn't flightworthy, but I do have a secure communication set up with Bonnaire in the morning to deliver the intel about Reyes. We'll be putting her in a dangerous position without any proof," replied Donovan, worried.

"We have to find a way to verify Karan's account about Arendal."

"Agreed. I'll advise her to keep this information in the strictest confidence and see what she wants us to do," Donovan said, finishing his drink and standing. "We aren't going to figure this out tonight, and you look like you could use some sleep. I'll be in touch."

"Very good, sir," Derek answered.

"Derek, you've earned this win. I know it came at a terrible cost. It always does. But I'm proud of you."

Derek cleared his throat. "Thank you, sir."

When Donovan left, Derek stood staring at the closed door for several heartbeats before grabbing his jacket and heading to the hospital.

Hands shoved in his pockets, he jogged the few blocks to the back entrance. He felt winter's approach in the biting wind against his face and in the smell of snow lingering in the air. Sliding his keycard into the reader, he waited for the click and entered the warm building.

He found Caeli behind a workstation, tapping notes into a portable tablet. A strand of blonde hair escaped its tie, and she brushed it behind her ear. Derek leaned against the wall, watching her from a distance.

He knew the second she sensed him. Her body shifted, and her head tilted as if she were listening to some distant music. Turning, she gave him a weary smile.

"Hey," he said, approaching her with his own tired smile. "Things seem quieter around here."

"We're at capacity with patients, but it's under control, finally," she replied.

"Will you come home tonight?" he asked, holding her gaze.

"Yes. I'm almost finished, if you want to wait."

Nodding, he found an empty chair and sat. He loved watching Caeli work. She was in her element, confident yet gentle with both her patients and her staff. Healing was more than just what she did, it was who she was.

True to her word, she finished in less than a quarter hour. After giving brief final instructions to another doctor, they left the ward.

"We need to stop downstairs," Derek said.

"Okay," she answered. He felt her tense slightly and heard the question in her voice, but she kept walking.

Instead of exiting through the back, they made their way to a lift. The security panel required a handprint and a retinal scan. Derek leaned forward, allowing the beam to sweep across his left eye. When the door slid open, they stepped in.

Derek and Finn had repurposed much of Marcus's underground bunker space for the military's operational command, but it was an extensive network, left over from Almagest's first civilization, and it ran underneath a good portion of the city. When the casualties poured in from the battlefield, they'd quickly converted this space to a hospital wing and locked it down. Only a select few people knew about the patients being cared for down here.

"Sir, ma'am," the security guard inside the ward greeted them.

"Anything I should know?" Derek asked.

"No, sir. Everything's quiet."

"Very good."

"I was down here for a couple of hours today," Caeli said. "All of them are stable and most are conscious."

"Good," Derek answered.

"What are we doing?" she asked.

His mouth compressed into a thin line. "I need an answer."

Caeli cringed. "Derek, I don't want to question him."

"I know," he said. He stopped and put a hand on her arm. "You won't need to, but I do have to know if he's telling the truth."

She sighed. "Okay."

They walked through a corridor and entered a quiet room. Dim overhead lights cast dull shadows on the sleeping patient's face. One hand was secured to the bed with a heavy metal cuff.

When Caeli and Derek approached, the Drokaran opened his eyes.

CAELI

CHAPTER 28

Caeli softened her expression as she leaned over the prisoner and checked his vitals. "How are you feeling?" she asked.

The Drokaran glanced nervously at Derek and then back at Caeli. He didn't answer. Unperturbed by his lack of response, Caeli continued her cursory examination.

"You're healing nicely," she said.

When Drokaran survivors were discovered alongside their own injured, Derek recommended they be isolated. Caeli went further, insisting their presence be kept from Alliance Command. After they shared an abbreviated version of Karan's revelation with Ben Glas and Finn, the others agreed the wounded Drokaran prisoners should not be turned over to the Alliance, at least not right away.

In her interactions with them, Caeli sensed the Drokarans' fear, something they'd previously worked hard to hide. Likely, they no longer had any reason, other than pride, to conceal their desperation.

Derek must have felt this shift as well, at least from the injured man in front of him. He pulled a chair up to the Drokaran's bedside. "I'm going to ask you a question, and don't bother lying."

The Drokaran stared back at Derek. Caeli placed a gentle hand on the man's shoulder. His eyes darted back and forth from Derek to Caeli, finally settling back on Derek.

"Was the last of your military fleet destroyed in this battle?"

Caeli watched the man struggle to keep emotion off his face. Finally, he closed his eyes and turned his head away from Derek. "Yes."

"Do you have civilians hiding somewhere?" Derek asked.

Caeli had witnessed Derek interrogate prisoners before. She dreaded those encounters. The change in him, his ability to show icy callousness or contained violence depending on the scenario, always unsettled her. There was none of that in his demeanor now.

"Yes," the Drokaran answered, still facing away from them.

Derek sat back in his chair. Caeli raised her eyebrows at him, questioning.

Before Derek could say anything else, the Drokaran spoke again, his voice soft and strained. "They are all that's left of our people."

Derek looked pointedly at Caeli. "I have to know if he's telling the truth."

Caeli gave Derek a slight nod. Unlike Karan's wall of defense, this man's crumbled easily. She pushed her way into his mind, searching only for the answer to Derek's question. In the Drokaran's mind, she found the truth of his words.

***

Caeli sipped hot tea laced with something strong and biting. It burned going down, but warmed her insides. Dorian Bell had wordlessly set the steaming cup in front of her and handed

Derek his own drink as soon as they'd entered the tavern.

"Long day?" he asked, returning with two bowls of stew and a fragrant loaf of bread.

Caeli dug into the bread, handing a warm chunk to Derek and inhaling the comforting aroma. She smiled at Dorian. "Want to sit with us for a little while?" she asked.

He pulled out a chair. "Are you two taking care of yourselves? You both look exhausted."

When Caeli's home had been destroyed and the small group of Novali survivors had arrived in Almagest broken and bleeding, Dorian's was the first friendly face Caeli had encountered. A cook at the hospital who also owned the tavern in which they now sat, Dorian had been a resistance member, his tavern a safe meeting place for the group.

"We're heading home after this. I'm ready for a good night's sleep," Caeli said.

"Good. That drink will help," he said, nodding at her tea.

The background hum of chatter, the subdued laughter, the smell of cooking food, all felt normal. Dorian, still caring for people in his way, felt like home, safety. Caeli needed that now, and she knew Derek did too. They talked about simple, ordinary things for a few minutes before Dorian left, tending to more of his hungry customers.

Derek reached across the table and ran his thumb over Caeli's wrist.

"What are we going to do about them?" she asked, her thoughts returning to the Drokaran prisoners locked in the hospital.

"I don't know. Tomorrow we'll talk to Ben." Derek took a long swallow of his drink. "Donovan came by earlier."

Catching the tone of his voice, Caeli put down her spoon. "What did he have to say?"

"Reyes is trying to convince Minister Bonnaire to go after the remaining Drokarans and finish them off."

"Does Reyes know there are no military targets left?"

"Yes," he answered.

Caeli swallowed, processing the implications. "Why would he want to do that?"

Derek shrugged. "He's trying to convince the Assembly that the Drokarans still pose a significant threat when he knows they don't. I don't fully understand what's going on either, but I think we're going to have to do something soon. We have to find a way to expose him."

Caeli's eyes widened, her mouth suddenly going dry. "Why does it have to be us?" she whispered. But even as she spoke the words, she knew the answer. They'd invested too much, lost too much, to let this corruption go unchallenged. And they were the only ones who knew the truth.

***

The next morning, Derek spoke to Ben, who confirmed that the Drokarans should remain in custody on Almagest until he knew they'd be treated fairly as prisoners of war and not tortured or killed. Worried about the civilian refugees being tracked down by Reyes, Derek suggested they try to make contact with them. Ben agreed.

Derek and Caeli returned to the underground hospital wing and approached the same Drokaran they had the previous night.

"Your civilians are in danger," Derek told him bluntly. "If the admiral of the Alliance fleet discovers their location, he will destroy them."

The Drokaran flinched.

"Can you communicate with them?"

The Drokaran's expression went blank. "Why would I do that?" he asked.

"You can give them a message. Tell them to stay on the move until they hear directly from you again."

Open suspicion now clouded the prisoner's face. "You are Alliance. Why should I believe you want to help us?"

"The war is over. We won. There is no justification for wiping out civilians," Derek said. Caeli could feel his growing frustration.

"We want to save your children, but you have to help us," she added, holding the man's gaze.

She could sense his inner struggle. Despite his effort to hide his feelings, a glimmer of hope fought its way into his eyes.

"We're telling you the truth. If you want, I can prove it to you," she offered.

His head sank back onto his pillow. "No. I'll send them the message."

Derek stood. "Can you walk?" he asked.

The Drokaran nodded.

Derek opened the door and gave quiet instructions to the guard. A few minutes later, a heavily armed detail secured the Drokaran's hands behind his back and, weapons drawn, marched him out.

Finn met them in the operations center and motioned for the Drokaran to sit. One guard freed the man's hands and then put a gun to the back of his skull. A muscle twitched in the Drokaran's cheek; otherwise, he was still.

"Go ahead," Derek said.

Glancing at Derek, the Drokaran entered a stream of data.

An artificial voice prompted him to begin his message. Caeli watched him swallow hard and close his eyes, as if this decision to speak were the most important of his life, which, in all likelihood, it was.

"This is Commander Jai Aakash of the battleship *Antim*, fifth squadron," he said.

***

So much remained unsettled. Between the prisoners in the bunker, the unrest within the Alliance, and the toxic information she carried about Reyes, Caeli could barely concentrate on her patients. Finished with her shift but knowing the apartment would be empty if she went home, she hid out in her tiny office, trying to stave off her growing dread.

The blink of her communication tablet caught her eye. A long-range message. Encrypted.

Curious, she tapped it open. It was Sean Asher. He'd brokered a deal to produce a limited amount of a trial medication that needed testing on live subjects. "*What do you want me to do now?*" he asked.

She typed a message back. "*Come to Almagest.*"

When he arrived a week later, Caeli had already spoken with Dr. Gates, who agreed to oversee the trial with her if the Drokaran prisoners agreed to it. Caeli wanted to read the reports and analyze all the information before she was willing to approach the Drokarans about a potential therapy. Sean brought everything with him to the apartment where he, Caeli, and Derek were now having a quiet dinner.

"What the hell is happening on Cor Leon?" Sean asked, shoveling food into his mouth.

Passing Sean the serving platter, Derek told him what they knew.

"Reyes is up to something," Sean said. Derek agreed. The conversation trailed off, everyone lost in their own thoughts.

"How's Nysa?" Caeli finally asked, breaking the silence.

Sean's expression softened, and he pulled a small handheld tablet from his bag. An image of a young girl appeared on the screen, a broad, carefree smile lighting up her face.

Caeli took it, looking from the screen to Sean and back again. "I don't know how to thank you for this," she said, swiping a tear from her cheek.

He took the tablet back. "You don't need to thank me. For all the shitty things I've had to do, maybe giving Nysa her life back evens things out a little."

Caeli started to speak but stopped herself. She trusted Sean, believed him to be a good man, but she also had no idea what he'd done in order to survive this war. Instead of offering empty words, she refilled all their cups and sat back down.

***

By the next day, Caeli had reviewed enough data on the drug therapy to understand the developers' approach. She found herself back in the room with Jai Aakash.

No longer cuffed to his bed, the Drokaran sat in a chair in the corner of the room. His expression blank, he barely looked at Caeli when she entered. An armed guard stood at the door.

"I'll be fine," she said to the guard.

The soldier hesitated. "You can stand just outside the door," Caeli insisted. With a curt nod, he left the room.

She sat in the chair opposite Aakash, placing her tablet on the table between them.

"You aren't afraid?" he asked, tilting his head.

"I'm the one who healed your wounds with my mind. You don't think I could do the opposite if I felt threatened by you?" A brief flicker of surprise passed over his face and disappeared quickly.

"You know who I am? Who my people are?" she asked, more gently.

"Yes."

Nodding, she continued, "When I was on Mira, I began researching a therapy, not just to treat your symptoms, but to actually repair your damaged DNA."

Caeli placed the tablet flat between them and tapped. A three-dimensional image materialized above the screen. Aakash leaned in.

"Here are the damaged nucleotides, and here are their healthy counterparts from my own DNA," she said, pointing. "I never got a chance to experiment with synthesizing compounds, but we found someone who could. I have the first round of trials here, ready to be tested. I've analyzed them, and as far as I can tell, they're promising."

She sat back, waiting for Aakash. His eyes lingered on the spinning models a moment longer before looking up at Caeli. "You want to test them on us."

"Yes."

He stared at Caeli, his piercing brown eyes boring into her. "Do it."

DEREK

CHAPTER 29

"The Assembly just enacted Section Seven and removed Minister Bonnaire from office," Donovan grimly told the group seated at the back-corner table in Dorian's tavern.

Kat swore softly. Drew and Sean both clutched their drinks tighter, and Derek ran a hand over his head. "Shit."

Caeli looked between Donovan and Derek. "What does that mean?"

"Section Seven is essentially a vote of no confidence that immediately removes the sitting minister from office," Donovan explained. "It's hard to pull off and requires a four-fifths majority from the Assembly. Reyes convinced them that Bonnaire's refusal to pursue the remainder of the Drokaran fleet will lead the Alliance back into war."

"That's why he was pushing this bullshit so hard. Removing the minister must have been his endgame," Derek said, tapping his fingers on the rim of his glass.

"And the vice minister resigned in protest," Donovan added.

"Who gets the seat?" Kat asked.

"The Assembly has the authority to appoint someone. They went with Reyes's recommendation, someone named Athanas.

I don't know him," Donovan answered.

Kat snorted. "Convenient."

"That name sounds familiar, but I'm not sure why," Sean said, frowning. "I'll do some digging."

"We have to find a way to expose Reyes," Derek said.

"Agreed. I was able to give Minister Bonnaire a report, but we were never able to communicate again after that. We have no idea who else is complicit. This is ugly territory," Donovan said, sighing.

"There's no point in going up against Reyes about the Drokarans. We've been at war for too long and emotions are too high. The Assembly trusts him. Hell, we all trusted him. We have to prove he could have ended this war twelve years ago but didn't," Derek said.

"Arendal is the proof," Drew said, staring into his glass.

Rubbing his thumb along the rim of his drink, Derek thought. "We have to bring back evidence that there's no biological contamination on Arendal. The Assembly won't be able to ignore it. They'll have to open an investigation."

"*Horizon* has been ordered back to Cor Leon. Our repairs are nearly complete. We won't be able to stay off the grid for very long," Donovan said.

"It would be a bad idea to use Alliance assets. Reyes can't get so much as a hint about what we're doing," Derek said.

"What *are* we doing, Derek? How are we going to get to Arendal?" Kat asked.

Meeting her gaze, he replied, "Almagest has a ship. It was going to be the third one in the fleet. She was ready for launch before the battle, but we didn't have a command crew trained on her yet. She can be flight-ready in a matter of days."

"She's not an Alliance ship, so her whereabouts won't be

tracked by the Alliance," Kat said, a hint of a smile on her face.

"We won't be able to enter Arendal's airspace undetected. If there's something to hide, that could be problematic . . ." Drew's voice trailed off, but he'd made his point.

Leaning back in his chair, Donovan ran a hand over his chin. "*Horizon*'s stealth shielding could be integrated onto your ship, Derek."

"I don't want to leave *Horizon* vulnerable," Derek answered, shaking his head.

"Vulnerable to what? The war's over. We shouldn't need that tech anymore, not immediately, anyway."

"Are you sure, sir?"

"Something corrupt is taking root in the Alliance," Donovan said, his face grim. "Maybe it's been there all along. If we have a chance to kill it at its source, we have to take it."

"We can fly with a minimal crew," Derek said, his mind already rushing ahead.

"I'll lend you whoever you need," replied Donovan.

Derek looked around the table. "I can't ask any of you to do this . . ."

"Don't be ridiculous," Kat cut him off. "Of course you can."

"I have to know the truth," Drew said, his jaw set.

"I'm in too. No one's looking for me right now anyway," Sean said.

"I'm coming," Caeli added. Derek hesitated, but knew this was an argument he wouldn't win.

"Get me a shortlist of additional personnel," Donovan said.

"Thank you, sir." Turning back to Caeli, Derek said, "We have to ask Ben Glas. I don't think he'll refuse us this, but he's already risking Almagest's membership status by hiding the wounded Drokarans and agreeing to run the drug trials here.

He deserves to know what we're up to. And I don't want to steal his ship."

***

They'd voted on the name of the first ship in Almagest's new fleet. It started out as a fun, competitive contest among the pilots and ended with a run-off between the two most popular choices. Ben Glas, as the first elected president, got to name the second ship, and Derek had been honored with naming rights for the third.

He'd chosen *Equinox*, after the small ship he'd crashed on Almagest years ago. He'd thought twice about it, not wanting to confer bad luck on its namesake, but his friend and copilot had died on the first *Equinox*. This seemed one small way to honor Tommy and to commemorate the mission that had changed the course of Derek's own life.

This *Equinox* was nothing like the first. He stared at her in awe. A battleship with a full fighter complement, she rivaled *Horizon* for speed and agility, but her engine design promised more power. Built to help protect the planet, she carried all the latest Alliance technology and weaponry. Even craning his neck, he couldn't see the bridge from where he stood.

Derek had only planned to have the first three ships built on the ground. Design work was already underway on an orbiting facility that would handle all future, large-scale construction. He was glad they hadn't started work on it yet, since, in all likelihood, it would have been destroyed in the battle. At least this was one thing they wouldn't have to rebuild.

Wandering through the large, empty hangar, Derek struggled with leaving Almagest. There was so much work to do, and his devastated pilots and ground crew needed him. If he was honest, he needed them too. He needed to do the work of healing right alongside them.

But he had to find the truth, for the sake of everyone who'd fought and died in this war.

***

"We started the drug trial today," Caeli said, her head resting on Derek's chest.

"Do you think it's going to work?" he asked.

"I do. The delivery vector targets the damaged sequences precisely. It's elegant. The nitrogenous base pair in the first nucleotide . . ." She stopped and lifted her head. "You aren't listening."

"Sorry. It's riveting," he teased.

"Next time you want to tell me about the engine specs of a battle-class cruiser, I'm going to start snoring."

"Sorry," he repeated, pulling her in and kissing her hard. "I *am* interested, and I do hope it works. I'm just distracted."

"I know. Is the stealth shield integrating smoothly on *Equinox*?" she asked.

"It is. We're running the last set of diagnostics tomorrow." He paused and let his head sink back onto the pillow. "I wonder what we're going to find on Arendal?"

"Answers," Caeli said softly.

"Or maybe more questions."

CAELI

CHAPTER 30

Caeli wandered through *Equinox*. The ship's layout was similar enough to *Horizon*'s that she didn't get lost, but the quiet corridors and empty rooms felt strange. She stayed away from the common areas, which should have been alive with noise and humanity but instead looked new and shiny and empty.

The sparse crew included officers handpicked by Derek or Captain Donovan. All had been briefed on the sensitive nature of the mission. All had been given a chance to decline without repercussions. Donovan's leadership instilled loyalty and trust among his crew, and Derek's service record spoke for itself. Everyone had accepted.

When Caeli returned to the bridge, she found Derek pacing. From her limited interplanetary travel experience, she'd learned that once the ship had cleared the system, it functioned nearly autonomously. Unless something went wrong, there wasn't much to do during this part of the journey but wait. And Derek hated waiting.

"Hungry?" she asked him. "We can take a walk to the mess hall."

He shook his head.

"Want to give me an official tour?" she asked.

He stopped pacing. "Are you trying to distract me?"

She smiled. "I am. I could feel your agitation all the way to sick bay."

Rubbing the back of his neck with one hand, he acquiesced. "I want to check on Reece anyway."

On their way out, Kat caught Caeli's eye and mouthed a *thank you* behind Derek's back.

"I may have been driving them a little crazy," Derek admitted.

Caeli smirked. "You may have."

She followed him through the desolate corridors to a workspace outside engineering. Reece sat on the ground with tools, scanners, and some kind of mechanical parts spread haphazardly around him. Muttering to himself, he didn't notice Derek and Caeli enter.

Grinning, Derek cleared his throat. Reece jumped to his feet. "Sorry, sir. I didn't hear you."

"It's okay. I just came to see how you're doing with the sensors."

"I'm retrofitting the bioscanners into the drones now. I don't want to compromise camera function, or any other data collection, so I've had to make some modifications. Almost finished."

Caeli smiled at the skeptical look on Derek's face as he surveyed the mess. "These drones look much larger than the little ones you like to use," she said.

Reece's face lit up. "Yes. They carry all kinds of sensors. Everything will tuck inside the outer shell neatly for atmospheric entry, and then open up when it's time to start reading data. But they're small enough to behave like space debris. No one will look twice, if anyone's looking."

"Great work, as always, Reece," Derek said, clapping his hand to the man's shoulder.

"Thank you, sir."

Caeli and Derek headed for the door when Reece cleared his throat. "Dr. Crys?"

Caeli stopped and turned.

"I'm, uh, really glad you're okay. We were all worried. When we heard you were missing . . ." he stammered.

The sting of tears caught her off guard. Swallowing back the lump in her throat, she said, "Thank you, Reece. I've really missed you."

The young officer blushed a deep red.

"That boy has a serious crush on you," Derek said when the door slid shut behind them.

"He's sweet," Caeli said, smiling.

"And smart. The sensor he's rigged will pick up spores, viral pathogens, bacteria, pretty much any biological or chemical contaminants. If anything's on that planet, we'll know."

As they walked in silence back toward the bridge, Caeli felt Derek's mood darken.

"What is it?" she asked gently.

"Is it wrong that I hope we find something?" he asked.

She knew he didn't expect an answer, so instead she gripped his hand.

"Things are fucked up when I'd rather the Drokarans had used a bioweapon on Arendal than find out our own people firebombed the planet." He ran his free hand over his head.

She couldn't argue with him.

***

"Engage the stealth shield," Derek ordered.

"System engaged. Green lights across the board," Drew said.

An alarm sounded over the com system, sharp and urgent.

"It's the automated warning from the satellite markers," Sean said.

A message followed the alarm, the disembodied voice repeating its critical warning. "This area is under a level one quarantine. All ships prohibited."

Caeli watched the distant planet grow closer by the minute, her breath catching in her throat.

"There's a lot of activity in this system for a planet under quarantine," Drew said.

"Can we identify any of those ships?" Derek asked.

After a few silent moments of working at his station, Drew shook his head. "It's not just ships. There's an orbital station."

"What the hell is going on?" Derek paced between workstations. "Kat, take her into geocentric orbit and keep us out of the way. Drew, see if you can figure out who these ships belong to, and Sean, monitor any communications you can pick up."

A chorus of "yes, sirs" followed, and the small bridge crew got to work.

Derek caught Caeli's eye, his expression stony. Tense silence filled the space until Kat announced they'd achieved orbit.

"Let's start looking around," Derek said, tapping the com. "Reece, deploy the drones and begin mapping the surface."

"On it, sir," Reece replied.

"Send all the data directly to the bridge," Derek added.

Time crawled by. Caeli wandered the deck, trying to stay out of the way. Tension hit her in waves. Outwardly, everyone did their job and held their emotions in check, but she felt their

EQUINOX 201

inner angst. Something corrupt was happening here, and now they all knew it for sure.

One of the monitors on a workstation chirped, and Caeli rushed over. "Preliminary readings." She squinted at the screen as the data scrolled. "This probe is in the lower troposphere over the southern continent. It's not picking up any chemical or biological hazards."

Derek rubbed the back of his neck. "Let's make sure we have readings from multiple sources and various locations on the planet. Caeli, compile everything into a secure file. We'll add the map images when they come through, and then we'll have to authenticate our coordinates."

Glad to have something to do, Caeli sorted and saved. Absorbed in the work, she startled when Drew's voice interrupted the silence.

"There's a ship leaving the system," he said.

"Can you identify it?" Derek asked.

"It's a cargo transport. She belongs to Trident Enterprises."

Caeli watched the emotions play over Derek's face. "Trident is one of the Alliance's largest private defense contractors."

"Do you know who the founder of Trident is?" Sean asked, his eyes wide.

Derek shook his head.

"Yannis Athanas, son of the Alliance's new minister, Vasili Athanas."

"Oh, shit," Derek said.

"I knew I recognized the name, but I couldn't place it," continued Sean, his eyebrows furrowed. "Trident supplies the Alliance, but they also sell to the highest bidder in other regional conflicts. Before Elista, I was in deep on Kirs during their revolution. Trident, using subcontractors to keep their name clean, sold to both sides."

"What are they doing here?" Derek wondered aloud.

"The ship launched from the surface. I can track it back and get a location," Drew said.

"Do it," Derek ordered. "Once we have coordinates, send the drone down to take pictures. Sean, dig into Minister Athanas and his son. We need to know as much as we can about them."

Her stomach churning with dread, Caeli returned to work.

Several hours later, two things became clear. There was no biological or chemical contamination on Arendal, and Trident had built a huge, presumably secret, manufacturing facility on the planet.

"We have to get this information to the Security Council," Derek said.

"Not the Security Council," Sean interrupted, looking up from his screen, expression tight. "This is the current roster of Security Council members, and Vasili Athanas is listed as co-chair."

"Damn it," Derek said, pacing again. "We really have no idea how deep this thing goes, and we have to find out before we try to release the information. This group was powerful enough to cover up a war crime and overthrow the sitting minister. They're certainly powerful enough to take us out if they know we're a threat."

DEREK

CHAPTER 31

They needed a plan, and quickly. Derek ordered Kat to move *Equinox* out of Arendal's airspace. He then turned the bridge over to their relief crew with instructions to interrupt him if anything out of the ordinary, no matter how seemingly innocuous, happened on their watch.

His team sat assembled around a conference table, brainstorming ideas. Derek felt backed against a wall, but the familiarity of having *this* team around him, working through strategy like they were prepping for any other mission, offered him a modicum of comfort.

"Minister Bonnaire has supporters, both in the General Assembly and in the military. If we can get this information to her, she could compel an investigation, even if she is out of office," Kat said.

Derek shook his head. "I agree that she could, but if we go to her now, with incomplete intel, we'll put her life in danger. We have to identify the network of corruption first so we can work around them."

"And we have to do it without tipping our hand," Drew added, tapping his fingers on the table.

"It's usually about money or power. If we can figure out who in the government has vested interest in Trident and its subsidiaries, we'll know who might be compromised," Sean said.

"How do we get close enough to Trident to access those kinds of records?" Derek asked.

"Buy something from them?" Sean suggested.

Derek stared at him, an idea forming. "I have bought from them. Not me personally, but Almagest, through the Alliance, for the new fleet."

"The fleet that was just decimated," Drew said.

"And needs to be rebuilt," Kat added.

"But with the unrest in the Alliance, Almagest might now be looking to deal directly with Trident, negotiate their own terms," Derek finished, sitting back in his chair.

"It's plausible," Sean agreed. "If we hint that Almagest doesn't want to play by all the rules, I bet the higher-ups at Trident would at least take a meeting to see if a new kind of relationship is worthwhile." Pondering for a moment, he added, "Trident's headquartered on Kythira. It's a non-Alliance world. Safe. Secure. But outside Alliance regulatory control and oversight."

"Shrewd," Derek said.

"Yeah."

"Money or power," Derek repeated Sean's words from earlier. He opened the com and ordered the bridge crew to set course for Kythira.

When he looked over at Caeli, who sat quietly next to him, she tilted her head. "Even if you can set up a meeting, how are you going to steal files from a defense contractor? They probably invented the security technology."

Derek sighed. "Not easily, but I'll get Reece thinking about it."

From her corner seat, Kat tried, and failed, to stifle a yawn. Fatigue slowed Derek's own thinking. They all needed sleep. He stood. "This is a good start. Get some rest. I need everyone sharp in eight hours."

He and Caeli stumbled into the bed in his quarters. His mind raced even as his body shut down.

"I just want this to be over," she whispered.

He pulled her against him, burying his head in the back of her neck. "Me too."

She rolled over. "I'm scared, Derek. Somehow this mission feels different."

Her breath misted his cheek, and when he brushed his mouth along her chin, he tasted salty tears.

"You didn't have to come, Caeli. I'm sorry."

She cut him off with a firm, "No." Her head shook, splaying her hair against his chest. "I need to see this through as much as you do. And I need to be here with you. I feel like I have to steal every moment I can."

Tracing her fingers along his arm, she settled her head on his shoulder. "When Drew and I left for the Drokaran base on Mira, he told me that every time Kat left, he wondered if it would be the last time he saw her. I feel that way now. I know bad things can happen. My parents left for work one day and never came back. But this . . . this is different."

"I'm sorry," he said again, and again she stopped him.

"Stop apologizing. You have to do this. *We* have to do this. There's no other choice. You and I are the same that way. We can't walk away."

Leaning up on her forearm, she stared him in the eyes. "I

wanted a life with you, Derek. I wanted it more than I've ever wanted anything. I thought we were going to have it, and now . . ."

"Here we are again," he said.

"Here we are again," she repeated softly.

He didn't have words powerful enough to tell her how much he wanted that life too, so he told her with his body.

***

"Captain Markham." Yannis Athanas offered his hand and a controlled smile.

"Please call me Derek. I'm not here as an Alliance officer."

They shook, and Athanas pointed to a chair opposite his desk. Derek sat, surveying the well-appointed office and the arms dealer who inhabited it. Tall and thin, with thick, dark hair that reached his collar, Athanas exuded confidence. While a smile may have curled at the corner of his lips, his eyes were cold, calculating, and didn't miss much, Derek was certain. He'd need to watch himself.

"Drink?" Athanas poured himself a glass of amber liquid and filled another for Derek.

"Thank you." Derek sipped, and the smooth liquor warmed his throat.

"I must admit, I was quite curious when I received your request to meet," Athanas said. He opened a hand, as if he could coax Derek's answer with only a gesture.

Holding the other man's gaze, Derek kept his expression blank and took a longer swallow. After several heartbeats, he finally spoke. "You may have heard Almagest lost most of her newly constructed fleet."

Athanas inclined his head.

"The planet's leadership wants to rebuild quickly," Derek said.

"Isn't that why you're there, captain? I believe the Alliance contracted with Trident Enterprises on behalf of Almagest. That contract is still in place."

"With all the unrest inside the Alliance and their hardware mostly decimated, Almagest feels vulnerable."

Athanas raised his eyebrows. "And just like that, they're willing to nullify their relationship with the Alliance?" he asked skeptically.

"Not at all. They simply don't want to be dependent on the Alliance exclusively."

"So, they sent you?"

"And they'll deny it." Derek took another drink.

Athanas gave Derek a measured look. When he spoke, his words were a challenge. "You've been an Alliance soldier for almost fifteen years. Your service record is impeccable. You'd have me believe you're suddenly willing to cut a side deal on behalf of a planet that's only been on the grid for a couple of years?"

Derek sat back and crossed his ankle over his knee, cradling the glass between his hands. "My service record is mostly redacted. I've spent almost all my career in intelligence, working black ops and doing things the Alliance could never admit to. For the greater good, of course."

"Of course," Athanas said, his grin a thin line.

His attitude had visibly shifted from doubt to self-serving interest, but Derek knew he had to take things a step further. "Five years ago, the Alliance, with weapons and tech supplied by Trident, backed the Kirs government. At the same time, a small company called Janus Industries backed the Kirsian insurgents." Derek silently thanked Sean for that piece of valuable intel.

Athanas quirked an eyebrow. "I'm impressed. How did you figure it out?"

"It's my job to figure shit out," Derek answered. Truth be told, he had no idea how Sean knew Janus was a secret subsidiary of Trident, and he hadn't asked.

"Arming the insurgents prolonged the war on Kirs by at least eighteen months. Almagest is still unstable. The warring factions are barely at peace," Derek added, letting the implication hover between them.

"War can be profitable," Athanas conceded.

"Indeed it can be."

"So, that's really why you're here," the other man said, an eyebrow raised in amused interest.

Nodding, Derek raised one corner of his mouth in a smile. "Almagest makes a side deal, and I make an even better side deal."

"And how much are you expecting out of this?" Athanas asked.

"A small percentage of total negotiated sales. I'm hoping we'll both find the arrangement worthwhile in the long run." Derek tossed back the rest of his drink and waited.

Leaning back, Athanas watched Derek with a glint in his eye. "I suspect it will be."

Derek leaned forward and placed his empty glass on the desk. With his other hand, he stuck a micro-drone to the underside. He smiled at Athanas. "I hear you're working on a new raptor design."

"Once a pilot, always a pilot," Athanas replied, chuckling

indulgently. "We're already working on the final test flight simulations. Interested in having a look?"

"Definitely."

He followed Athanas out of the room.

***

"I think he bought it," Derek said.

"Oh yeah, he did. He's already setting up an account for you," Reece told him. "Nice job planting the tracker. I matched our signal to other outgoing noise, so it shouldn't call attention to itself."

He threw a nervous glance over his shoulder as Derek hovered over his workstation. "Sorry," Derek said, backing off.

"I should have access to their files in a few hours. I won't need to waste time on decryption when I can watch Athanas access his data from here," Reece said, smiling.

"You, my friend, are a genius," Derek said, clapping the other man on the back.

CHAPTER 32

"Sir, we have a problem," Reece said over the com.

Derek sighed. "I'll be right down," he said, waving at Sean to join him. Reece had been sorting data and running algorithms on the stolen files for the past two days while *Equinox* hovered on the edge of the Kythiran system, monitoring ship patterns and unencrypted communications with her stealth mode fully engaged.

"What's up, Reece?" Derek asked when he arrived, mildly alarmed at the dark circles rimming the young officer's eyes.

"I can't find anything improper in these files," Reece replied, rubbing at his eyes with a knuckle. "All the payments, contracts, and affiliations on record are legit. When I search for any of the keywords Commander Asher suggested, including Janus Industries, or even the new account Athanas set up for you, the same gibberish-looking code appears."

"What the hell does that mean?" Derek asked, more bite in his tone than he intended.

Reece cleared his throat. "I'm not sure. When I search for any of the other illicit accounts we know about, this comes up." He pointed at a series of numbers as they flashed across the screen, then ran a frustrated hand through his short hair and looked nervously at Derek.

"The files exist," Derek said, tapping the number set on Reece's screen.

"I agree. But where are they, and why can't I access them?"

"Clearly, they have one set of records for their legitimate business deals and another for the stuff they don't want anyone to know about," Sean said.

"They have to track the dirty funds somewhere, though," Derek said. "With an entire hidden manufacturing plant off the grid and off their legitimate books, they have to be hiding huge amounts of wealth and transactional data. Someone keeps track of that."

"No doubt," Sean agreed.

"But who, and where?" Reece wondered aloud.

Drumming his fingers on the table, Derek stared at the number set that appeared in place of the Janus Industries file. "Reece, does the same number sequence pop up when you search for any of the missing files?"

"Yeah, it's the same. Look," he said, pointing. "I think this is how they tag the files they want to remove and keep them separate, but unless you know exactly what you're looking for, you wouldn't know anything's missing." Reece shook his head in frustration. "They're probably keeping these files at an air-gapped site."

"What?" Derek asked.

"If they don't want anyone to access this information, either internally, because there are probably people working for them who think they're totally legit, or externally, like us hacking into their shit, then they'll want to keep it isolated. An air-gap system will do that. This stuff won't be linked to any network, anywhere," Reece explained.

"So, they tag the files, pull them out, and move them

somewhere isolated where they can't be tracked," Sean said.

Reece leaned back in his chair, rubbing his hands on top of his head in frustration. "Yes, and that means I can't track them either. Damn it. There has to be a way."

Derek rubbed his eyes. "Get some sleep, Reece. That's an order. You can pick this up again tomorrow."

***

Twenty-four hours later, they stood around Reece's workstation again. This time, a wide smile split the young man's face.

"Yesterday, you mentioned dirty funds, and that got me thinking," he said.

"Go on," encouraged Derek.

"Funds have to be moved. Payments are made to Trident for weapons sales, and funds are paid out to those entities profiting from the deals. While transaction records and project files can be kept isolated and together in one place, money moves."

"And you're able to track the money," Derek said, slightly in awe of Reece's sharp mind.

Reece grinned again. "Yeah. We knew for certain Reyes and Athanas were involved. When I added in the other questionable deals Lieutenant Commander Asher told us about, I had more information. Payments from those sources end up in a different place than the ones we know to be from legitimate business deals. And funds track out of that same source."

"Can you tell where?"

"These coordinates," he said as a three-digit number sequence appeared on his screen. "Let me load a global map of Kythira and see where they are." Reece started tapping, renewed energy in his fingertips as well as in his expression, and then pointed at the screen. "Here we go."

"Zoom in closer," Derek ordered.

As Reece manipulated the data, detailed satellite imagery appeared on the screen. "Doesn't look like there's much there." A small farmhouse seemed to be the only main structure, with scattered outbuildings surrounding it.

"My guess is if something's there, it's underground," Derek said, thinking about the bunkers on Almagest and the rail system on Mira. Hidden. Protected.

"True. And if so, it's perfect for a black site. Remote, only one visible access point in and out. Excellent for security purposes," Sean said.

Stepping back from the screen, Derek started for the door. "We need to get down there."

***

Surveillance gear, weapons, and various pieces of tech belonging to Reece lay strewn around the small cabin. Derek wasn't sure how long they'd have to be there, so he'd sent Sean and Drew out to stock up on food.

The suspected Trident black site was in a rural location a few miles from the nearest town. From their remote surveillance thus far, the only structures appeared to be the farmhouse and a few outbuildings. A nature preserve surrounded the area, with rental cabins and campsites scattered throughout the neighboring forest.

When the small team had arrived back on Kythira, they'd covered their tracks carefully, using one set of identities to dock their shuttle in the capital city and entirely different ones to rent the cabin. Reece had already done a good job of setting up the place as a command center. Derek tolerated the young officer's brand of organized messiness, and he knew better than to touch anything. Instead of getting in Reece's way, he busied himself studying detailed maps of the region and locating strategic points where they could obtain real-time surveillance. He'd left Kat in command of *Equinox*. In the back of Derek's mind, he knew if something went wrong down here, Kat was the person he trusted most to find a way to keep the mission going.

He'd left Caeli behind as well. Although she probably could have survived out here with nothing but her pocket knife, there really wasn't anything for her to do. He missed her, though. The team had gone completely dark and weren't in communication with *Equinox* at all. He hated being so out of touch. It made him edgy.

Drew and Sean provided a welcome distraction when they returned with the supplies. Falling easily into the role of friends on a camping trip, they laughed and joked with one another while sorting and unpacking. Later, while they sat around the table to eat, they talked strategy.

"Our first order of business is to figure out if there really is a facility here. We'll assume there is, so we'll also need to get eyes on the access road and on the farmhouse itself. See who comes and goes," Derek said.

"I'll rig up the small drones," Reece volunteered. "They'll look like birds. I'll add some ground-penetrating radar to their package so we'll know if anything's under there."

Derek grinned at Reece, appreciating his cheerful attitude and resourcefulness. "Good. We'll set up some ground cameras too."

"This stew is really good, Commander Asher," Reece said, mouth full.

"Yeah, it is," Drew agreed. They both turned to look at Sean.

"Thank you," Sean answered. "Brescia, the capital of Kirs, was a high-end vacation destination before the war. When I was stationed there, my cover was as an apprentice chef in a restaurant. Turns out, the whole resort was a front for the insurgency, but I learned a little about using proper spices."

Derek let out a short laugh. He'd come to appreciate Sean both for his skills as an operative and for his sharp humor. Over time, Sean had revealed bits and pieces of his history, both personal and professional, and Derek had learned to trust him as much as anyone he'd ever worked with.

"Okay, Reece," he said. "After dinner, I want to get the drones ready to deploy. Drew and I will head out and set up the perimeter camera surveillance. We can monitor everything from back here over the next few days."

An hour later, after finishing their meal and cleaning up, Derek and Drew checked their weapons, slid on their night vision gear, and shouldered packs containing surveillance equipment. "Sean, make sure Reece is covered while he gets the drones up."

Sean nodded.

"And then keep the shades drawn and the doors locked until we get back."

"I've got this," Sean assured him, tucking a gun into the back of his pants.

"Call if you need us," Derek said, tapping his com.

"Be careful."

"Always." With that, he and Drew disappeared into the darkness.

Boots crunching on dried leaves, they followed the access road and worked their way toward the farm, keeping far enough away from the edge of the street to duck into the woods and out of sight, if needed.

In the cool silence of the night, with unfamiliar stars twinkling overhead, the scent of dirt and leaves triggered a powerful memory. He remembered lying under another canopy of stars with Caeli outside her hidden camp while recovering from his injuries. He'd reached for her hand like it was a lifeline.

"I think we should set one up here," Drew said, and Derek shook off the memory before he lost himself in it.

"Agreed. This is the last crossroads before the farm. Anyone coming in has to pass by. I'll cover you."

Shrugging off his pack, Drew knelt down to remove one of the small cameras. When he'd finished setting it up, he carefully covered all but the lens with sticks and brush.

Derek tapped on his com. "How does it look, Reece?"

A few seconds later, Reece replied, "Perfect."

"Okay, we're moving."

They melted further into the forest as they approached the farm, taking even more care to move slowly and deliberately. Derek had no idea what kind of perimeter security might be in place. They planned to fly the surveillance drones overhead, but the stationary cameras would give them the continuous data they needed over time, making this approach on foot worth the risk. Or so Derek hoped.

"One here?" Drew asked.

"Yeah, that looks good. Then we'll circle around to the other side."

They repeated the process, Derek standing watch as Drew set up the equipment, and then cautiously moving to the next site.

A couple of hours later, they retraced their steps and returned to the cabin.

Reece sat at his makeshift workstation, bleary-eyed. "We've got eyes everywhere now. I've also set perimeter alarms around the cabin. No one will surprise us here," he said.

"Good. Now go to bed," Derek ordered.

All four stumbled into their bunks.

***

Imagery from the drones confirmed that there was, in fact, an extensive underground facility. As they collected data from the cameras, a pattern emerged. Every fifth day, a vehicle approached the farm. Someone carried a case to the front entrance. After a security protocol, which included a retinal scan and handprint, the door opened and the person entered, only to re-emerge less than twenty minutes later, leaving the same way he came.

"Looks like a courier," Sean said.

"Makes sense that they have to hand deliver files. It seems like a lot of effort, but if they really want to isolate all their off-book activities, this is the way to do it. A simple human operation like this leaves no digital footprint to trace," Reece explained.

"We need to intercept the next run," Derek said.

Tense silence filled the room. He could feel them thinking, weighing the risks, uneasy.

"I know none of you like the idea. I don't either, but this is a way inside, and we have to take it. They aren't going to hand us the proof we need," Derek said.

Reece spoke first. "The courier arrives within the same two-hour window. We'll have to assume that if he's late, it would trigger some kind of alarm."

"That doesn't give us much time to extract intel from him," Sean said.

"No, and we need him to physically open the door," Derek said.

"I don't need to tell you how much can go wrong," Drew said, exhaling uneasily.

"Can you think of another option? We've been here for weeks."

Reluctantly, Drew shook his head.

***

Three days later, Derek waited by the side of the street, about a quarter mile ahead of the crossroads leading to the farm. He desperately hoped the courier would arrive on the early side. They needed every extra second they could get.

Moments later, as if Derek had conjured it, the vehicle appeared.

Derek trotted into the middle of the road, frantically waving his hands. The vehicle slowed to a stop.

"Can you give me a hand? We were out hiking, and I think my friend broke his leg," Derek said, approaching the driver's side.

"I have someplace to be. Can't you call for emergency help?" the man answered, eyeing Derek nervously.

Derek didn't miss the gun on the passenger seat, within easy reach of the driver.

"Get out," he ordered, pulling his own gun from his waistband and pressing it against the man's temple.

The courier glanced at his weapon.

"Don't even think about it," Derek growled.

Jaw set and looking very pissed, the driver opened the door. Derek grabbed a fistful of his shirt and yanked him out.

"Hands behind your back."

"Who are you? What do you want?"

Beads of sweat formed on the man's forehead. Derek cuffed him before shoving him into the back of the vehicle and sliding in next to him. Sean materialized from the forest, jumped into the front seat, and shoved the driver's weapon into the back of his pants.

"Start the clock," Derek said.

Ten minutes later, they had him secured to a kitchen chair in the cabin.

Reece sat in the back corner of the room, pale and jittery. Drew stood behind the prisoner, sidearm pressed to the back of his head. Sean leaned back in another chair, his weapon draped casually but menacingly over his thighs. Derek squatted down so he was eye to eye with their unwilling guest.

"We don't have much time, and I don't have any patience, so please, answer my questions and you'll get to walk away from here."

The man stared back at Derek, disbelief written on his strained features.

"You work for Trident," Derek began, the words a statement, not a question.

A hesitant nod of the head.

"Every week you bring something to this facility."

Another nod.

"Files."

"I don't know what's in the case. It's locked. I get paid to deliver, not to look."

"The security protocol at the door to the farm. Retinal scan, handprint. That's it?"

"Yes. The door automatically unlocks when it confirms my identity."

"Where do you go when you get inside?"

"To a lift. It takes me down. I don't know how far."

"And then . . ." Derek coaxed.

"And then someone meets me at the bottom. I deliver the package. He checks to make sure the lock hasn't been tampered with. I leave. A bonus shows up in my account."

"Only one person meets you? Every time?" Derek asked, insistent.

"Yes."

"Is he armed?"

"Probably."

Standing, Derek looked between Sean and Drew. Their grim faces told him they still weren't happy with this mission, but grabbing the courier had committed them to the course.

"Time?" he asked Sean.

"Thirty minutes."

"Good. Let's go."

They rode back to the farm in silence. Derek kept his nerves in check by reviewing the plan, what little there was of it, step by step. When they pulled up to the field adjacent to the farm, he tapped his com. "Reece, we're here."

Derek dragged the courier out of the car and hurried him to the entryway. Drew and Sean followed.

"Uncuff him," Derek ordered.

After Drew unlocked the restraints, Derek grabbed the man's sweating hand and pressed it against the pad. At the same time, the retinal beam scanned the man's eye. With a click, the door slid open.

Drew put a silent hand on Derek's shoulder. Derek gave him a slight, knowing nod.

"We'll be waiting," Sean said.

Derek watched Drew and Sean drag the courier back to the vehicle, then he stepped inside the farmhouse. The door slammed shut behind him.

CHAPTER 33

Derek's eyes swept through the empty building. Wood floors, no furniture, gabled ceiling. Simple, sturdy construction. He spotted the lift, built into the back right-hand corner of the room. Its gleaming metal door stood in stark contrast with the rest of the rustic interior.

He hesitated for a brief moment and then approached. Touching the call button, he took a breath.

"I'm heading into the lift," he said into his open com.

His stomach plunged as the car dropped. Reece's ground-penetrating radar had revealed an extensive underground structure and established that the farmhouse was one of two points of entry. The other was located a couple of miles away, somewhere inside a Kythiran military base.

The fact that Trident likely had someone in the local military on their payroll made the whole team twitchy. Derek could be walking into a data storage facility with a skeleton crew, or a full-scale hidden operations center. He prayed it was the former.

When the lift stopped, he already had his gun up and ready. The door slid open. A single person greeted him, just as the courier had promised.

"Hands where I can see them," Derek said, stepping out of the lift.

The man raised his eyebrows and his hands, but otherwise kept his composure.

"Very slowly, put your weapon on the ground and kick it over to me." The courier hadn't seen a weapon, but there was no way this guy didn't have one.

Dark, curious eyes bored into Derek's. Slowly, the man reached around to his back and pulled out his sidearm. He squatted, placed it on the ground, and kicked it over to Derek.

With one hand, Derek fished a set of restraints from his pocket and tossed them over. "Put these on," he ordered.

The man complied. His cold gaze didn't falter. "You'll never get out of here," he warned.

"We'll see," Derek answered. He approached the man cautiously, staying just out of his physical reach. Even restrained, Derek knew he was still a threat. "I need access to the main data files. And obviously, I'd like us to avoid detection."

"Follow me. We'll take the long way around."

Derek followed through quiet, artificially lit corridors. They stopped in front of another metal door. Another panel and retinal scanner.

The prisoner stepped forward, but Derek pressed the gun against his skull. "How many people are inside?"

The man looked over his shoulder and gave Derek an appraising look. "Two analysts."

Derek couldn't hesitate. "Do it," he ordered.

As soon as the door slid open, Derek shoved the man inside with such force that he stumbled to the ground. Derek's eyes darted around the room. Two startled bodies jumped up from their chairs. With a steady hand, he shot first one, then the other. They crumpled to the ground.

He turned back to his prisoner. "Stay down until I tell you to move."

From the way the man studied him, Derek could tell he was reassessing, calculating. "You're a field agent," his prisoner said.

Derek didn't acknowledge him. Gun still up, he shook off his pack and lowered it to the ground. With one hand, he pulled out a tablet and thin cable. He briefly wished Drew were here. He needed a second set of eyes and hands, but he hadn't been willing to risk anyone else.

"Get up. Sit at one of the workstations."

The man did as he was told. With his hands still cuffed in front of him, he grabbed the body that had fallen backward over the chair, tossed it to the ground, and then took a seat.

"What next, boss?" he asked, the whisper of a grin curling his lips.

"I'm going to take off the restraints, and you're going to copy some files for me."

"Sure thing."

Derek unlocked the restraints, still one-handed, and kept the gun trained on his opponent's temple.

"Take the tablet and connect it."

Briefly, Derek thought he'd have to shoot his prisoner as soon as they entered the room, but he was counting on the fact the other man wanted to know what he was after. If the Trident operative made his move too soon, he might lose the opportunity to gather valuable intel in real time. So, the man was letting things play out a little longer. It's what Derek would do in his position.

"It's connected. I have access to the mainframe."

"On the tablet, there's a list. Search by those keywords only and copy the related files onto the tablet."

Reece knew there would be volumes of data to sift through, so he'd wisely created a list of names including members of the Alliance General Council, Security Council, Inter-Planetary Oversight Division, and upper-level military. If any of those officials had files from Trident's black site associated with them, they were likely suspect.

The operative keyed in the list of names, glancing once at Derek with dawning understanding in his eyes.

"The program is cross-referencing and downloading now. I'll let you know when it's finished."

Derek watched data scroll across the screen. By the number of hits, he knew they'd found what they were looking for. As the files downloaded onto Derek's tablet, the operative turned slightly in his chair, hands folded in his lap.

"Are you Alliance Intelligence? I was too for a while. You'd probably have more fun working for us. You'd make more money too. And I like your style," he said, looking back and forth between the two bodies.

"Shut up."

"Sure." He swiveled back to face the screens.

Seconds ticked by. Derek stayed frozen in place until the screen stopped blinking.

"There you go. All the files we have on the big, bad government officials."

"Disconnect the tablet and then back away from the workstation."

Before Derek could react, the operative's fingers connected with the keyboard. Just a few strokes, but it was enough. In the distance, an alarm began to blare.

"Fuck."

He could hear the grin in the other man's voice before he

turned around. "I told you you'd never get out of here."

A second security door slid into place over the first.

"Reece?" Derek knew his voice sounded more desperate than he intended.

"I've got everything," Reece said into his ear.

Derek breathed a small sigh of relief and turned back to the operative. "Even if I don't get out of here, the files already have."

The operative's face shifted from surprise to anger in a matter of seconds. Derek's brief moment of satisfaction transformed just as quickly when the other man sprang from his chair, knocked the gun from Derek's grasp, and tackled him to the ground.

Flat on his back and struggling to pull air into his lungs, he missed his chance to deflect the first punch. It came fast, connecting solidly with his jaw. The metallic taste of blood filled his mouth.

When his opponent drew back for another swing, Derek rolled hard to the right, throwing the other man off. He kicked upward and felt his boot meet with a kneecap. Scrambling to his hands and knees, Derek lunged for his gun, only to be tackled again. This time the operative rolled Derek over and put both hands around his neck.

Derek's first instinct was to grab at the hands, pry the fingers loose. Black spots dappled his vision. The grip around his neck wouldn't budge. He had no leverage to punch or kick. Forcing his mind to calm, he reached up and dug his thumbs into the other man's eyes.

It took longer than Derek expected for the hands to loosen. When they did, he pushed away hard and crawled toward his gun. Nauseous and dizzy, he blinked to clear his vision.

Grabbing his gun, he stumbled to his feet and turned toward his opponent.

His first shot went slightly wide, hitting the operative's shoulder. Derek moved closer, steadier with each step. The next shot blew a hole straight through the man's chest.

"Derek!"

Frantic voices echoed in his head.

"What the hell is happening in there?"

He backed up into the wall and let himself slide to the ground. As the adrenaline fled from his body, he began to shake.

"He triggered an alarm. I'm trapped in the server room."

"We'll figure a way to get you out of there," Drew said, the pitch of his voice an octave higher than usual.

"No, you won't."

"We're not leaving you," Drew insisted.

"Yes, you are. That's an order. There is no way you can get me out of here. But you can get those files to Minister Bonnaire."

"Don't make me do this," Drew pleaded.

"Finish the mission, Drew."

The silence on the other end of the com stretched for several heartbeats.

"Don't fucking die, Derek. We'll find you. Whatever it takes," Drew promised.

Picking the tiny communication device from his temple, Derek crushed it in his fingers. Then, placing his gun on the ground in front of him, he leaned his head back onto the cold metal door and waited.

CAELI

CHAPTER 34

"Commander Rowe, I've got an incoming message from Lieutenant Chase."

Caeli's eyes flew up to meet Kat's.

"They're rendezvous coordinates," the helmsman said.

"Set our course to meet them," ordered Kat.

Kat wore her command easily, with both resolve and finesse. Caeli had seen her friend in action as an undercover operative and as a pilot, but never as the person in charge. It fit her, and Caeli told her so often.

"You have the bridge, Benin." She gestured to Caeli, and the two hurried out.

As planned, the team hadn't made contact during their entire mission. They didn't want to do anything, however innocuous, to give away either *Equinox*'s presence or their own. It had made for a nerve-racking couple of weeks. The tedium of living on a ship, one that was essentially in a persistent holding pattern, wore on the whole crew. Caeli functioned as the ship's doctor and treated minor illnesses and injuries, but that took up very little of her time. She tried to fill the remaining hours documenting more of Almagest's recent history, including the final battle against Marcus and her tenure as coleader.

As she trotted alongside Kat, her heart thudded in her chest. When they reached the landing bay, the deck officer informed them that the shuttle was on approach. Caeli stretched out her mind.

Panic filled her out of nowhere. "Kat. Something's wrong."

Kat's brows knitted with worry. They stood in silence, waiting.

Drew emerged from the shuttle first and looked agonizingly between Kat and Caeli. Caeli wrapped her arms around herself, shaking, and took an involuntary step backward.

"We got what we needed," Drew said, his voice barely audible. Sean and Reece appeared behind him. The shuttle door slid shut behind them.

"Where's Derek?" Kat asked.

Drew closed his eyes and shook his head. Kat paled.

Caeli's vision dimmed and the darkness closed in on her. She felt her legs give out, but before she crumpled to the ground, Drew had her in his arms. "I'm so sorry, Caeli. I didn't want to leave him. He could still be alive. I promised him we'd find him."

She tried to breathe, tried to follow Drew's rambling words. Derek could be alive. There was a chance he was still alive. She held onto that small hope, allowed it to pull her back from the abyss.

"We need to debrief," Kat said, voice strained.

Drew kept his hand on Caeli's arm as they left the bay. When they sat together a few moments later, he leaned back in his chair and took a shaking breath, then recounted the mission with careful detail. When he told Kat that Derek had ordered him to leave, he looked at her, pained. "Would you have done it? Would you have left him there?"

"Was there any chance you could have gotten him out?" Kat asked.

"None." It was Sean who answered. "Once the alarm triggered, the place went into full lockdown, and the only other egress was through a military base."

"Then, yes, I would have left him. Derek knows the only way we can help him now is by getting this intel to the right people. And that's what we're going to do."

Kat closed her eyes and rubbed them with her knuckles. Tapping her com, she sat staring at it.

"Commander?" The helmsman's confused voice echoed through the silent room.

Kat cleared her throat. "Take us out of here, Benin. Set course for Cor Leon."

Caeli let out a small whimper, and Kat gripped her hand.

***

Equinox hovered just outside the Cor Leon system, stealth shielding activated. Kat wanted to make contact with Captain Donovan before taking any next steps.

"Sir," she began after Donovan's image appeared. Her eyes were rimmed with bluish circles, and Caeli noticed the small tremor in her lower lip when she spoke, but she had on a fresh uniform and stood straight and tall before her commanding officer. "We've obtained proof that Arendal has no biological or chemical contamination, and further that Trident Industries has an unauthorized weapons manufacturing facility based out of Arendal. We obtained names associated with a hidden money trail, and we can link several members of the General Council, Security Council, and a few high-ranking military officers, including the newly appointed minister, Vasili Athanas, back to Trident."

"Damn it," Donovan hissed. "But now that we know who's complicit, we can inform Minister Bonnaire and circumvent the dirty officials."

Kat shook her head, opened her mouth to speak, and then clamped it shut again.

"What is it, Kat?" Donovan asked, waiting in silence.

"It's Derek, sir." She hesitated again.

"Tell me," Donovan demanded.

"Derek copied the files and uploaded them to Reece, but an alarm triggered in the bunker, and he was trapped inside. They have him."

Caeli caught the glimmer of pain on Donovan's face before he composed his features and spoke again. "That changes things," he said.

"I know, sir."

Caeli looked at Kat, confused.

Kat gave her a pained look. "Everything we know, they'll know."

"What? Derek wouldn't give anything up," Caeli whispered.

"Not willingly."

As a dawning realization swept over Caeli, bile rose in the back of her throat. She gripped the edge of her workstation until her knuckles turned white.

"Our plan was to bring this information to Minister Bonnaire, but we can't go to her now. They'll be waiting. *Horizon* is in danger too. They'll know you were working with us."

Donovan visibly blanched. "Athanas just placed Minister Bonnaire under protective custody, announcing there have been threats to her life. They must already know something."

Caeli's gut churned. She felt the horror and frustration of everyone in the room. No one spoke.

A moment of sudden clarity struck Caeli, and she looked at Kat. "I know where we can go."

***

Alone in her quarters, Caeli sat on the edge of her bed, numb. She recognized this detached feeling. It was the same protective response she'd had when she couldn't process the death of her loved ones, the devastation of her home, or the abuse she'd suffered under Marcus's regime. It was as if she'd cut herself off from her emotions and floated outside her body, listening, observing, even speaking, but with no real connection to anything around her.

Admiral Reyes had Derek. Caeli had heard rumors of enhanced interrogation techniques, of a place where the worst of the worst criminals and terrorists were sent. Was Derek there? What unspeakable things were they doing to him? What would happen when Reyes got what he needed? Would she even know if he were alive or dead?

The questions circled in her mind, driving her into a frenzy of panic and despair, until she simply shut down. She lost track of time staring at the ceiling in the dark, unable to sleep but not truly awake either. Minutes passed, maybe hours.

A light knock on her door. Kat didn't wait for a response before entering. She touched a sensor panel, and soft lighting cast a warm glow around the room.

Kat's eyes were bloodshot, and tendrils of dark hair escaped the tight braid at the nape of her neck. "Can I get you anything? Something to eat?"

Caeli shook her head. "I'm not hungry."

Looking unsure, Kat reached to put a hand on Caeli's arm but pulled back.

"How was he when I went missing?" Caeli asked.

"As wrecked as I've ever seen him," Kat admitted.

"I keep thinking about what they're doing to him," Caeli said, voice flat.

"Leaving him was the hardest decision I've ever had to make. I'm so sorry, Caeli." Shuddering, Kat hung her head.

Caeli blinked at her. "I don't blame you. Any of you. If there was a chance Drew could have saved Derek, he would have tried. If *you* thought there was a chance, you would have too. I know that."

Kat put her head into her hands, her shoulders shaking with silent tears. After a few moments, she wiped her cheeks with her sleeves. "Whatever it takes, we'll find him," she promised.

Caeli believed they would try, as soon as it was humanly possible. But the look on Kat's face and the tremor in her voice told her they might already be too late.

Kat's com chirped. "What is it?" she snapped into it.

"Ma'am, we're an hour out," the helmsman reported.

"Thank you, Benin," Kat answered. Now, she did take Caeli's hand. "I'll meet you in the launch bay in an hour."

"I'll be there," Caeli promised.

CHAPTER 35

"Commander Rowe, Dr. Crys, this way, please."

They followed the young lieutenant through a brightly lit, busy administrative office. They'd come alone. Caeli's hands shook and her stomach clenched as the door opened and they stepped into Admiral Markham's office.

Although Derek had his mother's deep blue eyes and thick, dark hair, he had his father's features, from the shape of his face to the line of his jaw. Caeli drew in a sharp breath.

The genuine warmth in the admiral's eyes when he saw her was instantly tempered with dread. He knew something was wrong. She couldn't keep the agonized expression from her face.

"Caeli," he said softly, holding his arms open. She stepped into his embrace, burying her face in his chest. When she pulled away, he squeezed his eyes closed for a moment and exhaled deeply, steeling himself for whatever she had to tell him.

"Commander Rowe, Caeli, come. Sit down," he offered.

They sat.

Kat cleared her throat. "Sir," she began, and then hesitated. The two held each other's gaze.

"Have I lost my son, Kat?" he asked, his voice ragged.

She took a shuddering breath. "In all likelihood, yes."

Caeli closed her eyes. Swaying lightly to her own internal rhythm of pain, she gripped the side of the chair. She held on to keep herself tethered to her own body, to keep from drowning in the darkness.

The admiral sat stiffly. His grief, sharp and searing, melded with Caeli's own. Next to her, Kat struggled to keep her composure.

When Admiral Markham spoke, his voice was gentle. "Tell me what's happening."

They shared everything, from the Drokarans' revelation about Arendal, to their part in the battle of Mira, to their off-grid mission to discover the truth. "Derek uploaded files containing the names of everyone in the government who has ties to Trident's illicit deals. I have that here," Kat finished, reaching into her bag for the tiny chip Reece had created for her. She handed it to Derek's father.

Admiral Markham stared at the piece of hardware now resting in his hands. Caeli heard his thoughts as clearly as if he'd spoken them aloud. His son might have sacrificed his life for this. "Whose names are on here?" he asked.

"Seven people, including Reyes and Athanas. Two are members of the General Council, and three are on the Security Council. Together, they wield a lot of power and influence. We're a small group. The evidence on there speaks for itself, but we have to make sure it gets into the right hands. We thought you could help us," Kat finished.

He nodded his head, then cleared his throat. "First, will you tell me what happened to Derek?"

Kat looked down at her hands and nodded. "I know his style. He went into that op knowing he might not come out.

He made sure everything he accessed from inside the Trident site would immediately upload to Reece on the outside. He knew he was entering an expansive underground bunker with only limited intel on what was down there, and he wouldn't let anyone else go in with him. He managed to extract the data, and then the Trident operative he'd captured triggered an alarm. The whole place went into lockdown. There was no way for Lieutenant Chase and Lieutenant Commander Asher to get him out. He ordered them to leave and finish the mission."

Kat paused and squeezed her eyes shut. In a hoarse whisper, she said, "We knew he was alive when we left him. He might still be, but . . ." Her voice trailed off.

"Kat," Markham said. She looked up. "Sacrificing yourselves wouldn't have accomplished anything. Finishing this mission will. This is about more than Derek, more than any one of us. He knew it. I know it. And you know it too." He paused and inhaled deeply. "If my son is still alive, we will move heaven and earth to find him. But the only way we can do that is to finish this," he said, holding up the tiny chip.

Kat briskly swiped a tear from her cheek. "Yes, sir."

***

The following morning, Sean, Drew, and Captain Donovan joined the group. Both *Horizon* and *Equinox* were now safely orbiting inside the Erithos Defense Network Array, a shield as powerful as the one surrounding the Cor Leon system.

"I've deactivated *Horizon*'s tracking system," Donovan informed them. "No one knows where we are, but that fact will trigger alarms in Alliance command."

"We have to work quickly. The more time we give Reyes and Athanas to consolidate power, the more difficult it will be for us to move against them," Admiral Markham said.

"Sir, I believe Reyes is going to kill Minister Bonnaire," Sean said.

All eyes turned to him. Clearing his throat, he continued, "Forgive my interruption, but Captain Donovan, you said he's already taken her into protective custody, and he's already established a narrative that her life is in danger. She knows he's corrupt. She's a loose end."

"I think there's a high probability you're right. He's kept her on Cor Leon under the guise of keeping her safe, but it's probably so he can keep her close," Markham said.

"She is the legitimate leader of the Inter-Planetary Alliance and the civilian commander of the Inter-Allied Forces. As Alliance soldiers, we're sworn to protect her," Donovan said.

"We have to get her to safety," agreed Markham. "But if we tip our hand before we do, Reyes and Athanas will likely eliminate her immediately."

"We were on our way to her, but we knew Reyes would be expecting us," Kat said.

Markham furrowed his brow in thought. "They were expecting *Equinox*, or possibly *Horizon*. They won't be expecting a routine diplomatic shuttle from Erithos."

"I see where Derek gets his tactical mind," Donovan said.

Markham gave him a tight smile. "While a team is extracting the minister, we can monitor the whereabouts of everyone on this list. We'll begin classified conversations with uncompromised Security Council members. They're well briefed on the location of most Alliance assets. And as a member of the Planetary Oversight Chamber, I'll notify the local leadership on member worlds. They can prepare their own forces if necessary."

Kat looked wary. "This could erupt into a disaster."

"Minister Bonnaire safely by our side would go a long way to averting that disaster," Markham said.

"I agree. When it gets out that Bonnaire was removed unjustly, member worlds will rally around her," Donovan said.

"Timing is going to be important." As he began to pace back and forth, Markham planned. "Based on this evidence, Donovan and I will petition the Tribunal for emergency arrest warrants. We need to secure the minister, and as soon as we have her, we need to take down Reyes, Athanas, and everyone on this list. We can't give them any time to start another war."

Donovan looked between Kat, Sean, Drew, and Caeli. "Ideas?"

"If we send a covert team on an Erithos shuttle to extract the minister, *Equinox* could follow with stealth mode engaged," Kat suggested. "The team can rendezvous with us once they've acquired the minister. We can keep her safe once she's on *Equinox*."

"Commander, I don't want you out there with only a minimal crew. That's a valuable battleship, and she'll need to be at full capacity just in case. I'd like to loan you a fighter squadron at minimum," Admiral Markham said.

"Yes, sir. I'd appreciate that."

"We'll be poised to act as soon as you have the minister," Donovan said.

"What if we can't get to her, or she's dead before we get there?" Kat asked.

"We'll act anyway. But there will be a vacuum of power, and people get excitable when that happens. There are a lot of moving parts. The faster we can reinstate normalcy, the less likely this will blow up into conflict," Markham said.

"Let's do this," Kat said.

CHAPTER 36

Caeli knew it was hard for Kat to sit out the covert part of the mission, but she needed to remain in command of *Equinox* in case conflict erupted. The small team of herself, Sean, and Drew stayed on Erithos to plan. Caeli hadn't needed to convince anyone she should be there. Her unique skills had come in handy many times before.

Admiral Markham handpicked the pilot, the copilot, and the two additional operatives that would join them, and had cover identities created for the tactical team. They'd worked out a rudimentary strategy earlier, but were anxious to leave. A deadly clock ticked in the back of all their heads. Fine-tuning the mission details would have to happen on the way.

Admiral Markham ushered them to a small, long-range shuttle and wished everyone good luck. The team boarded the shuttle, but Caeli lingered a moment.

"You know where he is, don't you?" she asked.

"I have a good idea," Markham answered.

"I can't stand the thought . . ." When her voice broke, she put her hand over her mouth, stifling the sob that escaped.

"He's strong. I know he'll fight to stay alive." Derek's father pulled her into his arms. "Focus on this mission, Caeli. I don't want to lose you too."

She nodded into his chest. "I will. I promise. Thank you. I knew we could come to you."

"I'm glad you did. Erithos is the most powerful member world in the Alliance. We *will* take down this corruption," he said. Then he kissed the top of her head, held her at arm's length, and looked into her eyes. "And then we'll find him."

"Yes, we will," she answered fiercely.

"Stay safe," he said as she stepped into the shuttle.

Usually, flying excited Caeli. When she felt the speed and the power beneath her, she understood Derek's love of it. But now, harnessed for launch, she leaned her head back on the seat and stared blankly at the cabin ceiling.

***

When they cleared the planetary system, everyone unbuckled and stretched. The pilot came back and sat beside her. They'd all been introduced to one another by name, rank, and mission assignment, but hadn't had time to exchange much beyond that.

"Caeli," the pilot said, and she turned to look at him.

"Captain Nolan," she replied, attempting to smile.

"Please, call me Julian. You're Derek's fiancé."

Her eyes widened in surprise.

"Admiral Markham told me," he explained. "Derek and I went to school together, and afterward, we flew together when he still served on Erithos."

Caeli's interest was piqued. Because she'd intimately shared her past with Derek through her gift, he knew much more about her life and history than she did his. Now, she longed for anything that would give her another piece of him to hold onto.

"You were friends?" she asked.

"Good friends for a long time. It was hard when he left, but it was the right choice for him. He needed more adventure," Julian said.

"And you didn't?"

"Flying was enough for me." He grinned and added, "And there was a girl."

Caeli laughed. "Of course there was."

"She ended up being my wife. We have two boys. It's a good life."

"That's wonderful."

"Derek definitely wasn't ready for that. He always seemed to find trouble, or make his own," Julian said, laughing now too.

"I'd say he still does."

"I've followed his career as much as I could. I know he works intelligence, so I'm sure there's a lot more I don't know, but what he's done has been impressive. As a kid, when he wasn't screwing around, you could see his potential."

"I heard he had a bit of a misspent youth."

"A little bit, yeah." Julian's smile faded, his expression turning earnest. "How are you doing, Caeli?" he asked.

She shook her head. "I'll hold it together. We have to finish this."

"I know you will. You wouldn't be on the team if you couldn't. I guess I just want you to know I'm here if you need anything."

"Thank you," she said, touched by his words.

"You guys have some planning to do, so I'll leave you to it," he said, returning to the cockpit.

Sean sat down in his place. "We do need to think about our strategy some more. I doubt we'll have any trouble getting inside with our Erithos credentials, but we could have a hell of a lot of trouble getting back out."

"We have to get the minister onboard and get this ship back outside the Defense Net without anyone knowing she's gone," Drew added.

"I can probably help with that," Caeli said.

"Yeah," replied Sean with a nod, "I was thinking you could."

"First, we need to find out where she's being held," said Drew.

One of the soldiers that had been assigned to the team by Admiral Markham spoke up. "The admiral put me on this team because I used to be stationed on Cor Leon. I did security work. I know who'll know where she is," she said.

"Will you be able to get the information without raising suspicion, or do we need to grab someone and ascertain the intel?" Sean asked.

The woman winced uncomfortably. "I'm not sure. But these guys are just doing their jobs. I doubt any of them have a clue about Reyes or Athanas."

"We have to get this information. I'd prefer we do it innocuously too, but we have to be prepared just in case, and we don't have time to waste. Will that be a problem?" Sean asked.

"No, sir. But I'd like to have a go at it first," she said.

Sean nodded. "Okay. We'll give Landis a chance to meet up with her old friends."

"Thank you, sir."

Caeli studied Lucia Landis for a few moments, reading her the way the Novali could. She felt the woman's intentions and essential character without intruding into her mind. Landis was apprehensive, as they all were, but also earnest and capable.

"Everyone clear with their cover identities?" Sean asked.

He was met with nods all around. "Let's keep things simple. We'll get through the security checkpoint, head to our accommodations, and regroup from there. If you can, I suggest you get a little rest now. Things are going to get busy pretty soon."

Leaning his head back against his seat, Sean closed his eyes. Drew folded his flight jacket up and tucked it into the corner, making a pillow for himself. The other borrowed agent from Erithos, Adrian Quinn, did the same. Soon, all three men dozed.

"I don't know how they do that," Caeli said, shaking her head at Landis.

The woman smiled and shrugged. "Necessity, I guess. I never could shut my head off that quickly."

"Me neither. I wish I could," Caeli admitted.

"You're from Almagest . . ." Landis began, but hesitated.

"It's okay," Caeli replied, "you can ask me about it."

"We've heard a little about your lost colony. A lot of rumors, some real facts. Before this mission, Admiral Markham told us a little bit about you, about the things you can do. I guess I'm just interested. I don't mean to be insensitive."

"Really, it's all right. I've done a lot of research since I've had access to Alliance records." She summed up the history of Almagest, of the illegal experimentation that had taken place there. "My people were the unintended consequences. I'm empathic. All the Novali are. Some of us can do more. I can see inside the body, even heal with my mind if I have no other choice."

"That's incredible," Landis said, eyes wide.

Caeli smiled. "It's come in handy."

"You saved Admiral Markham's son."

"I did. He crash-landed near my hidden camp," Caeli said, remembering the event with vivid clarity. "I didn't think I could save him, he was so badly injured."

"Why were you hiding?"

Caeli took so long to answer that Landis apologized again. "You don't have to talk about it."

"No, I want to. Good people, good *friends*, gave their lives for our cause. I want other people to know."

But it was still hard, and it took Caeli another few breaths before she found her voice again. "After the war that nearly destroyed our colony, apparently we tried to rebuild. But over time, the differences between those of us who had these changes and those who didn't became insurmountable. Two distinct civilizations formed. In Alamath, the other settlement, a charismatic, ruthless dictator rose to power. His army destroyed my home and killed almost everyone. The survivors, mostly children and young women, were assimilated into Alamath."

Caeli focused on a spot directly in front of her, pulled air into her lungs one breath at a time, and finished. "There were people in Alamath who knew Marcus had to be stopped. I joined their resistance, but I was caught. I escaped before they could make me give up my friends. That's when Derek crashed. When *Horizon* came to get him, he didn't want to leave me stranded in the middle of the wilderness. I didn't want to leave, but I couldn't help my friends either. So, I went with him and lived with his family for months, until things started to unravel with the resistance on Almagest and Derek took me home."

"But your people won," Landis said, searching Caeli's eyes.

"We did. It cost so many lives, but we did."

"I'm sorry," the other woman said simply. Caeli could feel that she meant it.

"More than anything, I want the life Derek and I started to build there," Caeli said, unsure why she was confessing something so private to someone she'd just met. But she felt raw, as if she were holding on by her last shred of strength, and when the other woman's empathy and compassion seeped into her psyche, she needed to say the words aloud.

"We'll make this right. So you can go home," Landis said.

"I hope so," Caeli answered softly.

They both sat in silence for several minutes, smiling at each other when one of the sleeping soldiers snored loudly.

"Tell me about you?" Caeli asked when it was clear neither she nor Landis would be getting any sleep.

With a shrug, Landis replied, "I joined the Inter-Allied Forces right out of school. I got assigned to do security, and eventually I worked protection details for some of the highest-ranking government officials on Cor Leon. I liked the work, and I was good at it."

"Derek started off doing something similar," Caeli said. "But as a pilot, he was usually transporting them from place to place."

"I know. He was a little before my time, but I know people that knew him. As Admiral Markham's son, he already had a little name recognition, but I hear he was good. That's how he ended up recruited to intelligence."

"You didn't stay with the Alliance?" Caeli asked.

"No. I'm from Erithos. My family lives on Erithos. I love my home, and I wanted to come back. But I also loved my job. I'm head of Admiral Markham's personal security detail now, so that worked out," she said.

"He's a good man," Caeli said.

"The best of the best. Seems his son turned out the same," Landis added quietly.

Caeli could only nod past the lump in her throat.

"We'll get him back."

CHAPTER 37

For the purpose of entering Cor Leon, Caeli's cover identity was that of a lower-level diplomat, Sean her assistant, and Drew, Landis, and Quinn posing as security for the small party. They passed through the checkpoint with ease and took the automated rail system to their accommodations.

Despite her worry, Caeli couldn't help but be awed by Cor Leon. Never a colony, the world had been designed as the seat of the Inter-Planetary Alliance. The buildings had been constructed to hold the Judiciary, the Assembly, and the minister and their staff, with a silent, efficient indoor rail system providing ease of transport.

As they rode, she stared out the floor-to-ceiling glass windows and watched as they passed by indoor shopping centers, residential apartments, and offices.

"It's impressive, isn't it?" Landis said, gesturing out the window.

"I admit, I haven't been on many other worlds, but this still seems like an amazing feat of architecture and engineering."

"It is. The whole city is indoors, under the glass dome. Cor Leon is hot. It's essentially a desert outside, so everything is inside and climate controlled. The dome lets in natural light, and there are greenhouses to grow crops on the premises. Even the residential areas are planned indoor communities, mostly for the families of the government officials stationed here."

Leaning close to the window, Caeli gazed up at the dome, then down at a river running beside the train, surrounded by lush greenery. "It's beautiful."

"No one who lives here is from here, but for many of the elected officials and support staff, this will be home for years. It had to be someplace they could bring a family."

"I was on my way here . . ." Caeli whispered, her voice trailing off. In the blink of an eye, her whole life had been turned inside out. Again.

The train slowed. Drew stood behind Caeli as they waited for the doors to open. He was still hurting. She could feel his guilt and regret like a cold, dark shadow enveloping him. When she turned to him, his face, as usual, didn't betray a thing.

There was nothing she could say to lift the burden from him, but she gently placed a hand on his arm. He looked at her curiously as she sent him a wave of love and gratitude, for their friendship, for all the times he'd stood beside her when the world blew up around them, and for his quiet strength.

For a brief moment, his mask of composure slipped. Pain marred his features and seeped into Caeli's mind. She accepted it, let it wash through her. "We'll finish this together," she whispered into his mind. He let her in. She felt him shift and allow her thoughts to move his, to soothe his suffering just a little. They both blinked when the train came to a full stop and the doors slid open.

The group followed Landis, who led them to their accommodations. Their simple yet comfortable suite had a central gathering space, a small kitchenette, and several private bedrooms off the main room. The group dropped their personal belongings, took a few minutes to wash and change out of their travel clothes, and met back in the common area.

Sean was already unpacking their equipment. While they couldn't bring weapons to Cor Leon, their tech, including coms, didn't raise suspicion.

"Okay, Landis, let's hook you up and get you on your way," he said.

Caeli reached for her own tiny communication device and affixed it to a spot on her temple. It blended seamlessly with her skin tone.

"Test, test," Landis said softly. Her voice echoed out of the receiver sitting on the table in front of Sean.

"Make the visit casual. You're here on a temporary mission and you wanted to check in on some old friends. See if you can find out where they're holding the minister, and if you can, what her security's like."

"Got it," Landis said.

"We'll be listening. Good luck," Sean said.

Landis gave him a slight nod and walked out the door.

The small group sat down together on the sofas and waited. Sean pulled out his tablet and set it next to the receiver on the table. He tapped a few keys, and a three-dimensional map of Cor Leon's major structures materialized above the tablet.

"This section here is mostly residential. These are the government offices and the chambers for when the Assembly is in session. This is the courtroom for the Tribunal. Shopping areas, entertainment, and gardens here," he said, spinning the map.

Caeli studied it, even more impressed now that she could see the city in its entirety.

"Security headquarters, where Landis is heading," Sean

finished, pointing to a centrally located area between the Assembly chambers and the Tribunal.

Within an hour, Landis's voice came over the receiver, warmly greeting the personnel she found at the command post.

"Lucia! It's great to see you," a male voice said.

"You too, Mikey. How are the kids?"

"Just had number five," the man answered, pride in his voice.

"Well, shit, Mikey, are you trying to populate your own colony?" she joked. "Seriously, though, where are the pictures?"

Landis carried on her conversation, catching up and making small talk with her old friends. Sean's left leg bounced impatiently on the ground, but otherwise they were all still and listening.

"So, what brings you back to Cor Leon?" another voice asked.

"Just doing security for a low-level diplomat. I volunteered. Missed you guys," she said, and Caeli heard sincerity in her voice. Then her tone turned to concern. "Crazy shit happening here though, right? I hear the former minister is under guard. Threats on her life?"

"That's what we've been told," Mikey answered without suspicion.

"You think it's credible?"

"Came from the top, so we have to take it seriously. We've got her in the south wing, though, and Jesse's team is taking point."

"His guys are good," Landis said approvingly. "How is Jesse? Wasn't he looking to transfer?"

"Nice," Sean muttered as Landis went back to the personal talk. He tapped and twirled the map until he pulled the south wing into larger focus. "Here we are."

When Landis eventually returned, they waited. Sean ordered food and made them eat, then sent them off to rest for a couple of hours. The plan was to grab the minister in the middle of the night, when far fewer people would be out and about.

Caeli let her head sink onto the pillow in the darkened room. Landis took the second bed. A few minutes later, Caeli could tell by her soft, regular breathing that the woman had fallen asleep.

The hum of distant voices played in Caeli's mind. She didn't try to tease out individual thoughts, but she could feel the emotions and intentions behind them. Sweeping her mind outward, she listened, comforted by the familiar sounds of humanity, and finally fell into a dreamless sleep.

***

Sean woke them a few hours later. "I've mapped out our route," he said, and everyone gathered around.

"We'll draw less attention to ourselves in smaller groups, so we'll split up into teams and meet here," he continued, pointing to the map. "When we approach the south wing, Caeli's going to keep us hidden."

She caught a look, a blend of interest and skepticism, between Landis and Quinn.

"Can you manage all five of us?" Sean asked.

"Yes," Caeli answered, nodding.

"What exactly are you going to do?" asked Quinn.

Caeli remembered Drew asking her the same thing on their first mission together years ago. "I'm going to visualize our group as a shadow and project that image into the mind of anyone around us. It won't hide us from surveillance cameras, though," she said, looking between Sean and Drew.

"We'll only need to worry about that when we've entered the south wing, and Reece hooked me up before we left. I've got it covered," Drew said, tapping the bag he held over his shoulder.

Sean looked pointedly at Landis. "Without weapons, the element of surprise and Caeli are what we've got going for us. We'll do our best not to cause any permanent damage to the security detail," he said.

Landis nodded tightly.

"Ready?" Sean asked, looking at Caeli.

"I am," she said, and headed out with Drew.

The interior lighting was softer throughout the corridor and even on the train, Caeli noticed. There were a few people out and about, but the daytime bustle had subsided. It was as if the city itself slept.

"Are you okay to do this?" Drew asked.

"Yes," she answered.

Once, Caeli had failed to keep her group hidden. When Amathi soldiers had overrun the resistance camp on her home world, she'd had a full-blown panic attack. Her control had slipped, and the shadow image she'd created had disappeared right along with it. Noah, a powerfully gifted Novali boy, had stepped in and saved them from capture. Caeli remembered the incident but felt none of that panic now, only a cold determination.

"Thank you, for earlier," Drew said.

Caeli glanced at him. "There's a chance we'll find him. I know it's a small one, but there would be none at all if you and Sean had sacrificed yourselves. Finishing what we started is the only choice we have. Derek knew it. I don't like it, but I know it too. Please, please, let go of your guilt," she pleaded.

"I'm trying," he answered. They walked the rest of the way in silence.

Drew led her to the meeting point. There was no surveillance in this small section of the indoor garden space. The stars twinkling through the overhead dome and the sound of flowing water made it seem as if they really were outside. Caeli stared overhead while Drew squatted down, reached into his bag, and pulled out a few small pieces of equipment.

"Presents from Reece," he said when Caeli looked over curiously. "This one will hack into the surveillance feed and create a loop, and this one will jam the security team's communication."

While Drew messed some more with his gear, Sean turned the corner and joined them, followed a few minutes later by Landis and Quinn.

"Okay, we have to go dark from this point on," Sean said.

"I've got the loop set for the security feed," Drew said.

Sean turned toward Caeli. "You ready?"

She nodded. "Stay close behind me. Don't make any noise if you can help it."

In her mind's eye, she pictured the space around them as they walked, imagining them as only shadows. She held her focus and kept the group moving forward until they reached the south wing. Two armed guards in full tactical gear stood outside the minister's suite.

Caeli moved to within a few feet of the first guard and held her hand up to halt the team behind her. Slowly, she approached him. When she was within arm's reach, she lightly touched his arm and pushed her mind into his body, choking off the blood supply to his brain.

His eyes opened wide with surprise and his hands flew to his throat. His companion turned with alarm and stepped closer. With her other hand, Caeli touched the second guard. In seconds, they both collapsed onto the ground in a heap. Caeli grabbed one weapon and handed it off to Drew, who was now beside her. Sean grabbed the other.

"Landis, Quinn, open the door."

They dragged one of the unconscious bodies close to the door. While Quinn hefted him up, Landis lifted his hand to touch the sensor pad at the door.

As soon as it slid open, Drew and Sean rushed in, weapons drawn. The other two startled security guards went for their guns.

"Don't even think about it," Sean said, and they both stilled.

Landis and Quinn dragged the bodies into the room. "Lucia?" one of the men at the table asked in confusion.

Landis didn't answer, rolling one of the large bodies onto his stomach and cuffing his hands behind his back. Quinn did the same.

"Up," Sean said, gesturing with the muzzle of his gun. "Hands where I can see them."

The guards obeyed.

"Landis, handle them."

She pursed her lips and cuffed her former colleagues while Quinn gathered their weapons. Next, she removed all their com devices and piled them onto a small cocktail table.

"Sit," she ordered, pointing to a couch. They sat.

Once they were settled, Landis and Quinn dragged the other guards, who were now gasping for breath and blinking themselves back to consciousness, to the couch, heaving them onto it.

"Caeli, Drew, get the minister up," Sean ordered.

The guards' expressions changed from confusion to utter panic. "What are you going to do with her?"

It was Landis who answered. "We aren't going to hurt her, Jesse. You have my word."

Caeli and Drew hurried into the minister's bedroom. Caeli ran her hand along the wall until she found the light sensor. The room brightened instantly to reveal the minister's sleeping form on her bed.

"Ma'am," Caeli said softly, trying not to startle the woman. But when the minister's eyes flew open and she saw Drew's imposing figure, she let out a shriek.

"Ma'am," Caeli said again, more forcefully this time.

The woman's eyes darted to hers. She stared for a second, squinting. "I know who you are," she whispered.

"Yes. I'm Dr. Caeli Crys, from Almagest. My ship was attacked while I was on my way here to meet you. I ended up on Mira."

"You and your team helped liberate that planet."

"We did."

"Then, what, may I ask, are you doing in my room, with a gun, in the middle of the night?" she asked, throwing Drew a scowl.

"Your life truly is in danger, but not from who you think. I can't explain now, but we have to get you out of here quickly," Caeli said.

"Dr. Crys, I'm inclined to believe you, but I need a little more," the minister insisted.

Caeli glanced at Drew, who shrugged.

"Minister Athanas and Admiral Reyes want you dead," Caeli said, inwardly wincing at the harsh words.

But the minister didn't look at all surprised. Her posture

stiffened slightly. Otherwise, she didn't react. "What do you need me to do?" she asked.

Caeli shrugged off the backpack she'd been carrying. "Put these on. You'll look like a member of my security team."

The minister slipped out of bed. She was a tiny woman. Short, graying hair framed her face. Intelligent brown eyes peered at Caeli.

Caeli gave the smallest of nods to Drew, who backed out of the room and shut the door behind him.

"While I dress, talk," the minister ordered.

"When we were on Mira, we obtained intelligence that the Drokarans did not, in fact, use a bioweapon on Arendal. There was nothing we could do with that information at the time, in the middle of battle, but afterward, we knew we needed to find out the truth. Reyes lied. He had an opportunity to stop the war with the Drokarans over a decade ago, but he didn't. Instead of a contaminated planet, our team discovered that Trident Industries built a secret weapons-manufacturing facility there. They have as many off-book deals as they do legitimate contracts. And I assume you know that Vasili Athanas's son owns Trident?"

The color drained from the Minister's face, but she continued to dress. "This is much worse than I thought."

"We have a list of all the government officials who have illegal deals with Trident." Caeli paused and took a shuddering breath. "Reyes knows we have it."

CHAPTER 38

"Ma'am," Sean said when the minister emerged from the bedroom, disguised as a security guard.

She surveyed the room, her eyes landing sympathetically on the bound men on her couch.

"It's all right, Jesse. They really are the good guys," she said.

Jesse looked pained. "My apologies, ma'am. They still shouldn't have gotten by me."

"What are we going to do with them?" Drew asked. "We need time to get to the ship and clear the Defense Network."

"If I asked you to give us an hour, would you do that?" the minister asked.

"You know I can't," Jesse answered simply.

"I'll stay," Quinn offered.

"What? No," Sean said.

"If this mission goes to shit, we're all dead anyway. I'll stay until you give me the all clear, then I'll surrender to these guys," Quinn replied, nodding at the couch. "I trust you won't forget me once you've cleaned house."

Caeli could tell Sean didn't want to leave anyone behind, but he didn't see a better option. Running his free hand through his hair, he said, "Okay. Stay. If they move before you get the all clear from us, shoot them. That's an order."

EQUINOX   259

"Yes, sir," Quinn said.

Landis winced. The minister was clearly displeased with the exchange too, but she didn't countermand Sean's order. Instead, she stood in front of the guards and said, "I have to leave. Please trust that this is the right thing and don't move. I don't want to see you hurt."

A muscle in Jesse's jaw twitched, but eventually he gave her a curt nod.

"Let's go," Sean ordered.

Caeli kept everyone hidden behind her while they exited the south wing. When they reached the surveillance-free area in the garden, they stopped, and Caeli released the shadow image.

"It's dawn. The city will be waking up soon. Let's wait here for a little while. The crowds will actually make us less conspicuous," Sean said.

Time slowed to a crawl, but eventually the corridors, train platform, and common spaces began to fill with people. Caeli's small group moved out from the cover of the garden and blended into the crowd. They took the train to the launch bay and hurried toward their docking port.

"Nolan, we're here," Sean said into his com. "Get the ship flight-ready."

"Welcome back," Julian's voice answered.

They had to pass through a security checkpoint on their way out. The screening wasn't nearly as thorough as on the way in, but their flight plan indicated they'd be on Cor Leon for another week.

Caeli took the lead in the conversation with the official at the gate. "I've been called back for a family emergency. I'm terribly sorry to miss the conference, but I have to get home."

Her brows furrowed with worry, and she allowed her voice to catch on the words.

Very subtly, Caeli pushed a thought into the man's mind, coaxing him to let them go through.

"I hope everything will be all right," he said sympathetically, and waved them along.

"Thank you," she said, giving him a small, sad smile.

They approached the ship. "You're getting good at this," Drew said, raising his eyebrows.

"I've had a lot of practice," she replied, her stomach clenching with guilt.

Aboard the shuttle, they strapped in and waited in tense silence. The ship cleared the hangar and lifted into the morning sky. Caeli gripped the edge of her seat, a bead of sweat trickling between her shoulder blades. The minister leaned her head back and squeezed her eyes shut. Landis chewed a fingernail, and Drew sat staring out the window. Sean's heel tapped nervously on the floor.

They cleared the lower atmosphere and waited in a queue for the next opening in the Defense Network. If the seconds had crawled by while they'd hidden in the garden outside the south wing, time seemed to stand still now. Finally, the shuttle's engines engaged again, and the ship sped away from Cor Leon.

"We've cleared the system," Julian said over the com.

Everyone in the cabin let out the breath they'd been holding.

Sean's face split into a wide smile. "We did it," he said incredulously.

Julian came out of the cockpit. "Ma'am, it's very good to have you here," he said to the minister, and then turned to Sean. "We'll rendezvous with *Equinox* in less than an hour. Where's Quinn?" he asked.

Sean's smile faded. "On guard duty. We preferred not to take out the minister's security team. They have no idea what's really going on. I'm sending him a message that we're out and he can stand down."

"What's the plan?" the minister asked.

"We're meeting up with *Equinox*. Once we have you safely on board, we'll communicate directly with Captain Donovan and Admiral Markham. They're standing by to trigger arrest warrants for everyone on the list I mentioned earlier, but we needed to get you to safety first," Caeli explained.

"Ma'am, you are the legitimate Minister of the Inter-Planetary Alliance and Inter-Allied Forces; therefore, you are in command here," Sean said.

After a moment's pause, Caeli could feel rather than see the minister collect herself. "Thank you, all of you. We'll make this right," she promised.

***

A little over an hour later, they stood on the bridge of *Equinox*.

"Ma'am, I have Admiral Markham for you," Kat said.

"Please," the minister replied.

On the screen in front of them, his image appeared. "Minister Bonnaire, I'm very relieved to see you."

"Thank you, Admiral. My rescue party has given me a detailed accounting of events. Where do we stand right now?" she asked.

"Arrest warrants have been issued in secret for all seven officials, including Athanas and Reyes. Donovan and I have also informed key members of the Security Council about the situation, and I've advised leaders of member worlds to put their militaries on high alert. We think we can take down everyone without a fight, but we have to be prepared for one. We'll need to provide proof of your illegal removal to the General Assembly as soon as we put things in motion so there can be no question that you're calling the shots from here forward. We'll execute those warrants simultaneously on your order," he said.

"Consider the order given," she said.

"Very good, ma'am," Markham answered.

Before he could end the communication, she held out a hand, as if she could catch his arm. "Admiral?"

He paused to look at her.

"We'll find your son."

CHAPTER 39

Sean, Drew, and Landis had gone off to rest and clean up, but Caeli stayed with Kat. The two escorted Minister Bonnaire to one of the more well-appointed staterooms on *Equinox*, and then Kat invited Caeli back to her quarters. Events were in motion, but it would be hours before they'd hear anything from Admiral Markham or Captain Donovan.

"I don't want to wait this out alone," Kat said.

"I don't either," Caeli said, grateful for the company. She sank onto the sofa in the common area of Kat's suite and let her head fall back onto the cushions. "Nice quarters," she said with her eyes closed.

"Yeah, I could get used to them," Kat admitted, pouring hot water for tea.

She carried two cups to the sofa and handed one to Caeli, who wrapped her hands around the warm mug appreciatively. Bone-deep exhaustion made her limbs heavy, and she couldn't seem to get warm.

"Do you think this will end it?" Caeli asked.

"I hope so. I don't want to think about the alternative . . . the Alliance tearing itself apart," Kat said, her voice trailing off.

"We did the right thing, didn't we?" Caeli asked, whispering.

"Of course we did." Leaning forward, Kat put her hands on top of Caeli's.

"It's cost us so much."

"I know."

"Kat, I'm tired. I don't want to fight anymore. I just want to go home. I just want . . ." She choked on the words.

"I miss him too." Kat took the cup from Caeli's hands and pulled her into an embrace. Caeli gave in to the pain and let the tears flow. Her shoulders heaved as she tried to pull in enough air.

Kat held her and let her cry herself dry.

***

Caeli woke to the insistent chirp of Kat's com. They'd fallen asleep on either end of the sofa, a shared blanket covering their legs. Sitting up, Caeli blinked and rubbed her eyes. Kat answered the call.

"Commander, we have a communication from Admiral Markham," Benin said.

"Have the minister, Sean, and Drew meet us on the bridge. I'll be there in ten," Kat replied.

After a quick moment to adjust their clothes and neaten their hair, they hurried out. Caeli was surprised to learn they'd been asleep for over eight hours. She could have slept for another eight.

Once the command team and Minister Bonnaire were assembled on the bridge, Kat ordered Benin to establish the link with Admiral Markham. Caeli's stomach clenched when she took in his worn appearance. Dark circles rimmed his eyes, and his lips were pulled into a tight line.

"We have everyone in custody except Reyes," Markham said.

"Where is he?" the minister asked.

"As careful as we've been, someone must have tipped him off. His flagship left Cor Leon a few hours before the warrants were served. He's disengaged his locater," Markham said.

"Best guess as to where he's heading?"

It was Sean who answered. "Kythiros."

Admiral Markham nodded. "That's what we're thinking too. It's a non-Alliance world. We have no jurisdiction there. If he makes it into their airspace, he's as good as gone."

"Not only will he escape justice, but he'll have weapons of war at his disposal," the minister said. "We can shut down Trident operations on Arendal, but we can't touch them on Kythiros."

"We're close enough to get there first," Kat said.

All eyes fixed on her.

"*Equinox* is a fast ship, and she has fully integrated stealth tech. We can beat him there and force him to stand down."

"Commander, you're carrying the Minister of the Inter-Planetary Alliance. We can't put her life at risk," Markham said, shaking his head. "I'll send one of my own battleships."

"They won't make it in time," Kat argued.

"Admiral," the minister said. "We need to take Reyes out. I am ordering Commander Rowe to Kythiros. If anything happens to me, Vice Minister Kalertis is a more than capable leader."

The admiral's eyes widened slightly, and he looked as if he wanted to argue with her, but the command structure in the Alliance was clear. It recognized the civilian leadership as the ultimate authority, and this group had put their lives on the line for the sake of that legitimate civilian leadership.

Markham gave her a curt nod. "I'll inform the Security Council and Assembly of your orders."

"How are they all taking the news?" the minister asked.

"Many are stunned, but the evidence is overwhelming and conclusive. They're coming to terms," he answered.

"Good. Commander, we should be on our way."

"Yes, ma'am," Kat answered.

"I will not forget this," the minister said, first looking to Admiral Markham and then letting her gaze circle the room.

"Good hunting, Kat," Admiral Markham said before signing off.

***

"Commander, we're coming up on Kythiran airspace," Benin said from the helm.

"Bring us to a full stop and scan the area. Keep stealth mode fully engaged. Sean, take weapons," Kat said. She tapped her com. "Drew?"

"The squadron's ready to launch," he answered.

"Good. Stand by."

"Scopes are still negative, Commander Rowe," Benin reported.

"Any increased activity in Kythiran airspace?" she asked.

"None so far."

Kat paced. A piece of dark hair escaped the confines of her tidy bun, and she brushed it angrily away from her face. Caeli could feel her emotions churning just beneath the surface, but her friend held onto them tightly. She herself was back to feeling calmly numb, her own emotions in a holding pattern, circling just out of reach.

"Commander!" Benin's voice snapped them all to attention. "I've got him."

"Set a pursuit course," Kat ordered. "Get up on him nice and tight."

"Sean, target his engines."

After a few moments, he said, "I have a lock."

"We're five minutes from Kythiran airspace," Benin reported.

"Drop stealth shielding," Kat said.

"Stealth mode disengaged."

"Sean, fire," she ordered.

Caeli felt the vibration up through her feet as *Equinox*'s powerful weapons system fired. On the screen in front of them, they watched the pulses make contact with Admiral Reyes's ship. Chunks of debris exploded into space.

"Direct hit on their engines," Sean said.

"Lock on weapons system and fire," barked Kat.

"I have a lock. Firing," Sean said.

"Full stop, Benin. Scan the ship," Kat ordered as they closed in. "Caeli, can you tell if he's got a full crew over there?"

She swept her mind out, listening. The hum of human minds grew louder as she tried to resolve the collective noise into individual voices. "There are maybe a hundred or so people on that ship," Caeli said.

"Multiple heat signatures," Benin added in confirmation.

"That's his full complement. What the hell was he thinking? He's turned his whole crew into fugitives. Benin, establish a communication link."

"Com's open."

Kat pulled in a deep breath and released the curled fists she'd been holding at her sides. "Admiral Reyes, this is Commander Katarina Rowe of the Inter-Allied Forces. By order of Minister

Bonnaire, you are to turn over your security codes, surrender your ship, and prepare to be boarded." And because she was Kat, she added, "You motherfucking bastard."

Maddening silence followed.

"They're scrambling their fighters," Benin said, his voice strained.

"Damn it!" Kat slammed her hand down on the internal com button. "Drew, launch the squadron."

"Fighters incoming," Benin said.

"What is he thinking? His ship is damaged. He can't run. He can't fire on us. He'll sacrifice his pilots, and ours," she said, her voice tormented.

"Commander, we have another problem," Benin said, wiping sweat from his forehead.

"What?" Kat snapped.

"Three Kythiran battlecruisers are organizing just on their side of the line."

Kat looked to Minister Bonnaire. "That's it. He's buying time. He believes they're going to come to his aid."

"If they cross the line, engage them," the minister ordered.

"Yes, ma'am. Sean, acquire targeting solutions on those ships if they come into range."

Tension so thick it was palpable filled the bridge. The odds in this fight wouldn't be in their favor.

"Lieutenant Benin," the minister said.

Wide-eyed, he looked at her. "Ma'am?"

"I need to you to contact the Kythiran president. This is the frequency and the security confirmation code I want you to use. When he's available, please let me know."

Kat lifted an eyebrow, but her attention quickly turned to the firefight outside.

The two squadrons were evenly matched. Caeli couldn't help but search for Drew amidst the chaos. He was gifted with laser-like focus and a mind that could easily compartmentalize, Caeli knew, but now, she felt his hesitation. He was being forced to fire on fellow Alliance pilots, not some proven enemy.

The other side felt no such hesitation. They were cornered, and they had no reason to question the orders of their commanding officer.

"Stay alive, Drew. Stay focused," she coaxed. She wasn't sure if he could feel her or not, but he fired on his target and blew the other ship to pieces.

"Minister, I have President Kain," Benin said.

The minister nodded to Benin. "President Kain, this is Celeste Bonnaire."

President Kain couldn't hide the shock in his voice. "Minister Bonnaire! I'm so pleased to hear from you. I had heard you were no longer in office."

"That little misunderstanding has been cleared up. I am back in my full capacity as Minister of the Inter-Planetary Alliance and Inter-Allied Forces."

"Well, that's . . . I'm glad to hear that," he stammered. "What can I do for you, Minister?"

"You can keep your ships in their own airspace," she said, her voice low and threatening.

"I don't know what you mean," he lied.

"If they come to the aid of Admiral Reyes, who is now considered a fugitive, the Inter-Planetary Alliance will unfortunately view that as an act of war. I know you have considerable hardware at your disposal, but ultimately it will be no match against the combined forces of every member world in the Alliance. Kythiros has always had an amicable relationship with the Alliance. I'd hate to see that lost," she said.

While Caeli was too far away to sense anything from President Kain empathically, from the heavy silence over the com, she suspected he was weighing his options. There was only one legitimate conclusion he could reach, and he came to it quickly. "I'd hate to lose our valuable relationship as well."

"I'm glad we see eye to eye on this. Thank you for speaking with me, President Kain. Take care," the minister said, signing off.

Kat gave her a small grin. Within moments, the Kythiran ships began dispersing.

"Open the com again, Benin," Kat said.

He nodded to her.

"Reyes, recall your ships. Those pilots don't need to die. Your friends aren't coming to the party."

After another long silence, Reyes's voice sounded over the com. "Transmitting security codes now. The *Quest* is yours, Commander Rowe."

CHAPTER 40

When the *Quest* fighters broke off from the fight and retreated back to their ship, Kat dropped her head into her hands and let out a deep sigh.

"Drew, stay out there and form a perimeter," she ordered.

"Roger that," he answered.

"Sean, lead the boarding party."

"On it." Sean gave a curt nod and rushed off the bridge.

"Commander, I've received the codes. We have control of navigation, communications, and all weapons systems for the *Quest*."

"Very good, Benin," Kat said.

As the minister paced the bridge, Kat sat, leaning stiffly forward with her hands on her thighs. "I still don't trust this bastard," she said.

Caeli swept her mind out toward the *Quest*, listening. She predominantly felt confusion and apprehension from the minds of the crew. Trying to tease out Reyes's thoughts from the collective hum was impossible, and even if she could, she still wouldn't be able to sense anything but his strongest emotions. She'd never made a connection with him before, and she wasn't in close enough physical contact now.

The boarding team awaited Kat's confirmation. "Sean, I'd

like to bring him in alive, and I'd like to spare his crew, but if they don't fully cooperate, put them down," she ordered.

"Understood," Sean answered over the com.

They watched from the bridge as Julian Nolan guided the shuttle into the *Quest*'s landing bay.

The noise in Caeli's mind grew louder, more frantic.

"We're on the deck," Julian reported.

Through the open com, they heard Sean give instructions to his well-armed boarding team. Then, suddenly, the tenor of thoughts from *Quest*'s crew transformed from confusion and panic to fear, and it wasn't fear of the incoming boarding party.

"Kat! Something's wrong!" Caeli cried.

She froze in place, her mind flooded with chaos.

"Get them out of there! Get them out!" she begged Kat.

Kat didn't hesitate. "Nolan, abort mission. Repeat, abort mission. Get out! Get out now!"

Caeli's heart thudded against her ribs. "Please, please, please," she repeated under her breath. She didn't know what the danger was, but she knew with absolute certainty it was coming. The voices in her mind knew it too.

Just as the shuttle cleared the launch bay, the *Quest* exploded into a brilliant display of quick-burning flame and flying debris.

Screams ripped through Caeli's mind, blasting her with a split second of excruciating pain and absolute terror. She felt herself fall, as if she were moving in slow motion. The agony of a hundred souls, immolated in an instant, shot through her brain and wracked her whole body. Their cries fell silent long before her own.

***

Her face pressed against the cold floor. Dark silence enveloped her, protected her. She wanted to stay safely hidden in the blackness, but an insistent voice nagged at her conscious mind and pulled her to the surface.

Minister Bonnaire knelt down next to her and placed a warm hand on her forehead. "Dr. Crys?"

Caeli focused on the woman's commanding voice, using it as a lifeline to pull herself reluctantly from the darkness. Around her, other noises filtered into her head.

"Nolan! Status report!" Kat shouted over the com.

No answer.

Caeli lifted herself to her hands and knees, the minister's small but strong hands guiding her up. Head pounding, she swallowed back stinging bile and fought the urge to vomit. She blinked. Black spots peppered her vision, and waves of vertigo threatened to knock her back onto the floor.

"Drew, can you see the shuttle?" Kat asked.

"They were definitely caught in the shock wave from the blast. I'm approaching now. The ship is in one piece, but I don't know how much damage they've sustained," Drew answered.

"Nolan, come on. Answer me!" Kat demanded.

"I think their com is fried," Benin said.

Caeli tried to shake the haziness from her mind. Kat turned her way. "Is she all right?"

"She's coming back to us," Minister Bonnaire answered.

Caeli inhaled, filling her lungs and focusing on her breath, then exhaled, counting the heartbeats in between. Her body trembled violently.

"How can I help?" Minister Bonnaire asked gently.

"I just need a minute," Caeli whispered.

"I need to know if there are survivors. Benin, bring us in tight," Kat said.

Caeli tried to get to her feet. Minister Bonnaire held her around the waist and helped her find her balance. She swayed, but gradually her vision focused and her head cleared enough for her to stretch her mind out to their damaged ship.

Faint whispers echoed back at her.

"Survivors," Caeli said, glancing at Kat.

"They're adrift, but they must have some life support function. Benin, get us alongside them and extend the bridge. Let me know when we're locked and sealed," Kat said. She tapped the internal com and ordered a medical team suited up.

"Let me go help," Caeli said.

"No," Kat answered, looking at Caeli with concern. "You can meet them in sick bay."

Caeli wanted to argue, but her body shook and her weak limbs barely supported her weight.

"Come on. I'll help you there," Minister Bonnaire said.

As they made their way to sick bay, Caeli stretched her mind out again, this time frantically searching for Sean. Because she'd healed him before, she could more easily recognize his consciousness among the background noise. When she found him, the tightness in her chest loosened a notch.

They waited in sick bay for the medical team's report.

"Are you feeling better?" Minister Bonnaire asked, her brows furrowed.

"I'll be all right soon," Caeli answered.

"You felt them die, didn't you?"

Caeli managed a nod.

"I can only imagine the horror."

"Reyes killed his own crew. Why would he do that?" she asked, her voice catching.

Shaking her head, the minister replied, "He was willing to sacrifice hundreds of thousands of soldiers and civilians in a war he had the power to end. His actions defy rational understanding."

Caeli touched the older woman's arm, and the minister covered her hand with her own.

A voice interrupted from the open com. "Commander, we have severe injuries but none dead. They didn't have time to strap in, but it looks like their combat gear and helmets gave them some protection. We're triaging and transporting now," the medic reported.

Caeli closed her eyes and let relief wash through her. The minister squeezed her hand. "What can I do to help?" she asked.

"I'll let you know when they get here," Caeli said.

***

Several hours later, Caeli finally tended to Julian Nolan's broken arm. He hadn't allowed her, or anyone else, near him until the boarding team and the rest of his crew had been treated. His face paled when she touched him, but a strong painkiller did its job quickly.

His head sank onto the pillow while Caeli set his arm. She hadn't needed to use her gift much with all the advanced medical equipment and trained personnel on *Equinox*. In fact, she'd avoided doing so to conserve energy, but once she realigned Julian's bones, she closed her eyes and coaxed his cells to mend.

When she finished, he gingerly rubbed his uninjured hand over the site of the break. "So, this is what all the fuss is about," he said, smiling gently at her.

"I'm glad you're okay," she replied.

Kat was making rounds in the sick bay when she spotted Caeli and Julian. "Nice job getting out of there so quickly," she said to Julian.

He acknowledged Kat with a sluggish nod, his eyes drifting closed. "It was close. I thought the shock wave was going to break the ship apart."

"Yeah, me too," Kat admitted.

"He blew his crew to hell, and he would have taken us with him," Julian said, the catch in his voice at odds with his calm features.

"It's time to get you home," Kat said, giving his shoulder a gentle squeeze as she turned to leave.

"Sounds good," Julian mumbled before giving in to sleep.

CHAPTER 41

When *Equinox* dropped into orbit around Erithos, Kat piloted the shuttle carrying Caeli, the minister, and the troops they'd borrowed from Admiral Markham down to the planet. After a formal debriefing and a break to wash and rest, Kat and Caeli were invited to a private dinner with only Markham, Donovan, and the minister.

Celeste Bonnaire was quick to praise them. "Because of you and the brave crew you assembled, I'm still alive, Reyes is dead, and we may have the opportunity to salvage the Alliance."

"You have the full support of Erithos," Markham answered.

"I need to return to Cor Leon as soon as possible. I'm sure the Assembly is reeling, and they'll need to be reassured that all branches of the government are fully functioning."

Nodding, Markham assured her, "I'll have my flagship take you there as soon as you're ready."

"Very good. Thank you." She paused and looked between him and Caeli. "And now we need to talk about Captain Markham."

Caeli stilled, her spoon frozen halfway between her bowl and mouth.

"Do you have any idea where he might be, since we can't ask Reyes?"

It was Donovan who answered. "My guess would be Dorscha Prison," he said, exchanging a glance with the admiral.

"The existence of that place goes against every value we hold," the minister said, her mouth compressing to a thin line. "I was convinced we needed it, but now I want it shut down. We have no idea who is being held there. Some are likely dangerous criminals, but others may have simply gotten in Reyes's way. Transfer all the prisoners to Cor Leon, and we'll sort them out there."

"*Horizon* will be ready to go in twelve hours," Donovan said.

"As will *Equinox*," Kat added.

"Good. Admiral Markham, it is my fervent wish that we find your son alive, but if we do not, his sacrifice will not be forgotten, nor will it have been in vain," the minister promised.

Caeli's heart thudded against her ribcage, her appetite gone. She wanted to leave immediately, her urgency bordering on frenzy. At the same time, she dreaded the coming days. She couldn't face the possibility that Derek might already be dead.

Uncertainty squeezed her chest like a vice. She hadn't yet fully processed the events of the past several months, and she couldn't look to the future with any sort of hope. Pain, as deep and dark as anything she'd ever experienced, threatened to crush her.

Subdued conversation circled the table, but she couldn't engage. She placed her shaking hands carefully on her lap, staring down at her plate.

When Kat looked over, her eyes widened in alarm. She grabbed Caeli's hand under the table and squeezed.

"Captain, Admiral, Minister Bonnaire, I'd like to get back to *Equinox*," Kat said. Caeli breathed a sigh of relief.

"Of course," Admiral Markham said, standing.

Pushing up from her chair, Caeli followed Kat around the table to say their goodbyes.

"We'll see each other again soon," Derek's father said, hugging her.

He pulled Kat into a tight embrace as well, and Caeli could hear his soft words. "He trusted you to get the job done, and you did. Whatever happens now, remember that. He's always thought the world of you."

"Thank you, sir," Kat said, choking on her words.

"See you out there," Donovan said, and Kat saluted her captain.

Numb, Caeli followed Kat back to the launch bay.

***

Dorscha Prison was a man-made facility orbiting an inhospitable rocky planet. As *Equinox* closed in, the bridge crew fell silent. They'd all known of its existence. They may have even approved of a place where the worst criminals would be justly punished and prevented from causing any more trouble. But now, knowing it operated outside the law, that Reyes may have used it to make witnesses to his treachery or threats to his operation disappear, made them sick. Caeli felt their unease grow with each passing second.

Over the open com, they heard Captain Donovan initiate contact. "Dorscha Command, this is Malcolm Donovan, captain of the *Horizon*. By direct order of Minister Bonnaire, you are to surrender operation of this facility immediately. I am transmitting her decree now. Stand down and prepare to be boarded."

"Here we go again," Kat said under her breath.

Caeli glanced at her. "I'll know if something's wrong."

Kat gave a terse nod. "As far as we know, Dorscha doesn't have a self-destruct protocol. My worry is that they'll put up a fight. They know the facility inside and out, and we don't."

"Are we taking them all into custody?" Caeli asked.

"Yes, per the minister's orders. She's not feeling generous toward anyone who might have been working with Reyes. The war crimes tribunal can investigate and figure out who knew what."

"I need to get onto that facility," Caeli said.

"I know. As soon as the guards and command crew are secure, we'll send our security team with the medics to help handle the prisoners. You can go over then with Sean and Drew."

They waited and listened. As the team from *Horizon* approached the docking port, Caeli stretched her mind out. Pulling in a calm breath, she focused all her attention on Dorscha. She desperately wanted to search for Derek's familiar psyche among the background noise, but she needed to have the boarding team's back first.

At this distance, she could only interpret the strongest impressions from the collective hum. She picked up anxiety and dread, but no real defiance from the guards and crew. Lurking behind the strong current flowing from their minds, another stream trickled in the background. Despair, so cold and dark her body shook with it.

Kat threw her a worried look.

"This place," Caeli started.

"Is a fucking pit," Kat finished for her.

Caeli felt bile rising in her throat. She tried to filter out the misery and concentrate on potential threats, but the undercurrent of suffering clung to her, seeped into her bones.

Kat stood beside her, still and focused on the conversation between the boarding crew and *Horizon*.

"They aren't putting up a struggle. We're doing a final sweep of the crew living quarters now," the team commander reported.

Within an hour, his voice sounded over the com again. "The facility is secure."

"Okay, go," Kat said to Caeli.

Caeli exchanged a long look with her friend and then rushed to the launch bay.

Once there, she met up with Sean and Drew, who, along with the rest of the team, were already armed and dressed in full tactical gear. While they assumed most of the prisoners wouldn't be in any condition to pose a threat, based on the partial manifest they'd acquired, they weren't taking any chances.

The medical teams finished their preparations, and the group boarded the ship. Caeli sat between Drew and Sean, drawing strength from their presence. When they launched, her heart raced. She tried every technique she knew to maintain control over her mind and body, counting the heartbeats between her own breaths.

Despite her efforts, tentacles of dread crept up her spine and bit into her resolve. She leaned forward, let her face fall into her hands, and sucked in air that now seemed too thick for her lungs.

Drew placed his steady palm on her back. "We'll do this together," he said.

"I know," she answered, when she could finally force the words from her mouth.

As the ship made its approach and touched down on the

deck, the entire group steeled themselves for the work ahead. Caeli looked around at the grim faces, feeling the tension radiating from them.

When the door slid open, she unbuckled her safety harness and followed Drew out of the craft. *Horizon*'s transport ships were docked beside them, with armed soldiers already loading a group of Dorscha's crew onboard.

They entered an area that looked like a supply loading dock. More *Horizon* soldiers stood guard around another group of Dorscha's crew-turned-prisoners. Lined up in two neat rows, they were on their knees with their hands bound behind their backs.

Drew approached *Horizon*'s unit commander. "We're ready to go in," he said.

The other officer shouldered his weapon and pulled a small tablet from his pocket, tapping at the screen. Drew looked over his shoulder at the facility's schematics. "This is the regular block," he said, pointing. "And these are the cells for prisoners still under active interrogation."

Caeli stole a glance at Drew, whose face tightened at the officer's words.

"As soon as we get this group loaded up, some of my guys will join you to help. The manifest says there are one hundred and ninety-six inmates. Some are identified by name, others just have a number. Here are the override codes for the locks."

"Roger that. Thanks," Drew said.

He turned and gathered the *Equinox* group. "We'll split into three teams. I'll lead one into the interrogation block. The other two will start on opposite sides of the regular cell block. I want all medical personnel to hang back. Keep your coms open. We'll call when we need you. Be careful, everyone."

When he finished giving instructions, he put a hand on Caeli's arm. "Stay with me."

"You think this is where he'll be?" she asked.

"He's been an intelligence officer for over a decade. There's a lot of information in his head."

Caeli blew out a long breath and nodded. "If he's here, I'll feel him," she said.

Sean and several other soldiers fell in line behind Drew and Caeli as they made their way through dimly lit, deserted corridors. The soft rhythm of their footsteps on the tiled floor broke the silence and produced the only sound in the vast expanse of hallway.

"They must have noise-dampening materials in the walls," Drew said.

Caeli wouldn't let herself think about why they'd needed soundproof material in this wing. Instead, she swept her mind out and concentrated on distinguishing each human voice from the chorus humming in her mind.

In seconds, she found him.

"Drew," she said, nearly breathless.

He stopped and turned.

"He's alive." She squeezed her eyes closed, focusing her whole consciousness on Derek, stretching her mind out to touch his. She knew she was physically close to him, but she couldn't sense anything more than his life force pulsing against hers.

"I can't feel anything, Drew. He's alive, but . . ." She couldn't finish her thought.

"We'll follow you," Drew said.

Her heart slammed into her ribcage as she stumbled forward, finally stopping at a cell near the end of the block. She stopped and put a shaking hand against the solid, windowless steel door.

Drew stepped forward, squeezed her shoulder, and entered the override code into the lock.

CHAPTER 42

The smell hit her first. Vomit, sweat, the pungent tang of blood. She took an involuntary step backward. Light from the corridor cast its dim glow into the otherwise dark room.

The cell was essentially a square box with a hole in the floor on one side, presumably a toilet, and a slab of metal sticking out from the wall. Derek's unconscious body lay on the slab, naked save for a dirty sheet that barely covered him.

Caeli's hand flew to her mouth, but she couldn't stifle her cry. She took one tentative step toward him and then found herself falling to her knees by his side.

Behind her, Drew shouted into his com, calling for the medical team. She reached out to touch Derek. His body was cold, hypothermic. She needed to get him warm. She needed to do something. But for the first time since she'd been practicing medicine, she couldn't focus her mind, couldn't gather the information she needed to assess his injuries or even begin to work out how to treat them. She couldn't do anything but stare in horror at his abused body.

"Derek," she whispered, reaching out to him with words and with her mind. "We're here. Please, wake up," she begged.

At her insistent prodding, his eyes fluttered open. She saw a brief flicker of recognition before his expression blanked and he turned his head away from her.

"Derek," she pleaded again, but his eyes closed and he slid back into unconsciousness.

The medical team arrived. She numbly backed out of the way, allowing them to move him onto a stretcher. When she caught a glimpse of Drew, his ashen face and agonized expression matched her own.

"I have to stay here and finish evacuating the facility. Take care of him," he said.

The medics were already moving out of the cell. Caeli hurried after them.

Back on the shuttle, the pilot took one look at Derek and said, "I don't want to wait for the team. Let me get clearance from Commander Rowe, and I'll go back for the others later."

Caeli nodded her agreement.

The two medics who accompanied them back to the ship moved quickly and efficiently. Caeli grabbed a thermal blanket, covered Derek with it, and then moved up to his head to keep out of the way. One medic started pumping him full of intravenous fluid while the other began a preliminary scan for major internal damage and broken bones.

Caeli put a shaking hand on Derek's icy forehead and gently pushed her mind into his. "You're safe. We're here," she repeated over and over, but he was so deeply unconscious she wasn't sure she reached him.

***

The medical bay on *Equinox* was well equipped to handle any kind of trauma or illness, and the borrowed medical staff who had stayed on from Erithos were highly skilled. Caeli let them work. She stayed at her place by Derek's head, keeping both the physical connection and the empathic one.

Filtering out the conversations around her, she focused all her energy on him. She remembered moments they'd shared, from stargazing on the beach to laughing over dinner, and sent those vivid experiences from her mind to his.

Kat appeared. She stood by the door and wrapped her arms around herself.

"How is he?" she asked.

"I'm still assessing," the doctor answered.

"Please keep me informed," she said to the doctor, and then to Caeli, "I have to finish monitoring operations from the bridge. I'll be back as soon as I can."

An hour or so later, the doctor touched Caeli's shoulder. "I'm going to keep him in an induced coma, at least until we get to Almagest."

"Okay," Caeli said. She appreciated his mannerisms. He spoke to her as a colleague, but also took the lead, knowing she couldn't.

He pulled a chair over and sat eye to eye with Caeli, his face filled with compassion.

"Tell me," she said.

"He's suffered physical torture designed to inflict maximum pain but not to be fatal right away. Sensory deprivation and overstimulation. Starvation and dehydration. He has broken bones that have already healed incorrectly. There are drugs in his system, hallucinogenic and psychotropic, used for enhanced interrogation. Those will clear out in a matter of days."

Caeli's chest heaved.

"I'm sorry. I know this is hard, but you need to understand

what we're dealing with. We'll design an aggressive recovery plan when we get him to Almagest. For now, we're going to treat him for infection and build his fluid volume back. I'm also going to begin correcting the fractures," the doctor said.

"I want to help you."

The doctor reached out and took her hands in his. "I've got this part. You just be here for him, okay?"

"Okay," she whispered.

As the doctor turned away to begin work, someone presented Caeli with a more comfortable chair. She collapsed into it and closed her eyes.

Hours later, she heard the ship-wide announcement that *Equinox* was leaving the system. She remained at Derek's bedside until Kat reappeared and practically dragged her away.

"I'll stay with him for a couple of hours," Kat told her, settling into the chair. "Take a shower. Get some food."

Caeli leaned down and gave the other woman a hug. "Thank you. I'll be back soon."

"Caeli?"

She turned.

"I don't know what to do for Drew. He's taking this hard. Still blames himself." Her expression pained, Kat asked, "Would you try talking to him?"

"Of course I will. How about you, Kat? Are you okay?"

"I will be," she said, leaning forward to take Derek's hand. "Do you think he knows we're here?" she asked softly.

"I think so," Caeli said.

"Good," Kat said, closing her eyes and leaning back in the chair, still gripping Derek's hand.

***

Caeli took a quick shower. She couldn't bring herself to eat anything, but she grabbed an energy drink from the mess hall and then went looking for Drew.

She found him in the launch bay, running diagnostics on a fighter that had been damaged in the fight with Reyes's squadron. When he saw her, he climbed down.

"Hey. How is he?" Drew asked. His deadpan voice and neutral expression didn't counter the dread in his eyes.

"The doctor has him in an induced coma. Kat's with him now," she answered.

"That place was a nightmare. Most of the other prisoners looked like empty shells, no life left in them." Drew dropped his gaze to the ground. "How does anybody come back from that?"

Caeli knew he was talking about Derek now.

"You don't. Not really. But you learn to live with it, and you find a way to make sure it doesn't define you," she answered.

Drew studied her carefully. He knew her history, the bare facts at least, and he'd witnessed her panic attacks on more than one occasion. Likely, he'd filled in some of the details on his own.

"Human beings are strong, resilient creatures, and we take care of each other. That makes a difference," she said, giving him a small smile. "I'm not going to lie to you, Drew. It's bad, and I know he won't be the same after this, but I have to believe he'll heal."

"I want to believe it too," he said.

When she left Drew, she went straight back to the infirmary. Kat sat dozing in the chair, in nearly the same position she'd been in when Caeli left. Caeli put a gentle hand on her shoulder.

"I think you should go to bed. Doctor's orders," Caeli said.

"You too," Kat answered, blinking and then standing to stretch.

"Hmm," Caeli murmured, noncommittally.

Kat sighed. "Just take care of yourself, okay?" she said, hugging Caeli before she left.

Caeli stood over Derek, watching his chest rise and fall, brushing his dirty, matted hair off his forehead. The only time she'd seen it this long was when he'd come back from a deep-cover mission, and then only until he could schedule a haircut. She touched the scruffy growth on his face and traced her fingers lightly over the bruises around his eyes. Evidence of the brutality he'd suffered was painted all over his body.

She slid the door closed to give them some measure of privacy, then filled the sink with warm water. Rummaging through supplies, she found a washcloth. As she gently wiped away the blood, sweat, and grime caked to his skin, she pushed her mind into his body.

She easily found the newly mending tissue. While she washed him, she coaxed the fractures to knit and encouraged his torn muscles to heal. Finally, when he was as clean as she could get him and she'd exhausted herself from the healing, she sank down into the chair and fell asleep.

CHAPTER 43

"It's time to let him wake up," Dr. Kellan said, giving Caeli's shoulder a squeeze.

They'd arrived back on Almagest the previous day. Kat and Drew were scheduled to return to *Horizon*, and Sean planned to head back to his family, but all of them wanted to wait until Derek woke up.

Lia had already come and gone, bringing Caeli fresh clothes and keeping her company during the long hours of the night. Dorian Bell hand-delivered homemade stew and fresh-baked bread for her dinner and warm pastries and tea first thing in the morning. Finn and Jason had both stopped by, promising to return again soon.

Home, surrounded by people she loved, Caeli felt like she could at least breathe again.

"He'll be groggy, but all the psychotropic drugs have cleared out of his system," Kellan said.

Pulling her chair close to Derek's bed, Caeli put one hand on his chest. She wanted him to know she was right next to him the moment he opened his eyes. With her mind touching his, she felt his consciousness begin to surface, but it was almost another hour before he blinked up at her. His eyes widened in confusion, darted around the room, and finally settled back on her.

"Caeli?" he asked, his voice ragged and hoarse.

"I'm here. You're home," she said. Reaching for a glass of water, she lifted his head and helped him take a sip.

"Are you in any pain?" she asked when he settled back on the pillow.

"Sore," he whispered.

"Where?" she asked.

"Everywhere," he answered, wincing.

"I'll get you a painkiller," she said, moving to stand.

"Wait. Please. Caeli, what happened?"

She sat back down and took his hand. "What do you remember?"

"You were there. In my cell. I thought I was hallucinating."

"I was there. Drew and Sean were with me. We got you out and shut that whole miserable place down."

"I don't remember any of that."

"No. You didn't wake up again, and then we kept you in an induced coma. But you're home now. On Almagest."

"Home." He swallowed and squeezed his eyes shut. "I didn't think I'd ever get home again. I didn't think anyone would find me."

"I would have never stopped looking," she said, blinking back tears.

Derek gave her the ghost of a smile, likely recognizing his own words.

Leaning forward, she brushed her lips gently across his. "Let me get you that painkiller now."

"Okay."

She watched his features relax and his breathing slow as the drug took hold. In seconds, he was out.

When Derek woke again, Dr. Kellan gave him a thorough assessment.

"You can move around a little bit. Carefully, with Caeli's help. You can eat. Start slowly, but we need to get calories into you," Kellan said.

"Thanks, doc," he said, his voice still rough.

"And Derek, rest, as much as you need to. It's going to take a long while to heal completely."

Derek looked away from Kellan and nodded. He held his expression blank, but Caeli could feel his raw emotions rolling beneath the surface, threatening to break through.

Kellan left, and Caeli sat beside Derek. "Would you like me to help you wash? I cleaned you up a little bit when you were unconscious, but you must feel pretty awful."

"I'd like that," he said, relief filling his face.

She knew he wasn't ready to talk yet, and she wasn't going to push. She'd let him ask about the things he was ready to hear about, and share the things he was ready to share.

As she helped him stand on shaking legs, he gave her a sideways glance. "We've been here before. You putting me back together."

"The doc on *Equinox* mostly put you back together this time. I just tried to speed things along."

They moved slowly into the bathroom. "I'm dying to wash your hair," she said.

"I'm dying to brush my teeth," he answered.

"I think we can manage both."

By the time she guided him back to bed, he was clean, his face scraped of scruff. Caeli noted how much weight he'd lost, the dark circles under his eyes in addition to the bruises, and the angry marks all over his body. She didn't trust herself to speak.

He closed his eyes, but she knew he wasn't asleep yet.

Climbing into the bed, she carefully tucked herself around him.

"I don't want to hurt you, but I really need to be close to you right now," she whispered.

"You aren't hurting me."

She rested her head on his shoulder and placed a hand over his chest, comforted by the strong, regular beat of his heart.

***

When they woke several hours later, Caeli brought him a bowl of Dorian's soup. While Derek slowly spooned it into his mouth, she arranged a bouquet of fresh flowers that Lia had dropped off while they'd been asleep, bringing a bright splash of color into the otherwise sterile room.

"Are you up for a little company?" Caeli asked, watching Derek's face carefully.

He stopped and nodded, but not before she saw a flash of panic in his eyes.

"Just Drew and Kat. They have to leave soon, but if you aren't ready to see anyone yet, it's okay."

He shook his head. "No, I want to see them."

"I'll let them know."

Moments after she contacted them, they both appeared in the doorway.

"Wow, you look like absolute shit," Kat said, a huge grin splitting her face. Drew stood beside her, tense.

When Derek returned Kat's greeting with a genuine smile of his own, the look of relief on Drew's face was so profound it nearly brought Caeli to tears.

Kat hurried over to Derek. As boisterous as her greeting had been, when she leaned down to brush his hair back and kiss his forehead, it was with a trembling hand and a surprisingly gentle touch.

Caeli moved a couple of extra chairs into the room for Drew and Kat. When they sat around him, Derek looked pointedly at Drew and said, "Thank you for coming to get me."

Drew cleared his throat. "I promised you I would."

"I never doubted it," Derek said. Neither his expression nor his voice revealed the lie behind his words.

He looked between the three of them. "What did I miss?"

They spent the rest of the visit catching him up.

"Once they had you, we knew we couldn't follow our original plan anymore, so we went to Erithos. It was Caeli's idea," Kat said.

"You went to my dad?" Derek asked, eyes wide. "That was brilliant, actually." Then his expression turned somber. "He knows about me?"

Caeli nodded. "I already contacted him to tell him we found you. We can talk to your family together when you feel up to it."

Derek nodded back, and they continued the conversation. Caeli watched his expression when they told him about Admiral Reyes blowing himself, his ship, and his crew to oblivion, and knew the information hit him hard.

When they finally finished the story with their raid on Dorscha Prison, silence filled the small room.

Eventually, Derek spoke. "We did it," he said.

"We did," Kat affirmed.

***

Over the next few days, a steady stream of visitors filled Derek's room. Sean stayed for a few hours before he left

Almagest to go home to his family. Finn came by every day, as did Lia. Derek seemed to appreciate the distraction of company, even if he'd often sleep for hours after they left.

When they were alone, Caeli would sometimes catch him frozen in an unblinking stare. He'd come back to himself in a cold sweat, shaking and disoriented. She understood all too well the dark place he visited in his tormented mind.

She didn't want to leave him, but eventually he was gone for hours at a time with the hospital staff anyway, working his body back into shape. She'd received a message from Ben Glas requesting to see her when she could manage it, so when Derek left for one of his sessions, Caeli made her way to Ben's.

"How is he?" Ben asked as soon as Caeli joined him in his office.

"Getting stronger," Caeli answered.

"I'll be by tonight," Ben promised.

"He'd like that."

Sighing, Ben was silent for a moment, then said, "Caeli, we need to talk about the Drokaran prisoners."

Caeli nodded her agreement. "I can contact the minister and let her know we have them. Now that she's back in office, I feel confident they'll be treated fairly, and I believe she'll understand why we kept them a secret."

"Good. Do that as soon as you're able. I understand the drug treatment therapy has been promising."

"That's what Dr. Kellan told me. I haven't had a chance to look over any of the results or check on the patients since I've been back."

"No, of course not," Ben said. He ran his hands over his face and blew out a long breath. "We've been discussing the situation with the Drokaran civilians in the Assembly. There's growing support to allow them to settle here."

Caeli hadn't given the Drokaran civilians, who'd likely been on the run since Jai Aakash had delivered them the warning message, so much as a passing thought since she'd been back.

"I'd really like your opinion, and I know it will hold great sway with the Assembly," Ben said.

Despite the fact that the previous decade of war might have been averted had Reyes not taken matters into his own hands, Caeli had no illusions about the Drokarans. They'd proven to be a ruthless, relentless enemy. And now, because she'd insisted on pursuing a cure, they'd also be healthy. If she were honest with herself, bringing Drokarans to Almagest terrified her.

But then she pictured Navi's sweet face. He was a child, an innocent, and he deserved a future.

She sighed. "It scares me, Ben, but I think it's the right thing to do. I know what it's like to have lost everything. If it weren't for Nina, who opened her home and took care of me when I couldn't take care of myself, I don't know what would have happened. We have to do what's right and not act out of fear."

Ben gave Caeli a long look. "I think it's the right thing too. I'll throw my support behind the initiative. You can let the minister know this as well when you speak to her."

"I'll take care of it. She'll probably be relieved. Civilians or not, it would likely be a hard sell to convince any other Alliance member world to take in Drokarans after fighting a decades-long war with them."

***

When Caeli was able to schedule a communication with the minister just a few days later, the older woman didn't try to hide her relief that Almagest was willing to take the Drokaran civilians.

"We've been battling over what to do about them," she said.

"I understand. There's something else," she began, and the minister tilted her head slightly in expectation.

"We have Drokaran soldiers locked in an underground bunker."

"I see," the minister said, her eyes narrowing.

"I hope you understand why we didn't turn them over directly after the conflict ended."

"I do, but you'll need to now. They are enemy combatants of the Inter-Planetary Alliance." The minister looked as if she were bracing for an argument.

"If we weren't planning to turn them over to you, I wouldn't have told you about them," Caeli said.

The minister gave her a tight smile. "No, I suppose you wouldn't have."

"We're trusting they'll be treated fairly," Caeli said, the memory of Dorscha Prison still fresh in her mind.

"You have my word. There are strict protocols in place for the treatment of prisoners of war, and I intend to personally ensure they're followed."

Caeli felt her shoulders relax and the tension leak out of her body. "Thank you."

As much as she needed to assure their fair treatment, Caeli knew the Drokaran soldiers couldn't stay on Almagest. While she could make a case for the civilians, the soldiers who'd attacked their planet were another matter.

When she finished her conversation with the minister, Caeli headed back to the hospital, but instead of going to Derek's room, she slipped her security keycard into the lift and stepped on. Her stomach lurched as she descended into the underground bunker.

The young soldier standing guard outside the ward flashed her a look of surprise before his expression softened. "Welcome back, Dr. Crys."

"Thank you," she said, smiling at him.

"How's Captain Markham, ma'am?" he asked.

"Much better. Thank you for asking."

"Glad to hear. Please tell him we're all glad he's back home."

"I will. He'll appreciate that. I'm going to look over some of the latest test results, and then I'll be speaking with Jai Aakash," she said.

"Yes, ma'am," he said.

Heading into the quiet, empty office to look at the test results, she gave herself time to mentally prepare to see Aakash again. Starting with his file, she reviewed the notes. The therapy was working. More than simply masking symptoms, Aakash's damaged nucleotides were repaired and functioning normally. Her own healthy genetic material had done its job.

The proof of her shared common ancestry with the Drokaran stunned her. It shouldn't have. She'd read the recovered files, learned details of the unethical experiment that had forever altered her people, and filled in the gaping holes in her world's history, but staring down at the evidence before her, a wave of revulsion gripped her. Unprepared for the force of her own reaction, she sank heavily back into the chair, dark spots mottling her vision.

Resting her cheek against the cool surface of the work desk, she closed her eyes and focused on taking one slow, steady breath at a time. There was nothing she could do about the past. She could only do her part to help create a better future.

The words she repeated to herself rang hollow, but she had to pull herself together. She couldn't lose herself over a situation not of her own making.

Eventually, her vision cleared. A thin coating of sweat covered her forehead and neck, and she trembled lightly as her body tried to recover from this latest layer of emotional trauma. She and Derek would have to compare notes later, she thought cynically.

Knocking softly on the steel door, she waited several heartbeats before entering the security code to open it. When she entered his cell, Jai Aakash stared at her, his face unreadable. His body became absolutely still. She'd noticed this Drokaran quality before, but it left her disconcerted nonetheless. He looked fit, as if the last several months of confinement hadn't had any physical effect on him.

"May I come in?" she asked.

He lifted an eyebrow, acknowledging he really had no choice in the matter, and then gave her a slight nod.

The cell didn't look like a hospital room anymore. A small table with a single chair sat tucked into the corner. A cot had replaced the bulky hospital bed. Aakash motioned to the chair and sat himself on the edge of the cot.

"A lot has happened," she began.

He merely continued to stare at her.

"I've reviewed your test results. The therapy is working," she said.

"I know," he answered.

Clearing her throat, she shifted topics. "The admiral who wanted to pursue and destroy your civilian fleet is dead. Almagest has agreed to allow your civilians to settle here, and the Alliance minister approves." She paused to allow the information to sink in.

The careful mask of control Aakash had over his features slipped a little. Caeli could see, and feel, his emotions stirring.

"You'll use this cure on our children?" he asked, an unmistakable note of hope creeping into his voice.

"We will. They'll be allowed to settle here, Jai, and not as prisoners or refugees. In time, this can become their home," she said.

She watched his throat working. He opened his mouth to say something and then clamped it shut again.

"*You* can't stay here, though," she added gently.

His eyes locked on hers.

"Your soldiers are considered enemy combatants. We have to turn you over to Alliance command, but the minister has assured me you'll be treated fairly, and I believe her," Caeli said.

"It doesn't matter about us," Aakash said, flattening his hands by his sides.

"It does matter," Caeli whispered.

"Our children will live."

"They will. I promise you."

***

When she returned to Derek's room, Finn and Jason were there. They laughed together over something, and Caeli smiled at the sound. She hadn't heard Derek laugh since he'd been back.

They stayed for another few minutes, until Dorian Bell stopped in to bring Derek and Caeli dinner. "That smells so good," Finn said as Dorian placed the tray down.

"You boys come on down to the tavern in an hour or so and I'll have some waiting for you," Dorian said.

"We'll see you there," Finn promised as he and Jason headed out the door.

When the room cleared, Derek's good mood faded.

"You okay?" Caeli asked quietly.

He nodded, but wouldn't look her in the eye. "I just want to go home."

A few days later, he was well enough to go home. But he didn't. Not really.

DEREK

CHAPTER 44

Work was the only thing that made sense to him. As soon as he could manage to keep himself upright for an entire day, Derek threw himself back into it. Disoriented at first, it seemed like he'd just left Almagest yesterday to command *Equinox*, and also like an entire lifetime had passed. Surrounded by the familiar people and routines of his workday, he kept himself so busy he had no time to think about anything else.

If he wasn't working, he was pushing his body, running until his chest heaved and his clothes were soaked with sweat or working with weights until his muscles screamed. But even when he fell into bed at night, exhausted, the nightmares still woke him.

Caeli tried to comfort him, to offer a link from her mind to his, but he couldn't let her in. He'd throw off the covers, tell her to go back to sleep, and wander the apartment. Sometimes, he'd even wander outside.

Once, he found himself standing on the bridge overlooking the wide, rushing Kalanama River. As he stood staring into the swirling darkness, the violent current of the water called to him. He wanted so badly to lose himself in it that he actually leaned over the railing.

When he climbed back into bed that night, smelling of fear and the outdoors, Caeli clung to him. He knew he was hurting her, but he didn't know how to stop. If the protective wall he'd constructed around his damaged mind cracked even a little, he was afraid he'd split wide open and the last remnants of his sanity would pour out.

***

On the day the Drokaran civilians arrived, Derek stood in the open landing field with Caeli. Transport ships from Cor Leon had already arrived to collect the Drokaran soldiers, but Caeli insisted they wait until after the civilians were settled before leaving.

She'd taken charge of the effort. He knew her own memory of arriving in Alamath spurred her to action. She wanted to make sure the new arrivals felt safe, if not welcome.

Next to Caeli, Marta stood holding Navi's hand. The little boy held up his arms, and Caeli lifted him. "You're getting so big and strong," she said, smiling. He giggled and squirmed, ready to stand on his own feet again.

Caeli had thoroughly reviewed the test results from the adult Drokarans and then worked with the medical staff to adjust the therapy for pediatric patients. Navi had responded perfectly to the treatments. Derek knew fulfilling her promise to Karan brought Caeli some measure of peace.

He looked around at the vehicles lined up waiting to transport the new arrivals, at the medical teams and volunteer staff prepared to receive anyone not healthy enough to move on their own. "This is impressive," he said to Caeli.

"We don't really know what to expect, but the Amathi have

done this before," she replied. "Marcus had a process in place and an excellent record-keeping system."

Derek nodded, thinking back. He remembered Caeli's first days in Alamath almost as if the experience were his own.

He glanced at a small vehicle parked just to the side of the medical teams. In it, Jai Aakash sat watching. Having him here made Derek slightly uncomfortable, but it meant a lot to Caeli, so he'd implemented the security measures himself and handpicked the detail guarding the young soldier. Aakash stared silently out the window, still and expressionless.

When a ramp slowly extended from the first transport ship, Derek held his breath. Feeling Caeli's body stiffen next to him, he took her hand.

If he'd had reservations about the civilians settling on Alamath, they vanished the moment the first group stepped out.

With clothes hanging off their sickly, half-starved bodies, terrified children squinted in the bright afternoon sunshine. A few adults emerged behind them, carrying small bodies delicately in their arms. After a moment of stunned silence, the medical teams rushed forward.

Caeli turned to Derek. "I have to go," she said.

"Can I help?" he asked.

She nodded. He wiped at the tears that escaped down her cheek and followed her.

They approached an older woman with a toddler in her arms. "May I take her?" Derek asked, reaching for the baby. The woman tried to keep her expression neutral, but the exhaustion and desperation bled through and her bottom lip trembled.

"We'll take care of her," Derek promised.

The baby was so thin and fragile he was afraid he might break her. With the tiny body nestled into his arms, he cradled her gently against his chest and carried her into a waiting vehicle.

Hours later, he was still following Caeli around the hospital. He'd grab supplies, move patients, whatever she needed him to do. Her whole staff worked with practiced efficiency. The cafeteria had been cleared out and lined with cots and warm blankets, but as comfortable as the space looked, there was only one adult for every dozen or so children, and small, terrified faces peered up at him.

"This is so much worse than we expected. I need to go back upstairs and look in on some of the sicker patients. Will you stay and help get these kids fed?" Caeli asked. "We could use the extra hands."

"Of course. See you at home later?"

"I'm not sure. I might stay here," she answered.

The distance between them felt like a gaping chasm. Derek knew it was his fault. He'd closed himself off from her so completely that he couldn't feel her at all. She looked worn out, but otherwise he couldn't even read her expression.

"Thank you for all your help today," she said, turning to leave.

"Caeli."

He reached for her. She stopped and turned around, but he couldn't think of anything to say. He finally settled on, "Get some rest if you can."

She nodded and left. Blowing out a frustrated breath, Derek left to find Dorian and help serve dinner.

***

Within a few weeks, nearly all the Drokaran children had been placed with families, and all were responding positively to the drug treatment. But even as things seemed to settle down, Derek barely saw Caeli. Either she was working long hours or he was.

One afternoon, Ben stopped by the flight training facility to see him. Derek generally had a positive working relationship with Ben and often had to interface with his office for planning and funding purposes as he coordinated the building of the fleet. Today, however, Ben had something else to discuss.

"I received a communication from the minister's senior staff. She's coming here in a month," Ben said.

Derek raised his eyebrows in surprise. "What for?"

Ben smiled. "An award ceremony. She wants the *Horizon* crew here, along with you, Caeli, and Lieutenant Commander Asher. She also wants to finally, officially welcome Almagest into the Alliance."

Derek's chest tightened. He couldn't bring himself to smile back. "Wow," he said stiffly.

"Not exactly the reaction I expected," Ben said.

Unable and unwilling to put his thoughts into words, Derek forced a tight grin and shook his head. "It'll be great to see everyone."

Ben held his gaze for a few heartbeats, concern in his eyes, but didn't say anything more about it.

Later that day, Derek went for a punishing run, returning home after dark soaked and starving. Taking a quick shower, he fought to keep down his rising panic. He knew he was barely functioning. Only the rigid routine and grueling schedule he'd created for himself kept him from losing his mind. The thought of any disruption to his carefully managed world filled him with dread.

When he walked into the kitchen, damp and shaking, Caeli was there. He caught the flash of alarm on her face as she put down the kitchen knife and stepped toward him.

"Are you okay?" she asked.

"Fine," he lied. She stared at him, eyes narrowed.

He sighed. "You've heard the minister's coming for some kind of award ceremony?"

She nodded and he shrugged. "I'm just . . . I don't know . . . it feels like a lot right now," he said.

Reaching up, she placed a gentle hand on his face. "I think people need this. It's something to celebrate, a way to help them come together and heal."

He swallowed hard. He could feel her opening, offering herself to him, but when he didn't react, the silence turned uncomfortable. Caeli went back to chopping vegetables. "I heard you in the shower and I thought I'd make us dinner."

"I'd like that. Do you need any help?" he asked.

"No, thank you. Sit. Tell me about your day," she said, moving efficiently around the small space.

He lowered himself into a chair at the table and stretched his legs out in front of him. He told her about the new recruits, their training regimen, and his plan for the orbiting space dock. Tantalizing smells filled the room, and his stomach growled.

She smiled. "There's a familiar sound."

She brought their plates over and sat across from him. While they ate, she kept her attention on him.

"I love Dorian's cooking, but I've missed this," he said.

"Me too," she answered, and he knew she meant more than just the food.

When they finished, she cleared the dishes, took his hand, and led him to the sofa. Something in the steeliness of her expression and the set of her jaw put him on edge.

"We're doing this now," she said, looking him in the eye.

He suddenly felt like an animal caught in a trap.

"Derek, talk to me," she said, her voice soft but unyielding.

He shrank back from her, the noise in his mind growing louder. Shaking his head, he tried to clear it. "I'm okay."

"Good. All our friends and family will be coming for the ceremony in a few weeks." She paused and pinned him with her gaze.

"Marry me then, while they're here." Her words sounded like a challenge.

He couldn't pull in a breath. Beads of sweat prickled his forehead, slid down his back. Darkness closed in on him, and his vision tunneled to a single point of light.

Caeli slid from the sofa and knelt between his knees. She captured his face in her hands. "Derek, look at me. Focus on my voice. I'm right here."

He followed the sound, the tether that kept him from plunging into the abyss. He felt her consciousness brush against his. As much as he'd resisted in the past few months, he had to grab hold of it now.

"Breathe. Feel my heartbeat," she coaxed.

The comfort of her calm mind anchored him. He took a shuddering breath. Then another. Finally, he could feel the touch of her hands against his skin, focus his vision, pull enough air into his lungs.

"Caeli," he said. He felt like he'd swallowed glass. "I'm a fucking disaster."

CAELI

CHAPTER 45

She'd pushed him, and for a moment, before he blinked down at her and spoke, she worried she'd pushed him too far. But she was desperate, and he was drowning in his own pain.

"I know," she said, brushing her thumb over his cheek. Sitting back on her heels, she took his cold hands between hers. "We have to do this together. That's how it works."

She felt him try to pull away from her again, but this time, she wouldn't let him. "Remember when I once asked you who we would be when this was over? You said that if we were still alive, we'd figure it out. Well, this is us, figuring it out."

"I'm so tired, Caeli," he whispered.

"Surviving is hard work," she answered.

His expression softened. "I think a lot about what you survived and how strong you are. That keeps me going some days."

"Derek, even during the worst of it, I was never alone. I always had people who held me up when I couldn't hold myself. *You've* done that for me so many times. On Mira, you said you wished you could take away my pain, but if you couldn't do that, you at least wanted to help me carry it. Let me do that for you now. Let me help you carry it."

He went silent for several heartbeats, then took a breath and said, "I'm afraid to look at it too closely. I'm afraid I'll lose myself in it."

She felt his panic rising again.

"I won't let you. I promise."

Fear battled with relief in his tormented expression. Finally, his head dropped, his eyes closed, and she felt him open his mind to her.

***

When they threw him into the chair, every inch of his body screamed with pain. Metal cuffs secured his wrists and ankles. The damage they'd done to him so far was for later, for after they'd gotten what they needed. It was so there'd be no fight left, no will left in him. If death were offered when they were finished, he might take it. He might beg for it.

Now, they did need something from him, but he couldn't quite remember what.

Someone said his name. The voice sounded distant, muffled, persistent.

"Captain Markham."

Admiral Reyes. He knew Admiral Reyes. The admiral had done something wrong. Derek fought for the memory.

"I'm sorry about all this, son."

The acrid smell of blood burned his nostrils. His dry throat stung when he tried to swallow. Breathing hurt.

"Ah, Derek. You should have let it go. You should have gone home a hero, with the lovely doctor by your side, and enjoyed the life you earned. Instead, here we are."

Derek squinted through swollen eyelids, his pulse pounding in his ears. His body shook uncontrollably, and his teeth rattled so hard he thought they might break. Finally, he managed to choke out two words. "Arendal. Why?"

Reyes barked out a gruff laugh. "Even when you were a smart-assed kid, I knew you were going to be good at this job. So, you found out about Arendal, and now you want to know why I did what I did all those years ago?"

The noise in Derek's mind silenced. For a brief moment, his thoughts cleared, the pain faded into the background, and he listened.

"I did it to save the Alliance. You remember how it was back then. Petty grievances, power struggles, territorial disputes that escalated into chaos. The Alliance was on the brink of disintegration, impotent, barely able to do the job it was tasked to do, namely keep order. Suddenly we were under attack, and woefully unprepared for it."

Reyes paused, pacing back and forth in front of Derek. When he stopped, he squatted down, so they were eye to eye.

"I saw an opportunity, an opportunity to unite us around a common enemy. And the Drokarans were a fearsome enemy, like none we'd ever faced. They were not an innocent group of sick refugees begging for our help. They were an invasion force, willing to take what they needed at whatever the cost. I recognized them for what they were. So, yes, I double-crossed them. I had no authorization to do it, but it had to be done. I bought us time to prepare, to unite, to rebuild the Alliance."

Reyes stood again. Derek couldn't lift his head to follow the admiral's movements.

"Of course, war is costly, but for some, it's immensely profitable. I had to align myself with certain organizations so we could build what we needed, arm our forces, protect our homes. It's a distasteful business, but I made the necessary relationships, and had to promise things in return."

Derek felt his mind shutting down, every nerve ending in his body *on fire again. He couldn't focus on Reyes's words anymore, couldn't make sense of them.*

Something jabbed at the base of his neck, and then a soothing warmth flowed through him from his head, to his chest, to the tips of his fingers and toes. His muscles relaxed. The shaking stopped.

"That's better, isn't it?" Reyes asked.

He might have made some sound in response.

"We need to talk about the data you stole."

Data. He'd stolen data from Trident. Names, accounts, contracts.

"Who has it now?"

Was he supposed to tell Reyes this? He didn't think so, but the answers pressed against his brain like needles, the sharp ends pushing against his skull until they punctured it and inched their way out.

"Don't fight the drugs, son."

When Reyes asked a question, the answer appeared in Derek's head, and he was powerless to stop it from clawing its way out.

Eventually, silence filled the room. Derek's mind felt emptied, wrung out like a used dishrag.

"Keep him alive for now. Who knows what other useful information he has in his head?" the admiral said to the guards.

Derek tried to protest, but the words wouldn't form. He slid toward unconsciousness, welcoming the merciful darkness when it finally pulled him under.

***

When he let go of the memory, his body shook. First his rage, then the pain of deep, cutting betrayal flowed from Derek's mind to Caeli's. She allowed it to wash through her.

Derek spoke so softly Caeli could barely hear him. "They kept going, after Reyes left. I couldn't keep track of time, but they'd hardly let me sleep. My cell would be too hot, and then freezing cold. When they'd drag me out again, it was almost a relief. Every time I'd think, *maybe now they'll finally let me die.*"

He stopped for a moment, but she knew he wasn't finished. She kept her hands on him and inched herself closer.

"The physical pain wasn't really the worst part. I couldn't stop them from taking what they wanted out of my head. It's like they reached inside and scraped out my thoughts. I couldn't *stop* them," he repeated, his voice hitching.

When she saw the vulnerability and despair in his expression, she lifted herself off her heels and wrapped her arms around him. He buried his head in her neck. His shoulders heaved as wracking sobs tore from him in violent bursts.

With all her being, she wished she could heal his suffering mind the way she could his body. Instead, she whispered that she loved him over and over, holding him until his energy drained and he leaned into her, spent and empty.

Derek slept soundly that night, but Caeli lay awake. Derek's mind had been violated. *She'd* violated other minds. She'd lied and manipulated people. She'd killed.

Despite the countless people she'd saved because of her actions, despite her willingness to sacrifice herself for others, despite the battles she'd fought and the horrors she'd endured, she didn't know if the scales would ever balance.

DEREK

CHAPTER 46

It had been two weeks since the night in the apartment. Derek wasn't all that much better, but he didn't want to throw himself off the bridge anymore either, and that felt like enough of a win for the time being.

When the nightmares woke him, he didn't leave the bedroom. Instead, he allowed Caeli to help steady him. She'd find other creative ways to fill the long hours of the night too, and he very much enjoyed her efforts.

He spent more time with Jason, who'd been nearly tortured to death while imprisoned during the Amathi Civil War. Although they didn't talk much about their similar experiences, the unspoken understanding between them brought Derek more comfort than he expected. He continued to push himself physically, but not with the same manic intensity as before. And, instead of dreading the coming ceremony, he looked forward to seeing his friends.

As he stood waiting for Caeli outside the hospital, he zipped his jacket. The evening breeze now held the brisk bite of autumn. While he knew Caeli loved the long, hot days of summer, fall was his favorite season on Almagest. He breathed in the scent of leaves and dirt as he leaned against the wall of the building.

A moment later, she stepped outside. A smile lit her face when she saw him waiting. "Hi. I thought you were working late tonight," she said.

"Finished early and thought you might like to go for a walk," he answered, taking her hand.

"I'd love to."

"How was your day?"

"Really good. We released the last Drokaran baby today. His case was so complicated it took us a while to realize some of his issues weren't related to his compromised genetics."

"Glad you got that sorted."

"Yeah, me too. How about you? How was your day?"

Their conversation felt so shockingly normal, he couldn't answer her.

She glanced at him curiously. "You okay?"

He cleared his throat. "Yeah."

They walked in silence to the riverbank, stopping at a spot he knew she loved, where the stark peaks of the Orainos mountain range towered over the tree line. When she'd run from Alamath years ago after escaping from the military prison, she'd made camp beside a river like this one. He knew the sound of the rushing water centered her, calmed her mind.

He turned to face her. The setting sun's rays filtered through her blonde curls and framed her face like a glowing halo. Touching her cheek with the back of his hand, he stared at her for so long, she lifted her eyebrows.

"Yes," he said, breaking the silence.

She looked even more puzzled.

"Forgot your request?" he teased. Putting his hand behind

her head, he pulled her close and kissed her long and hard.

When he stepped back, he grinned at her flustered look. "Yes, I will marry you when our friends and family are here."

Her eyes widened. "Are you sure?"

"It's the only thing I am sure of," he admitted softly.

She threw her arms around his neck and buried her face in his shoulder. "I love you," she said, her voice muffled against his chest.

***

Derek sat with Sean and Drew in the back corner of the tavern. He hadn't realized how much he'd missed their easy friendship until they were here with him again. Donovan, now Admiral of the Inter-Allied Fleet, had since gone to bed, and Derek's parents wouldn't arrive until morning. Kat and Caeli were off with Lia, making last-minute wedding arrangements, Derek imagined, so it was just the three of them.

"Kat wears it well," Derek said, breaking the companionable silence.

"She does, and she's earned it," replied Drew.

"What does this mean for the two of you?"

Drew sighed and swirled his glass. "I'm not going to renew my commission with the Alliance."

Derek wasn't shocked. He knew something had shifted irrevocably in his friend since they'd learned about Arendal.

"I'm going home to Mira. There's plenty of work to do there," Drew said.

"Ten years of occupation leaves a mark," Derek said.

"Even if I wanted to re-enlist, I couldn't stay on *Horizon*. Kat would be my captain, and we can't go back to holding hands."

"Nope," Derek agreed. When he'd been their squadron commander, he'd overlooked the relationship, and they'd never behaved as anything other than consummate professionals. Even after Kat took over Derek's old job, it still hadn't really been an issue. But, as *Horizon's* new captain, Kat definitely couldn't date one of her officers.

"She needs to do this, and I'm proud of her. We'll see what happens," Drew said, his voice trailing off.

"How about you?" Derek asked, turning to Sean.

When Sean had arrived a day earlier, Derek and Caeli had waited with Noah in the landing bay. The pure joy on Noah's face when his younger sister emerged from the shuttle had been a sight to behold. They'd also met Sean's petite, dark-haired wife, and Caeli had instantly been taken with her.

Sean grinned and shrugged. "Sonia won't want to be far from Nysa, so maybe we'll end up as neighbors."

Derek's eyebrows shot up. "You'd settle here?"

"My commitment to the Alliance won't be finished for a while yet, and deep-cover work is what I'm good at. Sonia understands, but it would be nice for her to feel like she's got family around her."

Derek swallowed down the lump in his throat. This group was family, every bit as much as the one he'd been born into. They understood the darkness that chased him because it chased them too. None of them really knew who they were without the war that had defined their entire adult lives. They'd each have to figure it out the best they could.

"What about you, Derek? What are you planning to do?" Drew asked, as if reading his thoughts.

"Besides getting married, you mean?" he asked, grinning because he couldn't help it, and because he wanted to lighten the mood a little.

"Yeah, besides that," Drew said, taking a long drink.

"Finish what I started with building Almagest's fleet. Then, I'm not sure. I don't think I could give up flying, and I like teaching, so maybe I can still do that." He shrugged. He could only really think about one thing at a time.

CAELI

CHAPTER 47

Minister Bonnaire stood on the very same platform where Marcus had once stood in the center of town. With her gaze fixed on the stage, Caeli remembered her first days in Alamath with vivid clarity, and Marcus's speech to the Amathi people in particular.

Surrounded by armed soldiers, she'd huddled with a small group of survivors and been forced to listen as he'd spewed his lies. Nearly everyone she'd ever known had been killed, her home destroyed, because he'd convinced his people the Novali were a threat to their existence. On that day, she'd felt more alone than she ever had in her entire life. Blinking the memory away, she focused on Minister Bonnaire and thought about how much had changed in five years.

Derek sat to her left in his full dress uniform, the rest of the *Horizon* team in the row beside him. There were no outward marks left on Derek. He was physically as healthy and fit as he'd ever been. Only his eyes betrayed the inner battle he still waged in his mind. But next to him now, Caeli felt his calm contentment. By her side with this group around him, he seemed at peace, at least for the moment.

Derek's mother and father sat to her right. Miriam Markham's fingers threaded through Caeli's, her grip gentle but firm. Caeli had kept in constant communication with her over the last few months, even more often than Derek knew. Admiral Markham's solid presence next to his wife exuded an air of confidence and authority, but Caeli sensed an underlying sadness in him that she'd never felt before. The events of the last several months had taken their toll on everyone.

Minister Bonnaire's voice carried out over the crowd, strong and clear. Caeli lifted her eyes back to the stage and listened.

"It is my honor to officially welcome Almagest to the Inter-Planetary Alliance at last. I think it's fitting that today I stand here, on this world, where so long ago another war was waged. The conflict here put events in motion that would ultimately end where they began. The people of Almagest have fought many times for the principles we in the Alliance hold dear. You have shown resilience, courage, and a commitment to justice. You have paid a high price to assure all your people are valued and protected and to give future generations hope. You knew that peace without justice was tyranny, and you did not rest until you wiped that tyranny from your planet.

"Safeguarding this liberty will be an ongoing struggle. Forces which oppose you will threaten time and again. You must never let down your guard. As members of the Inter-Planetary Alliance, we will protect each other, stand together, and fight together when necessary. As a reminder of our commitment to you, and to the principles for which we all stand, please accept this gift."

Minister Bonnaire swept her arm out toward the back of the square, where an obelisk, similar to the one Caeli had seen on Mira, now stood.

"May this monument be a reminder that you will never be alone in your pursuit of freedom."

A moment of deep silence fell over the crowd. Then, they burst into applause. Caeli felt a rush of emotion she couldn't easily qualify. Relief, maybe. A sense of belonging. She didn't have time to sort it out, because she, Finn, Erik Kellan, and Ben Glas were needed on the stage to sign the official admittance documents, a ritual that held symbolic value even if the legality of Almagest's membership had been established many months ago. Another round of applause met their small group.

When this part of the ceremony ended, Minister Bonnaire spoke again, now in a more somber tenor.

"Sometimes an enemy comes from within, as the people of Almagest well know. An insidious enemy nearly destroyed the fabric of our Alliance. They may have been motivated by greed, power, some corrupted version of purpose. Maybe all those things. Whatever the case, on my watch, something ugly sank its teeth into the Alliance, and it is only because a group of courageous individuals chose to put their own lives at risk that we are able to stand together today. The personal cost to them was great, and no amount of recognition or reward can ever repay them for their sacrifices. I only hope the knowledge that we are grateful, that our future is more secure, and that the Alliance still stands will bring them comfort and satisfaction."

She turned the podium over to Admiral Donovan, who looked over his former crew with pride.

"The *Horizon* crew is one of the finest in the fleet, and certainly the finest I have ever commanded. Most of what they've done to protect our member worlds will never come to light. Their sacrifices will never be fully recognized. Today we will honor them for their part in liberating Mira, a planet occupied for nearly a decade, but even more importantly, we will honor them for upholding the principles of the Alliance and for uncovering a terrible truth despite the grave danger to themselves and the ruthlessness of their adversaries."

Donovan turned to Minister Bonnaire, who held an open box in front of her. The senior officers of *Horizon*'s crew stood to receive their commendations. Caeli watched Derek's face as Donovan pinned the medal to his uniform. He held his expression blank, but Caeli heard his voice catch when he said his thanks.

***

The morning of their wedding dawned bright and cool. Caeli and Kat had stayed at Lia's the previous night. There was no sign of either of the other women as Caeli wrapped a blanket around herself and stepped out into the backyard. No surprise, since they'd stayed up well past midnight laughing and talking. Caeli probably should have tried to get a few more hours of sleep, but that wasn't happening. Her stomach fluttered and her heart raced.

Tendrils of gentle pink and orange seeped over the horizon, promising the sun would soon follow. Caeli's mind wandered to Daniel, the man who would have been her husband if the Amathi hadn't destroyed her home. The sharp edge of that particular pain had dulled to a familiar, quiet sadness. Daniel had deserved a long, full life, not a brutal death at age twenty-five from a gunshot wound to the chest.

The demarcation in Caeli's life before the Amathi invasion and after was stark and absolute. Even the untimely death of her parents hadn't infused her world with the kind of violence she'd faced later. Now, watching the tree limbs gently sway in the morning breeze, she allowed herself to truly believe it was all behind her. Hope, warm and full of promise, spread through her.

It wasn't long before the household came to life. Clattering dishes, children's laughter, and the enticing aroma of breakfast drew Caeli back inside. Ben hurried to feed the boisterous group and then ushered the children out of the way. Lia and Kat fussed over her, forcing her to eat and then handing her tea, laced with something stronger, to calm her nerves. She soaked in the bath, brushed her curls, and pinned them into a twist.

Caeli's dress was simpler than the one she'd planned to wear years ago, but no less beautiful. The silky, cream fabric left her shoulders bare but flowed to her ankles. Kat tucked wildflowers into her hair. Lia clasped a sparkling necklace, a gift from Derek's mother, around her throat. Catching a glimpse of her reflection, Caeli barely recognized herself.

When they arrived in the late morning, the memorial garden overflowed with people. End-of-summer blooms splashed bright colors along the walking paths, and the sweet fragrance carried on the breeze. Derek had asked her to marry him in this place, knowing that her losses, as much as anything else, had shaped her into the person he loved.

With the names of the dead inscribed on the wall in front of her and the smiling crowd of friends and family seated behind her, Caeli took Derek's waiting hand.

DEREK

CHAPTER 48

One Year Later

The house was nearly finished. Derek wandered the perimeter, appreciating Noah's craftsmanship. Always an accomplished sculptor, the young man had turned his attention to architectural design, bringing Novali artistry into every new structure he built on Alamath.

The sloping backyard curved down toward a meandering brook nestled into the valley below. Floor-to-ceiling glass covered the back of the house, assuring a spectacular view of the water, the forest, and the distant mountain range.

Derek and Caeli checked on the progress of their new home every day, stopping by either before or after work. He heard her voice now, from the front of the house, chatting with Noah. Running a hand over the smooth trim on the back door, he walked toward them.

Caeli carried a basket and a blanket. When she saw him turn the corner, she waved with her free hand. "I stopped by Dorian's and grabbed us some dinner."

Noah greeted him warmly. "We're finished for the day. I

had a couple of questions, but they can wait until tomorrow. Enjoy your picnic," he said, smiling.

Derek took the blanket from Caeli. Together, they headed back to where he'd just been standing. Another hour of daylight awaited them before the sun slipped below the mountain peaks. He found a relatively flat spot to spread the blanket, and Caeli knelt to set the basket down.

"Hungry?" she asked.

"Always," he answered.

She caught his gaze and held it.

"What is it?" he asked.

She didn't answer, and instead began unpacking their dinner from the basket. Something was on her mind. He felt her thoughts humming against his.

Stretching out on his back, he stared up at the blue sky. As he inhaled the scent of damp leaves, earth, and late summer berries, he watched wisps of white clouds float by overhead. He still struggled at times to calm his racing thoughts and remember that the war was over. Even if his mind knew this truth, sometimes his body failed to follow suit. But with each passing day, he trusted this reality more and more.

Caeli joined him, her warm body pressed next to his.

"Derek," she said softly. He turned his head.

Her eyes glistened with unshed tears. She interlaced her fingers with his.

"What is it?" he asked.

"Listen," she whispered.

She closed her eyes, and he did the same. Her consciousness joined with his until there was barely a distinction between the two. He could hear the blood pulsing through her vessels, the breath flowing in and out of her lungs. He felt the beating of her heart inside his own body. And then, he felt another.

The End

ACKNOWLEDGMENTS

I want to express a heartfelt thank you to my readers. Your love of this series kept me writing to the end, through plot tangles and bad days!

It takes a village, or at least a good team, to bring a book into the world, and my team is first-rate. I stand in awe of Steven Meyer-Rassow and the beautiful cover designs he created for this series. Grateful thanks to Laura Zats and Graham Warnken, publishing pros, who guided me through the process once again. And of course, much gratitude to my amazing editor, Amanda Rutter, who helps me tell a stronger, better story every single time.

I also have outstanding beta readers who give me meaningful, finessed notes, often on a tight timeline. Thank you once again to Ron Delaney, Jr., Amy Hawes, and Lisa Messina. This book is better because of you three.

My family is tremendously supportive of my crazy writer's life. Thank you to my mom, dad, and baby sister. I feel your love behind me every day. I also have four creative, talented kids with whom I can hash out story ideas, plot twists, and action scenes. A special shout-out to Noah, kid number two, who always helps me find a fresh take on a plot tangle when I'm stuck. The "money moves" scene is all his!

Finally, much love to my husband Ray, who truly is my biggest fan. Thank you for the gift of your unconditional support.

Tabitha's *HORIZON* series has won several independent book awards including the Writer's Digest Grand Prize in 2016. In addition to writing novels and short fiction, Tabitha is a partner and senior writer for Book Club Babble and managing editor for the Inkitt Writer's Blog. She lives in Rhode Island with her husband, four kids, and lovable fur babies.

44835224R00198

Made in the USA
Middletown, DE
10 May 2019